THE REA

THE REALITY EXCHANGE

by James Vigor

FIRST EDITION

First published by Fantastic Books Publishing 2020

Cover design by Ramon Marett

ISBN (ebook): 978-1-912053-34-6
ISBN (paperback): 978-1-912053-33-9

To the people who inspired me.
Especially those who didn't realise it.

ACKNOWLEDGEMENTS

My thanks go out to my family, who have been a tremendous support throughout the process of writing this book. My parents have read the whole story several times in various states. My mum helped me to perfect some of the driving aspects of the plot, and my stepdad has been invaluable for smoothing off some of the rougher edges in my writing. But more than that, the amount of love and support they have provided me with has been immeasurable.

My girlfriend, Eve, has known me for almost as long as I've been working on this story. She has been incredibly tolerant of me for taking time away from her to work on the prose and I thank her for her patience. I only hope she has enough to last my future projects as well!

My sister, Beth, has always been there to show her own creative brand of support. She gave me a wooden block once, to help me write. It's been sitting on my desk ever since. Thanks, Beth.

Drew Wagar, fellow Fantastic Books author and creator of the wonderful Shadeward Saga (amongst other works) was kind enough to lend his experienced eye to The Reality Exchange and offer his feedback. Drew, you're a great friend and a treasure to the world of science-fiction.

Thanks to everyone at Fantastic Books Publishing who has had a hand in making this all happen. You've given me this opportunity and you've made this story shine. I will always be grateful for everything that you've given me.

And thanks to all the friends I've made in the Elite: Dangerous community. You're mad, but you've made me the man I am today. I wouldn't change the times we've shared for anything. See you in the black, Commanders.

CHAPTER I

Orange sunlight beat down upon the road. Fine dust permeated the hot air and soldiers in full-body armour struggled to keep the sweat from their brows. The light reflected off the gleaming white spires, surveillance towers and antennae of Port Jova, which stood tall behind the concrete wall that had been smoothed by the dust in the seasonal winds.

Corporal Baren waved on the latest visitors. His well-worn face creased to a yawn as he watched them roll on through the gate, scraping the grit from the corners of his eyes but only managing to cause further irritation.

He blinked through the tears that welled up in defiance of the hardy, authoritative presence he had hoped to impose and caught sight of a line of pale, blurry shapes approaching along the road.

The dejected fusion of a sigh and a groan slipped out as he clocked the incoming trade convoy, then quickly checked that none of his fellow soldiers were in earshot. The exhaustion was getting to them all, but he had to be seen setting an example.

He stood up straight, wiped the moisture from his forehead and took a swig of his tepid water. It would take some time to register and approve a convoy of this size, but he would do it with a determination and stamina that would make the other Aralians proud.

'Move up. I want to be done with this lot in five minutes.'

They began to dawdle along the side of the road, slumped

over and barely managing to keep their rifles held in two hands.

The great cargo haulers were a curious blend of form and function, with cabins that curved back at the top and merged seamlessly into the long cargo container. Such industrial elegance, once white but now soiled and yellowed by the sandy winds, held aloft by six individually articulated sets of caterpillar tracks. One by one, the haulers rumbled to a stop with the foremost vehicle a dozen metres short of the gate. Baren inflated his chest and held his rifle across his body as he marched confidently towards the cabin and looked up at the driver.

'Your business?' he barked.

A thin smile nested itself in the driver's black stubble. He swiped his fringe away from his eyes, leaned out of his window and looked back at the long line of cargo haulers behind him before turning back to Baren. He lowered his sunglasses to the end of his nose. 'Trade, I would imagine.'

'And what are you hauling?'

'Only the finest in perfectly legitimate renewables, officer,' he chirped with feigned enthusiasm. Baren fixed the driver with an unsmiling stare and watched the attempted levity deflate. 'Plant matter, fertiliser, et cetera. All suitably boring, I can assure you.'

Baren drew out a small device; a glass tablet with a holographic display. The interface was nearly invisible out here, blending almost perfectly with the sunlight.

'Thumbprint.' Baren held the device up.

The driver pressed his thumb through one of the holograms and on to the glass. A chirping noise, barely audible over the sound of rumbling engines, confirmed an identification match.

Baren held the device close to his chest to shield it from the sunlight. Even so, he had to squint to read the display. As he squeezed his eyelids together, drowsiness from the heat swept over him.

He skimmed the driver's file. Everything seemed to check out. 'Move up to the gate.' Baren stepped back and waved his hand in dismissal.

The driver pushed his sunglasses back up and made a toothy, almost cartoonish, smile as he edged his vehicle towards the barrier. Another soldier with a rifle across his chest held up a hand to signal him to come to a stop. Baren made his way towards the back of the convoy, taking a quick swig of tepid water.

It would take some time to sort through all the cargo, but once that was done the approval would be quick and simple.

Nearly halfway down the line, he glanced back towards the front. It took a couple of seconds too long for his weary mind to realise something was amiss.

He stopped abruptly and shielded his eyes from the sunlight. Why was the door on the lead transport open? Where were the guards?

Then, a distant call.

'Officer!'

It came from about a hundred yards away from the hauler where the transport driver stood leaning against the starport wall. He raised a fist above his head. Was he holding something?

A flash. A thunderous boom. The cargo hauler at the gate erupted into flames. The shockwave rushed out, kicking up an expanding wall of dust that slammed into Baren, punching the breath from his body and hurling him from his feet.

There was darkness. Silence. Then Baren's lungs forced a

sharp intake of breath and everything felt all too real. The heat of the ground beneath him. A throbbing pain in his chest and back. A piercing tone in his head, interrupted by rapid cracks in the distance. Gunfire.

He forced his eyes to open. All he could make out in his stupor was a dark column of smoke rising into the sky.

The gunshots became less frequent. Amid the chaos, yells turned to cries, shouts turned to screams. Then, the sounds of conflict came to silence and all Baren could hear around him was a whistling breeze and the rhythmic crunch of dirt beneath boots.

His breaths rapid and irregular, his heart pounding loud and fast, Baren struggled to lift his head. The footsteps fell silent. Looming over him, dark against the white sky, was the silhouette of the driver.

He felt a firm grasp around his ankles, then felt the ground scraping against the armour on his back, but it stopped after only a few seconds, once he had been enveloped by the shade between two of the cargo haulers that remained intact.

He felt a tug at his thigh as the man squatted over him and pulled his handgun from its holster. Baren found his own weapon aimed at him, inches from his face.

The ringing in his ears was too loud for him to hear what the driver was saying. The man began calmly, but it wasn't long before he was making wild gestures, waving the gun all over the place.

He was ranting. Something about fairness and justice. But Baren was in pain and too tired to listen. He let his head fall back and his eyes close.

'Hey.'

Baren just hoped that somehow this would all go away.

'… come on now, Aralian.'

This could still be a dream. It had to be.

'… not listening? Alright.'

A bang. Searing pain in his left hand. Baren let out a scream, his eyes snapping open as his gut convulsed and he lurched upright only to meet the sole of a boot that slammed him back into the dirt.

He brought his hand up in front of his face. An enormous hole had been carved through it. His fingers hung off by the thin shreds of meat that remained.

He couldn't stop crying out, clutching his hand to his chest.

He was aware of the ranting voice but all sense was drowned out by the pain. Occasional words slipped through '… the war … Aralian Pioneers … Solar Conglomerate …'

'… don't see the irony, do you?' The man raised a blood-spattered eyebrow. 'The one non-renewable resource … the most valuable …'

The butt of the pistol came down towards him. Baren tried to pull his hand away. He couldn't move.

The pain exploded as shrieks were ripped from inside him.

'I'm talking about you, dummy! The life of a person! Can't grow that back, can you?'

The ever-louder shouts made no sense. Baren pressed his eyes tightly closed, clutching at the fire in his hand, sobbing for home.

Something cool pressed against the bridge of his nose. He looked to see his own pistol lined up between his eyes, and stared transfixed. In his peripheral vision he was aware of the man's mouth moving. More words. He couldn't listen, couldn't hear, could only pull in another breath, his last, as the bullet left the gun.

* * *

The oceanside port Jova was perhaps at its most impressive from this distance. Mighty starships heaved themselves out of their moorings and into the sky with roaring engines. The sea lapped at its outer wall as dozens of smaller craft came and went, gliding above the waves before turning skyward and sailing out.

Jova came into view as the small craft sped past the last ranks of trees, but where many drivers would have stopped to admire the view, Winter maintained her speed.

The front of the vehicle was open-topped, as though a motorcycle had been encased in a car chassis; the pointed cockpit only had room for its sole occupant. Its cargo, a tower of small metal shipping crates, rattled behind.

Winter neared one of the many entrances to the starport. When she spotted the soldiers at the gate, she began to consider her next steps. Firstly, she would have to slow down on the approach. She needed to show them that she was neither nervous to enter, nor in a rush to be done with it.

She came to a stop just before the gate. Two soldiers had already left their positions by this time and were on their way over.

Winter pondered step two. It was important to get the look right. Most traders had had to endure this tedious procedure countless times, so it was normal to look bored.

One of the guards came up to Winter at the front of the vehicle, while the other walked around the back. She removed her helmet and shook her hair loose.

'What's your business?' The soldier panted, sweating under his helmet's clear visor. It almost seemed cruel to force them to wear such thick black armour on a day like this.

'Trade. Just a small shipment today.'

'And what are you hauling?'

'Trinkets. Boxes full of small market crap. All totally recycled, I've been assured.' It wasn't a complete lie, at least. Each crate contained recycled products designed to be visible when scanned, while the real load remained hidden. As long as she gave them no reason to find her suspicious, they wouldn't tear the boxes apart.

'Thumbprint.'

As he spoke, Winter's gaze was drawn by a line of heavy cargo haulers in the distance, behind the soldier.

'It sure looks busy over there,' she said.

'Yeah,' the guard muttered.

It looked like a trade convoy. There were a lot more soldiers over there, moving down along the line. The guard's face betrayed a flicker of relief.

'Place your thumb on the device please, ma'am.'

Winter was just reaching her hand out when she was startled by a flash and a bang. Her eyes jerked away from the device to see the hauler at the front of the convoy exploding into flames. She gaped as the shockwave rolled outwards, a thick cloud of dust engulfing the gate and most of the vehicles behind it. Flashes of light pierced the smoke. Screams and gunshots echoed off the starport walls.

Both she and the soldier stared wide-eyed. She was aware his lips were moving. Was he mumbling a prayer? Winter flinched instinctively as debris rained down, though it was too far away to reach them. Distant silhouettes emerged from the dust cloud only to jerk and fall as gunfire crackled.

She jumped at a sudden burst of static. The soldier grabbed his radio.

… all available units … Gate 04 …

Then he was sprinting away from her, joining a throng of uniformed bodies all racing towards the carnage.

She was alone.

With a quick backward glance, she rolled over to the barrier, dismounted to raise it, then drove straight through.

It didn't take long for her to reach the commercial area of the port. Crowds of pedestrians pushed through the streets, many of them trying to get closer to the walls, intrigued by the sounds of conflict. They slowed Winter to a crawl.

After a while the atmosphere was almost like on any other day, if a little more tense.

As she neared the docking zone for independent pilots, her vehicle's computer automatically located her client and plotted a route to his ship. She hailed the internal comm line.

'Winter here. I have your shipment. Care to let me in?'

After a beat, the computer announced the receipt of a reply. *Message Received*. Then on the screen, a smiley face. A familiar response.

The road sloped downwards into an underground tunnel, lit with a blue glow. Winter brought the vehicle up to speed, and felt the handling change as the road in the tunnel actively gripped her tyres to aid her cornering and lead her to the right bay.

It was an enormous chamber. Scaffold and walkways scaled the walls and sprawled high above. Protruding from the walls were crane arms with pointed claws hanging down by thick metal cables.

Any space overhead that wasn't occupied by metal structures had been filled with spotlights that shone on to a mighty freight starship. It wasn't the prettiest ship by any stretch of the imagination, but she wouldn't say that in front of its crew.

A ramp extended and a man emerged, his ginger hair slicked back and his short beard neatly trimmed. He removed his hands from his pockets, letting his jacket swing open, and he held his arms wide as a smile stretched from cheek to cheek.

'Miss Starling!' he called.

'Captain Short.' She powered down the vehicle, dismounted and met him in a warm embrace. She didn't believe that Short was his real name, but it was what his crew called him and it was the only name she thought he needed.

'That's a big delivery you have for me,' Short observed, rubbing his hands together. He worked one of the nearest crates loose and cracked open a concealed side panel.

The cover swung down on its hinges. Winter peered over Short's shoulder as a few chunks of asareyite tumbled out. Jagged lumps of deep blue rock, pearlescent and with a texture comparable to marble.

'These will polish up nicely.' Short took one and turned it over in his hands. 'You have bigger ones too?'

'The largest is about a cubic metre.'

Short widened his eyes, then put it back and closed up the box. 'Did you have much trouble getting it here?'

'Actually it went a lot smoother for me today. I don't suppose you've heard what happened out there?'

'News doesn't really travel down here. You've got me interested though.'

'I'll bring you up to speed while we get you loaded up. Come on, lend a hand.'

She made a move towards her haul and was about to loosen the clamps when the captain told her, 'There's no need.' Winter shot him a glance. 'My crew have been sat on their arses all day. They can sort the cargo. Why don't we go grab a drink? If I know you, you haven't taken a break all day. Besides, there's something we need to talk about.'

He wasn't wrong. Winter's day so far had consisted of six

hours of driving, loading and unloading. She'd brought some water for the ride, but even with frequent refills it quickly became too warm to be refreshing. The thought of sitting down to an ice-cold refreshment was tempting.

'Sure, but you're paying.'

CHAPTER 2

Winter sat gazing out of the window in a small café overlooking the sea. It was an excellent vantage point, providing a spectacular view of the waves that crashed against the cliffs below. She could feel the floor rumbling and hear the table rattling in a crescendo, which ended as a starship launched out from a tunnel beneath her and soared away over the ocean.

Captain Short soon returned with a tray, carrying a pair of cool beverages and a slice of iced cake which he placed before Winter.

'I told you I didn't want that,' she muttered. Short just smiled and took his seat.

He leant in towards her, slurping his drink noisily through a straw. Winter poked at the cake with a fork as she regaled him with the events at the gate.

After a pause he stopped sipping his drink and lifted his head. 'I've seen this before.'

'Yeah? Often?'

'A few times.' Short leaned back in his seat and stared into space.

Winter returned to prodding the cake. 'It's probably the Conglomerate. Of course they'd attack an Aralian hub like this.' She looked up to see Short shaking his head.

'The Conglomerate wouldn't attack one starport, at one gate, with one explosion. It would hardly be worth the effort.' He folded his arms and fixed his eyes on Winter. 'The Solar Conglomerate is an enormous governing body, not a small band of terrorists. If the Conglomerate attacked this starport, they would be trying to occupy it.'

'You don't think it was them?'

'I know it wasn't.' He made no effort to hide a smug smile as he lifted his drink back to his lips.

'Why not just be straight with me and tell me who it was?'

Short finished his drink. 'I'm trying to get you to work it out for yourself. The politics of this war are remarkably simple and very important for someone in your profession to understand.'

'Well, I don't care for politics.' Winter pushed her uneaten cake aside and fixed Short with a glare. 'I don't like watching people die and if you know why they were killed I'd much prefer that you just told me.'

Short looked at her as though to stare her down, but soon dropped his gaze and released a sigh. 'Sympathisers. Most likely Aralians working to aid the Conglomerate. Quite honestly, I'm surprised you don't know more about this.'

A flashback of corpses blending with burning shrapnel, bloody chunks of mangled flesh disintegrating in a hail of debris and ammunition. Armed guards charging through clouds of dust, killing to stop the killing.

'I guess I'm just lucky.'

'Lucky?' Are you joking? Step back and have a look at the big picture. These people may be terrorists, but they're on your side!'

'I have no side!' She leant across the table, pushing herself into his space.

'Think about it. Sympathisers don't win wars and they know it. So what are they going to do? Did they think they could decommission an entire starport by blowing up a single entrance?' He made a gesture towards the constant flow of space vessels entering and leaving. 'No, of course not. We close the gate and continue to function near peak efficiency while it's repaired.

'But in the moment of attack? Everyone panicked. The public, the security forces … everyone except the smugglers. And what did the smugglers do?'

'I drove straight in.'

Short smiled. 'For as long as it took for everyone to recuperate – about half an hour – every smuggler entering the starport could do so with next to no hassle. That's a lot of illicit goods getting through. In the end, all it cost was a few enemy soldiers and some willing volunteers, all to the benefit of the Solar Conglomerate and of course, the smugglers who supply them.'

It made sense when he put it that way. It had been a distraction designed to help her to do exactly what she had done, even though she hadn't known it. It didn't feel good to have been aided by an act of terrorism.

In her discomfort, Winter moved her hand to the back of her neck and fidgeted with her spinal implant. She could feel the metal strip stretching a couple of inches down her spine as she ran her fingers across it. Hidden beneath her skin, it was invisible save for a small patch of scar tissue on her neck. Besides her unconscious impulse to trace its outline with her fingers, it was almost as if it wasn't there.

'And I'm afraid I have more news for you,' he said. Winter sensed his discomfort as he sat back in his chair. 'I'm going to have to alter our deal.'

'You've never done that before,' she said. 'You've already got your goods. All I need is my money.'

'I'm afraid that's the stumbling block.' Short's tone lowered. 'We … I had a bit of a problem client on my last job. She managed to make off with most of the goods without leaving us so much as a penny. We should have been more careful, I know, but we'd been having such a good run of jobs and we just let our guard down for a second and then she–'

He took a deep breath, then cleared his throat and leaned forward.

'Look, you've done your job and now you deserve payment. And seeing as how you've pointed out that people have died to make your job easier, I'm even more obligated to deliver.

'I can pay for a third of your shipment. Let me take that and pass the rest along to a friend of mine. He's not a smuggler by trade but he'll take small loads like this for the Conglomerate. I'll tell him what the goods are worth and he'll take my word for it. I promise I will send the money straight to you.' He clasped his hands together and looked at her with pleading eyes. 'What do you say, Starling?'

Winter hesitated. He already had the goods, and maybe this was the only way she'd ever get paid.

'I could introduce you to him, if you'd like? He's not far.'

'It's getting late and I've got business in the morning.'

'Okay, well I can vouch for this guy. I've worked with him for years. I know it's not good business but …' He breathed deeply, pressing his palms tightly together. 'Just trust me on this one?'

Her eyes met his. She tipped her head towards her untouched cake slice. 'Thought you could buy me off with that, did you?'

'Can you blame me for wanting to butter you up a bit first?' He laughed a little. 'So, you accept?'

'I'll let it slide this time.' She pushed her chair back and rose to her feet. 'But I must be on my way. I'm still on the clock.'

Short stood with her. 'Excellent, thank you! I'll get those

goods passed along right away. You can head straight off and we'll get it all sorted while you drive. The money should be in your account by the time the blue sun rises.'

'It had better be.'

He waved a dismissive hand. 'I'll be in touch if there are any problems. If I completely screw you over though and you want to beat me up, you'll have to come back pretty sharpish. We leave early tomorrow morning.'

Reluctantly she nodded, and sensed Short's relief as he led her from the café.

'Tell me about this friend of yours. You said he's not a smuggler. Are you sure he's going to go for this?'

'Eddie Orson. He's not a smuggler, no. He's a general transporter. There's plenty of room in his hold for a good haul, but he'll take passengers too. He usually tries to keep it legit, but he'll carry a little contraband if it's for the Conglomerate.'

'Only for the Conglomerate, huh? The side that employs terrorists? Sounds like a great guy.'

'The Conglomerate doesn't employ terrorists, Starling, their ideals just resonate with the right people. Or maybe they're the wrong people. Anyway, you'd be crazy to think the Pioneers don't have the same kind of support on Earth. War is bloody.'

'And no business of mine. I'm glad I'm not the one dealing with him. He's all yours.'

'Having a firm political standpoint doesn't make him evil. He's from Earth and he's ex-military, so of course he's going to support the Solar Conglomerate. But this works for us. He'll take the goods to support his own cause and he'll give us the money because he's an honourable man. You come to expect that much of a soldier.' Short smirked. 'You couldn't dream of a better client.'

'Then you shouldn't have any trouble sending me the money tonight. As long as I get my money, I'll consider him a legitimate business partner. Until then I reserve my right to remain sceptical.'

They continued to walk in silence through the markets towards the shipyards. One of many lifts took them back underground into the enormous hangar that housed the freighter. Winter's transport rested by the starship's boarding ramp.

Short motioned towards the empty cargo rack on the car. 'Marvellous, look at that! You shall never see my crew of magical elves, for they work tirelessly in your absence that they might never be discovered.' He laughed, then turned to Winter.

She looked at him blankly. 'Yes, it's a miracle,' she replied, deadpan. 'Now maybe you could cut the crap and give me my money?'

'Ah, you're no fun.' He drew a small glass panel from his jacket pocket and poked at its holographic buttons. Winter checked a similar device of her own and confirmed receipt of the agreed sum. 'As I said, you'll have the rest in a few hours. You have my word.'

She gave him a hard look, mounted her vehicle and started the engine. 'If there's nothing more, Captain?'

Short shook his head. 'Take care of yourself, Starling.' She nodded, then turned the vehicle around and drove out of the hangar. She emerged from the steep tunnels, squinting in the blazing sunshine.

The panic of the crowds had subsided, which made forging a path through the starport far quicker. Before long she was back on the open road.

The drive home from Port Jova was a long one, but driving

past her parents' quarry was a sign she was getting close. Like many of the quarries in this region, it was dense with veins of deep blue asareyite, the same stone that she had just sold to Short. Digging it was legal, but exporting it to Earth was another matter. As that was also where they made a lot of their money, they had to be discreet about it.

She had passed the quarry and was nearly home when the screen in front of her lit up with an alert, confirming that further payment had been received from Captain Edward Orson. In fact, it seemed Short had managed to convince him the shipment was worth a little more than she had asked for. If this was Short's way of making up for the inconvenience, she was happy to accept.

As she drove, a star began to rise, casting a cool blue ambience over the landscape. Right now, in the middle of the Blue Season, it would rise and set within night-time hours, and light Winter's route home. In a few months, it would stray further and further into early morning until the Blue Season was over and she would have to make this journey in darkness.

By the time Winter arrived home, the sky was nearly at its darkest, the distant blue star climbing high above the horizon. The air and the heat forgot their daytime hostility and a soft breeze cooled the sweat on Winter's skin.

The house was dark. It wasn't that late. Someone should be up.

Perhaps they had gone out somewhere? Or maybe they'd just turned in early?

As she turned off the engine and dismounted, Winter caught the gleam of vehicles in the driveway. Both their cars were there. They'd turned in early. She tiptoed her way to the front door.

She peered at the thumbprint lock. It was offline. Cracks were visible in the casing, exposing wiring and circuitry.

A chill swept over her. Winter placed a hand against the door and gently pushed. It swung open, smoothly and quietly, then with a loud crack it collapsed from its hinges and thudded against the wall.

She stood silently and swallowed deeply. The fingers that had been hovering by the handgun on her hip, now tightened around the grip as she drew the weapon silently from its holster and disabled the safety. Raising it in front of her, she took a step inside.

In the hallway, tables and bookshelves had been yanked away from the walls, thrown over, pulled apart and smashed to pieces. There were holes in the walls from which bare strands of wire trailed out, fraying at the ends.

She inched forward. Was anyone in the house? Desperate to find her parents alive and well, she strained to listen for any noise.

There wasn't much in walking distance of this place and the only vehicles outside belonged to the family, so her parents probably hadn't escaped by themselves and anyone else who had been here had most likely driven off. She couldn't depend on probabilities though. She kept her guard up.

Winter pushed past overturned furniture, squeezing down the hall, then entered the living area. She was struck with a blast of cold air that punched through a wide crack in the window. Shreds of torn fabric lay amongst scattered feathers. They must once have been the cushions. The coffee table lay on its side with one leg missing and the others split apart. The walls were bare, and as she stepped further inside, the crunch of glass and wood underfoot told her what had become of the pictures that had once adorned them.

It looked more like a battlefield than a break in.

Winter didn't want to disturb the place. There was no-one in here and that was all she needed to know. She backed out into the hall, trying to keep her hands steady as she raised her weapon again.

She moved towards the back of the house, then froze. The quiet scrape of wood against wood. It was coming from the kitchen.

She adjusted her grip on the gun, her finger on the trigger. As she approached, she could see the door lying on the floor, torn off its hinges.

As she crossed the threshold, she detected a single faint clicking sound behind her, followed by a metallic whirring.

Winter braced herself, waiting as the mechanical hum drew nearer, then whirled to face it with her weapon outstretched. A heavy strike to the head stopped her short. The last thing she remembered was her gun clattering to the floor and a bright blue light in her eyes.

CHAPTER 3

A shock jolted Winter awake. She fought to catch her breath.

She was still dazed and a bruise throbbed on her temple. She was on her back, but elevated away from the floor. It took a moment to realise she was lying atop the kitchen table. The dim blue glow of the star in the early night shining through the window had moved. Before, the whole room had been bathed in its radiance. Now it had drifted, leaving much of the kitchen in shadow.

Winter couldn't feel anything below her neck. She could move her head but was otherwise completely paralysed.

She willed her arms and legs to move. She grew desperate, trying to kick and flail with every ounce of her being, frustrated and terrified at being left so vulnerable. Yet all she managed to do was jerk her head from side to side.

She scanned the room frantically, searching for something that might set her free.

Then, at the other end of the table, a light blinked on. A single pale blue point in the shroud of darkness. A faint clicking, the quiet humming of motors. It moved closer.

A metallic case emerged from the shadows. The dim light shining through the kitchen window settled on its sharp angles and outlined the silhouette of a hovering drone. Rare and expensive, this was most likely what had broken into Winter's house.

'Why can't I move? Let me go!' Winter tried to scream, but

her voice was too weak. There was no power from her chest. She could hear how feeble she sounded.

The drone flexed its thin, articulated metal arms to reveal saws, scalpels and claws. Winter gasped and strained to move.

'Please do not struggle,' it said in a soft synthesized female voice. 'You are recovering from a delicate procedure, but will be back to your usual self in just a few hours.'

'A *delicate* procedure? What part of bludgeoning me into unconsciousness do you call delicate?' Winter's voice was shaky and she found herself struggling for air.

'Modifications have been made to Miss Winter Starling's neural fibre-cluster implant. Until you recover, all but your vital functions have been temporarily disabled. Please accept our apologies for any inconvenience.'

'Fuck you. I said let me go.' It had disabled her, but it hadn't killed her. Not yet. And it was a robot, a machine. If she was careful with her questions, it might tell her what was going on.

She tried to relax. She measured her shallow breaths and asked, 'What do you want with me?'

The drone beeped loudly, then announced, 'Incoming communication. Opening channel.'

The next voice to come from the droid could not have been more different. It was deep, masculine and definitely not synthetic. The upper-class Aralian accent was strong and there was an authority to the tone that darkened the room further. A chill washed over the parts of Winter's body that she could still feel.

'Miss Starling. I'm sorry we have to speak under these conditions but I'm afraid I am in need of your full co-operation.'

'You could have just asked me,' Winter said, trying to assert some control.

'Hmm, I'm afraid that would have rather defeated the objective. I have more than enough individuals under me who would gladly have agreed to the job, but this is the only means at my disposal to ensure utmost secrecy. I'm sure you can understand the effort it took to incapacitate you, and to prepare you for what is to come. I assure you I would have employed simpler means, had they only been available.'

He gave the impression that this was a briefing he had prepared in advance.

'You're trying to convince me to do your dirty work? Of everyone you could possibly know, you want me to do it for you?'

'But of course, Miss Starling. After all, you are an extraordinary young woman with some unique qualities.'

'Then it seems you've given me the advantage. I won't do anything for you until you tell me everything I want to know.'

'Oh, you mistake me, Miss Starling,' he said, an air of amusement in his tone. 'I wouldn't dream of sending you out on such a vital task without a firm grasp of the basics. Be under no illusions, however. I have taken steps to ensure that the advantage remains mine.'

The drone floated around the edge of the table, drifting to a stop beside Winter's head.

'First and foremost, you will have noticed that I've been quite thorough in ensuring we're alone in your family abode. You'll be pleased to know that your parents are alive and well, living under my protection. They will continue to live in comfort, but if you fail to complete your assignment, you will never see them again. Furthermore, if you attempt to disrupt this assignment, well, let's just say that I'm no stranger to bloodshed.'

Winter began to realise how intricate his plans must have been. Her dread grew.

'Second, you will have also noticed that I have performed a rigorous inspection of your home and have discovered some rather unfortunate information about your activities of late. The kind of information that would be enough to have your family, your friends and even your good self thrown in prison, *smuggler*.' Winter could almost hear his lips curling into a sneer. 'Of course, all of this information can be forgotten if you play your cards right.'

Whoever this man was, he was good with threats. On top of threatening her parents, her smuggling links could be traced to dealings with each and every one of her contacts. Getting Short tossed in jail would hardly be a fair expression of gratitude for everything he had done for her over the years. A lot of people could be hurt if this guy made good on his threats.

'And finally, my medical drone has already informed you that it has accessed your spinal implant as a means of inhibiting your movement. By now, I'm imagining you're asking yourself what else was done to it while you slept.'

The thought of this man exploiting it was beyond disgusting. She felt violated. It took every ounce of willpower to prevent her from screaming at the stranger, but she was determined not to lose control.

'The answer is in fact twofold, as I have commissioned two additions to the device. Upgrades, if you will. The first addition is a capacitor, capable of discharging at an impressive rate. I won't pretend to understand the science myself, but I've been told that it should destroy the device, and your brain along with it. Your death would be quick. However, should you survive the initial shock, the lack of a functioning implant will entirely negate your ability to breathe. If you test me, I will destroy your friends, your family, and ultimately, you.'

Winter seethed with fury. He had all his bases covered. Everything she cared about. There was too much at stake to trade curses. She had no choice but to do the job, whatever it was. Clamping a lid on her anger, she said, 'This must be one hell of a job if you've spent so much effort covering your arse. Just what do you want me to do so badly?'

'That's the spirit.' His tone had lifted, echoing louder around the darkened kitchen. 'And it's a perfect segue into the second addition I had installed in your implant. It's a small data storage device, containing an encoded message. I need you to deliver it for me.'

A perplexing assignment. 'There are easier ways to send someone a message.'

'Indeed there are. Ideally I would simply transmit it, but as it would be limited to light speed, it would take around fifty years to get to Earth.'

'*Earth?*'

'Correct, Miss Starling. A superspace-capable vessel could reach the Sol system within a matter of weeks, far quicker than any transmission, and this is a matter of some urgency. You should have no problem hitching a ride at your nearest starport and sitting in a pod until you arrive.'

'You make it sound so easy. What's the catch?'

'Catch? There is no catch. In fact I couldn't have made things easier for you. You don't even need to find the intended recipient. All you need to do is arrive in a wide orbit and your little machine will do the rest.'

'Plenty of people have implants.' She flicked her glance towards the hovering drone. 'I'm sure your machine could have fixed up one of your own people. Why me?'

'You have a reputation for getting the job done, Miss Starling. This message could save millions of lives. We have one chance to succeed. Anyone from my organisation could have motives that would undermine our only opportunity. By giving it to you and telling you nothing about the nature of the delivery, you cannot willingly deliver it into the wrong hands, and you know exactly what I can do to you if you try.'

Despairingly, she could see no way out. 'When I get back from Earth, I am going to kill you.'

'So you have accepted the mission? Marvellous! I hope we get the chance to speak again, I have enjoyed our chat. I understand that we're both rather busy for the time being, but do come back when you have the chance.' The drone whirred back into motion, preparing a needle and pressing it against the skin of Winter's arm.

'Until we meet again, Miss Starling.' The communicator clicked off.

With no way to withdraw her arm, the needle punctured her skin and the drone pumped a clear fluid into her vein. Her eyelids fluttered shut, her mind slowed and she fell once again into a deep slumber.

* * *

When Winter awoke, she was lying on her side. Everything was still dark. When her thoughts came into focus and she remembered where she was, her body leapt. She rolled off the table and landed on a toppled chair on the floor. The wood snapped loudly under her and she screamed, throwing herself away from it and pressing herself up against the wall. She looked over her shoulder, searching for any sign of the robot.

But she was alone.

She allowed her body to slump, resting her forehead beside her hand on the wall. She measured her breathing and reflected on her conversation with the drone, or rather the man who spoke through it. His identity remained a mystery, though he had dropped a few clues.

For now, she had no choice but to deliver the mystery man's message. If she tried to fight, he could destroy everything she cared about in an instant. He'd gone to a lot of trouble. He knew everything about her and he had money behind him; that droid hadn't been cheap, and it had taken some doing to set up this ambush.

She flexed her fingers, stretched her arms, then her legs. The paralysis was gone. She shuddered at the thought of it, then picked herself up and retrieved her handgun from the floor. She moved around the kitchen, relieved to be able to walk again. It was strangely reminiscent of rehab after first receiving the implant.

Her foot knocked into something that clinked as it rolled away. A bottle, and it looked intact. She grabbed it and blew off a cloud of fine dust. Wine. Twisting off the cap she took a deep glug and felt the glow of the alcohol rush through her. She wiped a drip from her chin with the back of her hand.

It was tempting to lose herself in the rest of the bottle but she had to go, to leave everything behind, and find a way to get to Earth.

Short might still be in Jova.

She put the wine back on the counter, pulled out her communicator and sent a handshake signal to his ship.

The device emitted a tone. The signal was out, awaiting a response.

She waited impatiently. After about a minute with no results, the tone wavered briefly as the telecommunications array expanded the range of the signal. That this was necessary at all wasn't a good sign.

This time the response came within seconds and Short's voice was relayed through her communicator.

'Starling!' he greeted her warmly. 'What are you still doing up at this hour? You got the payment okay, right? Eddie told me he sent it.'

'What? No, no, I got the money, Short. Listen, I'm in some really deep shit right now and I need to get off this planet as soon as I can. I need to get to Earth. Can you give me a lift?'

'Aw man, I wish I could help you out there but we've already left dock and we're behind schedule as it is. We couldn't spare the time even if we didn't have to faff around with the bloody mooring fee. There's not a lot I can do, I'm afraid.'

Winter slapped a hand to her head and began pacing through the wreckage, racking her brain for another solution.

'How come you need to get off-world so desperately? No-one's caught wind of your activities, have they?'

'No. Well yes, they know, but that's not the problem. Well, it could be the problem if I'm not quick.'

'Slow down, Starling. Take it easy.'

'I can't slow down! I need to leave right now!'

None of her other contacts would be at Jova for a while. She could try and hitch a ride with a passenger ship, but they'd be far too slow. Stowing away on a transport ship with a free crew space would be better. For freighters, time is money.

Suddenly, a thought occurred. 'What about Eddie?'

'Eddie?'

'You told me he's a hauler in part, but also takes passengers, right?'

'Yes, he–'

'You dealt with him in Port Jova. Is he still there? When does he leave?'

'He should still be there. He was meant to leave today

though, not sure when. I can get in touch and see if he'll wait for you?'

She released a breath of relief. 'Thank you, Short! I'll be in your debt. Let him know I'm on my way.' Winter made a beeline for the door and sprinted out into the cold.

'I can't make any guarantees, you know, but I'll do my best.'

'That's all I need,' she shouted as she leapt on to her vehicle. 'Let me know how you get on.'

'I will.' His tone softened. 'Stay safe, Winter.'

The connection dropped.

Skidding away from the dead house, Winter squinted against the glare of her own headlights bouncing off the road surface. The cold hit hard as she accelerated into the darkness. She had to be in time to catch Eddie and had to trust Short to pave the way for her. Banishing all thoughts of her implant and the man who could control her like a puppet any time he wanted, Winter set her sights on Port Jova, and pushed the vehicle to maximum velocity.

CHAPTER 4

The two stars battled for supremacy in the sky, but as the blue light waned, the coming of the orange sun heralded the start of a new day.

On the drive back to Jova, Winter had received a message from Short. He had managed to convince Orson to reserve her a spot on his passenger manifest, and had even managed to haggle down the price a bit, but she didn't have the time to express her gratitude. For now, she kept her eyes on the road.

The surface changed gradually, from smooth and clean to gritty and worn, as she transitioned on to the main roads on the run up to Port Jova. Bright spotlights at the gates shone down on the road for the end of the night-time shift, picking out the soldiers moving back and forth between transports. But one of the gates was dark, the rubble scattered around the crater veiled by the shadows of the night.

The drive here had taken almost two hours and every minute that she stayed on Arali, Winter feared for herself and her family. Beneath that fear, she felt bubbling anger.

The bodies had been removed, but there were still people picking through the dust to clear away the remaining debris. She detoured to keep a distance between herself and the rubble-strewn gate, patience running thin at the extra time it took before she rolled up to one of the entrances.

Winter kept her eyes forward. She brought her vehicle to a stop and one of the nearby soldiers paced towards her.

He placed his hands on the side of her vehicle and leaned

on it. He had bags under his eyes. Winter was in no mood to tolerate his sluggishness.

'What's your b–?'

'I'm getting a ride to Earth,' she interrupted, already bored of the rigmarole. 'Please hurry, I'm in a rush.'

The guard drew out his glass tablet. The holographic display blinked on and the bright lights shone into his face. He took a moment to blink away the glare, then he slowly and deliberately tapped the glowing buttons.

Winter screwed up her face and tapped her foot against the side of her seat.

'Thumbprint,' he demanded, turning the device to face her. Winter stuck her thumb out and waited for the familiar chirp.

The device turned back to its owner. He brought it in close to his face and squinted as he read the name. 'Winter … Sterling?'

'*Star*-ling. Can we move this along?'

'Are you booked on to a ship?'

'I'm … not sure. It was very last-minute.'

'Do you know the name of the vessel?'

Short had sent her the key information. She double-checked the computer on her dashboard.

'It's the … uhh … *Redemptive Veteran*. Hangar 46?'

More buttons. More waiting.

Winter didn't imagine it would take long to search for one ship in their docks, yet the guard was typing for an irritatingly long time. She could hear muttered curses from under his helmet; watched him delete his input to try again. It was almost as if some divine power were playing a cruel joke on her.

Finally, he pulled up a record. He looked over it, then appeared to nod his approval. Winter had her hands back on the wheel, ready to drive on, when the guard asked, 'Do you have any other business?'

'What?'

'Well, ma'am, you're driving a freight vehicle with no cargo, and you're getting passage to Earth, but you're not carrying any luggage.' He gestured to the empty cargo pallet behind her.

Winter stared him down. 'I've had quite enough personal intrusion tonight, soldier.' She spoke darkly. 'Would I be breaking any laws by travelling light?'

'N-no.'

'Then I'd suggest you keep your curiosity to yourself and open the bloody gate.'

The guard hesitated, then scurried over to the control panel and raised the barrier. Winter drove on through without sparing him another glance.

She had troubles enough, but already regretted her impatience. He might have arrested her for that kind of attitude and her journey would have been over before it had begun.

She was going to need people on her side and as little attention on her as possible. She could save her fury for another time, when she would have the chance to get her hands around that bastard's throat.

Intruder. Kidnapper. Blackmailer.

She steadied her breathing. It wouldn't be hard to summon this hatred again, but for now she decided it should be made to stay dormant.

The on-board computer plotted a route to the entrance to hangar 46 and Winter navigated it with a haste she could only have dreamt of yesterday. The roads were almost empty, leaving her the space and freedom to gather some speed.

She arrived at a set of large metal doors blocking her access to the docking bay. She logged into the local comms system to announce her arrival.

'Hello, Captain Orson? It's Winter Starling.'

A response crackled back promptly. 'Oh, hello there, Winter. We were beginning to wonder when you'd turn up.' The accent was undoubtedly from Earth, but it clearly belonged to a woman. 'I'm your pilot, Sam Yuki. The captain's just seeing to some of the other passengers, but I'll let him know you've arrived.'

The doors began to part, revealing the steep, dimly lit incline down towards the hangar.

'We'll see you shortly. Please enjoy the flight.' Then, with a hiss and a click, the line closed.

More than familiar with this sloping descent, Winter reached the bottom in record time and left the tunnel to enter the hangar bay.

The starship was smaller than Short's box-like craft and much easier on the eye, but still far from sleek. It consisted of one enormous engine built through the middle of the main fuselage, supported by a shock-absorbing frame. Built around the engine was the primary hull, with two small pods on the port and starboard and the cargo bay bolted on underneath.

It wasn't a new ship, that much was obvious. The paintwork looked like it hadn't had any attention in a very long time, scuffed and scratched on all of the leading edges. It looked strong, though. Reliable.

Right beneath the ship's bow, a section of the cargo bay had slid apart to provide a large entryway into the belly of the ship. Winter could hear voices from inside and as she drove up to the base of the ramp, she saw a man, by estimate in his mid-fifties. He was busy helping a younger man to carry some of his luggage through a door to the right. As Winter drew closer, the older man glanced at her. He dropped what he was doing and descended the ramp.

'You must be Winter.' His voice was deep and rough. She shook his outstretched hand and he clasped his other hand firmly over the top.

He was muscular, but his belly bulged out more than a typical soldier. His face was youthful, despite his age, though his hairline had receded easily halfway over his scalp. He bore a friendly smile, but with his large frame and military bearing it was a little more intimidating than it was probably meant to be.

'Yeah, that's me,' she replied. Her part of the journey was already over. Now she could relax a little. 'I'm just glad I got here in time.'

'Well, I'm afraid you didn't give us much notice; we're leaving in just under an hour. I'm Captain Orson. Short told me you needed to leave the planet in quite a hurry. May I ask what's so important all of a sudden?'

Winter didn't know how much of her mission brief she was allowed to discuss, but he had been kind enough to let her on to his ship. It was only fair to tell him what he was letting himself in for.

'I have to take a message to Earth. There may be lives on the line so there's really no time to waste.'

The captain looked confused, but only for an instant. 'Ah, I understand,' he said, tapping the side of his nose. 'Say no more. We'll make sure you get to Earth in plenty of time, don't worry.'

Did he understand? How could he? She barely did herself.

Best not to ask. He'd agreed to get her to Earth and in good time. That was all she needed.

'Thank you, Captain.'

He bowed his head. 'Would you like any help getting your

belongings on board?' He looked past her, towards her vehicle, and his confused expression returned. 'Where is everything?'

Winter nervously fidgeted with her implant, running her fingers over fresh scar tissue. 'I left in quite a hurry.' She drew his attention to her clothes with some small hand gestures. 'This is all I brought.'

'And that.' Orson pointed at her vehicle.

'Well, yes, it is mine, but I can hardly take it with me. It's quite a bit bigger than a suitcase, after all.'

'The rest of the passengers have brought a lot of stuff. You'd be amazed how much people will bring when they're moving planet. Some of them are taking up far more space than your little hauler and I've got plenty of room left in my hold. If that's really all you have, you can bring it with you.'

'Sure, thank you.' She had a lot of fond memories surrounding that little motor, and it could make for a nice place to seek refuge during the flight.

A smile played at her lips. That might have been the first positive thought she'd had all night.

'You can bring it on one condition.' She should have seen this coming.

'Name it.'

'Assuming your … job, doesn't take up too much of your time when we make port, how about helping me unload some of this cargo? An hour or two of labour would go a long way towards justifying a third off your flight costs.'

'Deal.' She drew out her tablet and tapped on the screen. 'How much do I owe you then?'

Orson held up his palms. 'Don't worry about it for now, you can pay when we arrive. Everyone else paid with their booking, but obviously in your case there was no time for that.'

'Yeah, sorry for the trouble.'

'No trouble at all, young miss.' He leaned in closer and lowered his voice. 'Short sold me some of the goods you brought him. They're sure to bring in a pretty penny anywhere we can find the Solar Conglomerate, which is everywhere,' he whispered with a chuckle. 'Money isn't a concern between us; we look after our own.'

This was extraordinary behaviour for someone like him. He was being far too friendly. Too willing to usher her into his inner circle. No-one who illegally exported goods should say that to one of their passengers, especially in their first conversation.

Now wasn't the time for second-guessing, especially when he was doing her a serious favour. Instead she just smiled. 'I appreciate it.'

'Don't mention it. I'll get Julian to come and get your ride stowed away. Won't take a minute.'

And just like that, Winter was left with nothing to do until the ship launched. She had too much on her mind to feel comfortable sitting idly. 'Can I help at all?'

'No, you don't need to worry about a thing. Everyone else is on board and you'll be spending the next week or so with 'em. Might as well wander round. Make some friends and a lasting impression. Or just take some time to relax. Put your feet up.' Orson smiled as he strolled away. 'I'll see you again just before launch.'

Alone again, Winter felt a bit lost. The captain probably had the right idea though. She followed the passenger Orson had been helping when she arrived and went through the door on the right of the cargo bay.

She found herself in a corridor that turned sharply to the left, deeper into the vessel. Every surface was a whitish-grey, with a darker grey stripe spanning its length. Spotlessly clean;

far cleaner than on the outside. Winter ran a hand over the stripe on the wall. Spaced along it were inset handholds lined with rubber.

In front of her was a door labelled 'SSR #2'. The captain had made no mention of off-limits areas, so she decided there was no harm in having a look. Winter knew very little about space travel, but she was here now. She figured she might as well learn a thing or two.

She wandered towards the door and pushed a small button on the wall beside it. The door slid open with a hiss.

The room wasn't particularly large and the main floor was mostly empty. Set into the walls were a multitude of metal pods, easily big enough for a human. They were open.

The bulkhead on the right was bare, with no pods built into it. In the near corner was a computer terminal worked by a young woman, her hair stark-white and tipped in a pale pink. She looked around to see Winter.

'Hi there,' the woman greeted her with a high voice, with yet another accent from Earth – another that Winter couldn't put a name to. 'You must be one of our passengers. Are you okay? Are you lost?'

'Yeah. No, I'm fine. I'm just having a look around. I'm Winter.'

'Oh, you made it! We were a little worried you'd miss us.' She swivelled her chair to face her properly, which was when Winter saw her right leg, or rather her lack thereof. There was nothing save for a stump beneath her right hip. 'My name's Hayley. I'm the SSR technician.' She took up some crutches, placed them against the floor and stood on her single foot. 'Would you like me to show you around at all?'

'Are you sure you're up to it? With your …?' Winter pointed awkwardly towards Hayley's stump. It felt wrong to ask her to give a full tour.

Hayley looked down. 'Oh, don't worry about this,' she said. 'I've been this way all my life. Trust me, I'm fully mobile.' Her smile was wide, pushing her cheeks up such that they almost hid behind the bright locks that flowed down the sides of her face. 'So, can I show you the ship?'

'I think I'm okay, mostly. Actually, do you know where I'm staying? Where my room is? Well, I suppose it would be a cabin, wouldn't it?'

Hayley chuckled. 'That's an easy one. It's right here!' She raised a crutch to point at the pods in the walls.

'What?' It was a little different to the bedroom she'd had in mind. Winter wandered over to the nearest pod and took a peek inside. It was barely a metre deep, containing nothing but a seat made of what looked like a clear jelly, shaped to fit against the far side. 'I have to sleep in there?'

'Oh sorry, I didn't realise. You've never been into space before, have you?'

Winter shook her head.

'Okay, well let me give you the basics. We're going to be accelerating for the first half of the journey and decelerating for the second half. Those are some pretty harsh forces at work. These pods are designed to keep us safe until we reach Earth.'

Winter laid a hand on the pod's surface, feeling the cold smooth metal against her fingertips. 'So it's like cryosleep?'

'In a way. You'll be unconscious, but your mind will still be active. We'll spend the time living together in a virtual environment powered by the ship's computer. That's SSR. Suspension and simulated recreation.'

Winter hadn't touched virtual reality in any form since she was a child. She hadn't cared for that level of escapism before, but now it might be just what she needed.

'When do we begin?'

'We'll need to get ourselves in there before we leave. We'll still have access to all the ship's systems, so Sam can take us out of port from inside.' Hayley went back over to her workstation. 'Not long until take-off, so it wouldn't hurt to get prepared now. We'll all go in together though, as soon as everyone's set.'

'Right. What do I need to do?'

'Well, it's pretty much just the attire. You can't go in wearing that lot. All the straps and buttons, and that gun on your leg could do you quite a bit of damage with the gel pressure. You'll need something simpler. More minimalist.'

'I don't like the sound of that.'

Hayley giggled again. 'Nothing too revealing, don't worry.' She slid open a section of the wall and leaned against it so she could put one of her crutches down. She took out a long white robe made of a light cloth and handed it to Winter. 'See, it's not too bad. Don't worry, everyone will be wearing them. Of course, you won't notice when you're in there.'

Winter held it up in front of her and examined it. Then she draped it over her shoulder and began unstrapping her handgun holster. 'Where can I get changed?'

CHAPTER 5

The ship felt about as cold as it looked now. Winter re-entered the SSR room in her thin robe, its colour matching the frost-white bulkheads. She stood with her arms folded tightly across her body, standing on the rubber padding where she could. It wasn't warm, but it was far more comfortable than the metal that froze her bare feet to the bone.

Now that all the other passengers had arrived, she felt exposed. All she wanted to do was relax but she couldn't let her guard down. They kept glancing at her as she hovered near the door.

Maybe one of them was after the message she carried.

There were six of them – three men, two women and a young boy – and eight pods lining the walls. They were dressed exactly like Winter. Some looked to be as cold as she was, too, hopping from one foot to the other in an attempt at keeping warm.

Hayley was sitting at her computer terminal once more, now also adorned in the long white cloth that ended just above her ankle.

Taking occasional paranoid glances behind her, Winter stepped towards Hayley. She raised her arms and turned. 'How do I look?'

Hayley looked her up and down. 'Cold.' She smiled. 'You won't feel it when you're in the simulation though, so try to bear it for now. I think we're about ready to boot up the system. I just need to pop to the other room and check the crew's ready. I still don't trust Julian to do it without supervision yet.'

Hayley collected her crutches and stood. She went over to the door but paused before passing through.

'Go grab a pod and take a seat,' she said. 'I'll be back in a few minutes.' Then she left.

Winter looked at the other passengers. They had huddled into a group on the far side of the room, chatting and cackling together. She made her way towards the furthest pod from the crowd.

The interior walls and floor of the pod were a dull grey plastic with small holes arranged in columns. The seat was smooth and curvaceous. It almost looked wet, like an organ pulled from some kind of huge alien beast.

Winter gripped the sides of the pod, then lifted a foot and placed a toe on the floor inside. It was cold, but not as bad as the metal deck throughout the rest of the vessel. She stepped down and brought her other leg in.

There was a faint echo in here and it smelled sterile. She padded around in her limited room, turning and preparing to sit down in the strange gelatinous blob.

Taking a deep breath, she bent her knees and lowered herself down. The seat felt sticky as it contoured to her shape, but once it settled it was quite firm. She felt its surface with her fingers and found it to be dry, like the hide of a snake. It was a peculiar substance.

She ran her hands over its surface, poking and squeezing it to see how it would react. She was so absorbed by her experimentation that she almost didn't notice the figure standing just outside her capsule.

'What's it like?' he said nervously.

He was young. Fifteen, maybe sixteen. His dark hair flopped

down over his ears and swept over slightly at the front to leave his emerald eyes visible, gazing out from the shadow of his brow. Just like everyone else he wore the plain garment. His hands fidgeted with each other.

'Not as bad as it looks. A bit weird though,' she replied. 'You want to try it?'

The boy widened his eyes, then looked from Winter to the chair. Winter pushed herself away with her legs and felt the chair release her. It returned slowly to its original squat shape.

She smiled and gestured towards the seat, hoping to ease his discomfort. He hesitated, keeping his eyes on it as though expecting it to move. Then he stepped into the pod and lowered himself into the gel. His reaction was much the same as Winter's. He bounced on it and poked at it.

'First time in space?'

The boy kept his eyes on the seat. 'My mum's from Earth so she's been up before, but not me.'

'Why are you going? Holiday? Seeing family?'

'Moving. She says Arali isn't as nice as Earth. We were going to move before but we never ...'

He trailed off. There was sadness in his voice. His gaze dropped.

'This is my first time too,' Winter said. She moved her hands to the pod's outer shell and ran her fingers over its surface, examining the craftsmanship of the machine. 'I've never thought about getting on a spaceship before, never thought about visiting Earth. I never wanted to be here in the first place.'

Out of the corner of her eye she noticed the boy stop touching the chair. He looked up at her.

'But you know, it's not all bad,' she continued. 'I'm learning new things already. I hadn't even heard of an SSR before. And

I've met some nice people too. The captain, the …' She paused, trying to recall her name, waving a hand in the vague direction of the workstation on the adjacent wall. '… the lady at the computer.'

'Hayley?'

'Hayley! That's it. Yeah, Hayley, she seems really nice.' Winter turned to look at the group of passengers, still talking and laughing in their huddle. 'And I'm sure they're all nice too.'

'Yeah. Maybe.'

Winter looked back at the boy in the pod. 'You don't think so?'

'I didn't really talk to them. They're all swapping stories about being in space. They've all done this before, so my mum loves talking to them. But I have nothing to say.' He looked down at his feet. 'That's why I came to talk to you. Everything here seemed new to you and you were avoiding all of them.'

Winter went to speak, but this time it was her who couldn't maintain eye contact. 'I don't know about *avoiding* them. I'm just not really a fan of big groups.' Looking at them individually, she knew immediately who the boy's mother was. Her hair was as dark as his, stark against the white of her gown. Her wide frame bounced as she laughed along to the anecdotes they shared. He was the spitting image of her.

'You feel lost.'

'I guess. It's not easy to feel like an individual when you're surrounded by others. Trying to get everyone to like you at once.'

'That's not what I mean.'

She looked back at the boy. His head was tilted and his piercing eyes were fixed on hers. 'You feel lost. You weren't ready for space, but you came anyway. No, not space. It's something else.'

He paused, his mouth hanging open slightly. His eyes narrowed, but never blinked. 'You're not sad to go. You're afraid to leave.'

Winter stared back at him.

'Afraid to leave, but afraid to stay,' he continued. 'Terrified that you'll regret your choice no matter the outcome. But you've made your decision and now you're scared.'

She looked at him, but there was nothing to read. Nothing etched into his face that would divulge anything about him. His anxiety and loneliness were gone. Now he was like a mirror, a reflection of the thoughts and feelings Winter had been trying to ignore. Impressive was not the word to describe his keen insight.

'How do-?'

'Hey, guys!' The door slid open Hayley entered the room. 'The crew are set up and raring to go. Are you all ready to get started?'

Some of the other passengers cheered their approval, perhaps too enthusiastically.

Winter looked back to the boy and saw him staring at Hayley with wide eyes. His fear – if that was what it was – had returned, but Winter could glean nothing more from him.

'If you sit yourselves down inside your pods, I'll get you all plugged in.' She smiled. Looking around, she caught the boy's gaze. 'This kid's ahead of the game! I'll start with him and work around to you all.'

She swung forward on her crutches. Winter moved aside to make room for her then offered to assist but was declined.

'Have you ever done anything like this before?' Hayley asked the boy.

He shook his head.

'Okay, not to worry.' Hayley propped one of her crutches up

against the wall to free a hand, reached inside and opened a small panel above the seat. Inside were four small metal boxes with suction cups. She pulled at one and it came away, trailing a thin cable that kept it wired into the wall.

Hayley held it between her fingers and showed it to the boy. 'This is an electrode with a tiny computer in it,' she said. 'I'm just going to stick a few of these to your head and they'll help you into the virtual world. Okay?'

He didn't react.

She pulled the electrode further out and affixed it to the side of her own head. 'See? No need to worry, it doesn't hurt.' She tugged at it and it came off easily. 'Will you let me put them on you?'

The boy looked at the electrode, then up at Winter who stood behind Hayley. She smiled reassuringly and gave him a small nod. He looked away, back to the device in Hayley's hand. Then he lowered his head and squeezed his eyes shut.

She moved to stick one device to each of his temples, one to the middle of his forehead, and one to the back of his neck. All the while he sat rigidly, as if anticipating a shock that never came.

'Job done! See, that wasn't so bad, was it?' Hayley gave him some room as she retreated to reclaim her discarded crutch. 'If you just hang tight for a few minutes, we'll start very soon.'

He opened his eyes slowly and began to move his head around. The weights of the electrodes wobbled up and down and the slack in the cables swung with them. He seemed apprehensive, but otherwise alright.

Hayley turned to face Winter. 'Go and get yourself a pod. I'll sort everyone out and get round to you in just a minute.' She moved on to the next pod and put down her crutches again.

Winter recognised the occupant of the next pod over as the boy's mother. While Hayley prepared herself, Winter told her, 'He's all fine now.'

'I know.' The woman hardly spared her a glance.

Winter hesitated, unsure how to respond. In the end she decided it was best just to move away. She was on a short fuse and it would be best not to make a scene.

She found another pod a few steps away. She stepped inside and sat down. From this pod she could see the boy sitting with his eyes closed. He looked more relaxed now, but she was sure he must be eager to be done with this.

Hayley made her way around the pods. As many of the others had done this before they were familiar with the process and were able to do part of the job themselves.

When she got around to Winter, she smiled, then silently reached for the electrodes.

Hayley placed one on the right temple, one on the left, and one on her forehead. Then she reached around and Winter could feel a finger probing around the base of her skull before the final electrode was pressed into place.

Hayley withdrew and gave Winter one more smile. She retrieved her crutch and hopped back towards her workstation.

Winter felt the electrode and found that it had been placed right on top of her implant. She placed her fingers where Hayley's had been and felt the edges of the neural device beneath her fingertips.

She hadn't considered the implications it would have on the SSR system, but Hayley must have noticed it and she didn't say a word. Surely it was fine.

'Alright then, everybody!' Hayley turned to face the passengers. 'You're all plugged in and I'm just about to launch the system. After a few seconds the pods will close and you'll begin to drift to sleep. Just a quick warning; when you wake up at the end of our journey, you may find yourselves feeling a bit weaker than you do now. It's a perfectly normal symptom of space flight. A little bit of exercise and you'll be back to your old selves in no time.'

There was a murmur from the passengers but no sign of any objections. Hayley wobbled as she stood up with the aid of a single crutch, then tapped a button on her screen before taking the second crutch and making her way towards the last empty pod. She took a seat, storing her crutches in a compartment on the inside.

Hatches began to lower in front of each pod. They slid into line with the openings, then clunked into place.

The seal was airtight and the metal panelling and glass window of the door were thick. The only thing Winter could hear was the sound of her own breathing echoing off the plastic walls.

Then another sound filled the chamber – a metallic hissing, coming from behind her. It stopped abruptly, then each of the holes in the walls and floor began to produce a clear, thick liquid.

It dripped and dribbled to the bottom of the pod and began to pool around Winter's feet; a sticky, viscous substance that very slowly seeped its way into every crevice. It rose rapidly, but by the time it reached her knees, she could feel her electrodes buzzing gently.

She grew light-headed. Her neck felt weak and her eyes became heavy. She allowed her head to roll back and felt her consciousness slowly leaving her body behind.

* * *

Winter felt different when she woke from her slumber. She felt lighter and well rested.

Her eyes fluttered open. She was still encased within the pod and everything on the other side of the window looked the same.

As her thoughts cleared, she became aware that the gel that had engulfed her legs was now gone. As she rubbed her head she also came to realise that there were no electrodes anywhere on her body.

She allowed the echoes of her breaths to calm her nerves. Then she jumped as the door popped out sharply and rose into the ceiling with the sound of whirring motors. She was about to pick herself up when Hayley stepped in front of her.

'Let me lend a hand,' she said, offering Winter an open palm. She took it and Hayley pulled her to her feet, then moved aside and allowed Winter to step out on to the metal deck plates. 'See? I told you you wouldn't feel the cold in here.'

Winter looked down at the floor that before had felt ice-cold, but now felt as warm as a soft carpet. Hayley turned away and Winter's attention was drawn to something that took her entirely by surprise.

Hayley had two legs.

She knew how to use them, too. She walked confidently into the centre of the room and bounced happily on the spot. Winter found herself staring at the new leg a little too intently.

Around the room were the other passengers, looking exactly as they had before. They stood in front of their respective pods, waiting for Hayley to speak up once again.

'We're up to the exciting part now! Have a look around you. We are now inside the computer. From now until the end of the line, everything you see, hear, touch, smell and taste, is entirely digital.

'Your real bodies are right where they were, protected from the stresses of space travel, encased in suspension gel. They'll be treated carefully with everything they need to keep them healthy, so don't worry. They'll be right there waiting for you when we arrive at Earth. We, on the other hand, are free to live for the next two weeks in this simulated reality.

'But that's just the start. Waiting for you right outside this door is a wondrous collection of realms, both possible and otherwise. Outside this door you can find your own personal heaven. Why don't we take a peek?' A wide grin spread from ear to ear, then she spun around and skipped towards the portal to paradise.

CHAPTER 6

Wind swept softly through the leaves of the willow tree and the branches swayed. The long blades of grass joined them in motion, fluttering in waves by the lakeside. The water was peaceful, rolling tenderly up and down the banks.

The entire scene was stained a soft orange by the bright star that lingered on the horizon. Its rays picked out the edges of the clouds that wafted past with a gorgeous luminosity, then channelled through the sky and highlighted the ripples of the water with a warm glow.

Clad in her sandy jacket and cargo trousers, Winter rested against the tree trunk. Her combat boots nestled in a patch of white flowers off to one side. The various belts and straps around her arms, legs and waist were left loose.

It felt good to be back in familiar clothes, even if they were just a close virtual approximation based on what Hayley was able to find in their database of garbs. The technician had outdone herself though, having delved into the source code for each piece of the outfit to tweak the colours and tones to almost exactly match Winter's old smuggling ensemble.

Despite the return of her favourite apparel in the simulated world, she felt out of place. Things here were remarkably serene, in stark contrast to every event these clothes had seen. Whenever she had worn this particular selection there had been high-speed driving, illegal trade deals and, very occasionally, a firefight.

This outfit was her. Designed for practicality, but Winter felt it had a pleasing appearance nonetheless. The black straps stood out against the brown fabric and added a dynamism that was otherwise lacking. It was a look that conveyed confidence and experience; something that would make her more troublesome clients think twice about double-crossing her.

She had a catalogue of other clothing options at her disposal in this simulation, guaranteed to fit her like a glove. If she had ever been invited to a place as beautiful as this on Arali, she would most likely wear something thin and light, made of Aralian fibres. Something bold and bright. Something that would let her feel the weather on her skin.

She could wear something like that now if she wanted, but something about that idea didn't feel right. She wasn't ready to distance herself from the job just yet. Maybe in a day or two she would feel differently, but everything was far too new and alien to her. Anything could still go wrong.

She had sought the serenity of this lakeside setting immediately upon her arrival. Relaxation was the first thing on her mind, but before she had been able to shake herself free of the crowd, there was something of a celebration surrounding the ship's take-off.

With everyone safely encased in their protective gel, the ship was ready to leave. Hayley had guided everyone from the SSR suite they had awoken in, to the ship's bridge, or rather the virtual reconstruction of it. She assured the passengers that it was accurate down to the last detail.

When they arrived, the crew was already there. Captain Orson stood behind a woman, who was sitting in the chair closest to the front of the vessel. On the right-hand side of the bridge, another man sat at a console.

Orson, Hayley and two others. Apparently this was a big enough crew to command a small passenger ship.

The captain couldn't have been in his pod much longer than Winter, but already he was dressed in the sharpest outfit on the deck; clean-cut, bright white and with thin accents of crimson. Orson turned to face the passengers as they entered and addressed them as a group. He briefly introduced himself, moving on to introduce the woman in the central seat as Sam Yuki. Winter recognised the name. They had spoken on the intercom when she first arrived.

Sam appeared to be older than Orson, with silver strands snaking their way through her dark hair which had been tied neatly into a bun. She didn't speak during her introduction, instead offering everyone a smile as the captain outlined her role as the ship's pilot.

He then moved on to the final crewmember, who sat off to the right-hand side. The engineer, Julian, was a skinny man, and tall even when sitting. While Hayley was the ship's technician, Julian was described as an engineer. Winter wasn't entirely sure how their jobs differed, but it didn't sound like this man had much to do with the SSR technology.

He sat remarkably still except for his eyes, which darted from one of the new passengers to the next.

When the introductions were over, the captain directed everyone's attention to the dock outside. The view through the glass was a perfect rendering of their real-world surroundings. They were flying the real ship from inside this virtual ship, the only difference being that no-one could feel its movements.

Hayley stood with the other passengers, still wearing their thin gowns having come straight from the digital replicas of their pods, and the rest of the crew manned their stations.

Winter heard a rumbling start to build beneath the deck. The docking bay outside seemed to wobble as they left the ground behind. The ship inched forward, leaving the hangar and turning into a long causeway with a light at the end.

Winter looked at Sam to see her operating a combination of touch screens, switches and levers. With the vessel holding its position aloft in the enormous tunnel, Sam reached for the biggest lever she had and eased it forward.

The lights in the walls flicked past as they gathered speed, powering down the length of the causeway. The light at the end grew larger and brighter, until soon the whole bridge was flooded with its radiance. As Winter's eyes adjusted, she saw the familiar ripples of the ocean below, stretching out far into the distance. The *Redemptive Veteran* skimmed above the waves for a short time, much to the delight of the cheering audience.

Even Winter had found she could spare a little energy to feel somewhat impressed by the spectacle.

The horizon soon fell away as the ship pitched upwards, arcing towards the sky. White clouds filled Winter's view, growing larger and larger. They thinned and faded leaving a spotless blue in their place. That didn't last long either, and soon the bright hues darkened to an inky blackness.

A few minutes passed while the captain performed something he must have rehearsed many times, explaining at some length how superspace worked, but Winter was both tired and uninterested and had allowed the entire lecture to pass right over her head.

Her attention had snapped back as everyone joined together in chanting a countdown, at the end of which Sam made a show of hitting a particular control. The space in front of them appeared to shiver. Thin ribbons of light cascaded from a single point ahead of the ship's bow, spreading out and around the sides of the wide glass canopy of the bridge. Suddenly, the space around that point tore open and the *Redemptive Veteran* forced itself though the opening.

The black of space had vanished. Everything now shone purple. There were no stars. Instead there were wispy spirals of pink and blue that danced in the distance, spinning against the dark, blurry clouds behind them.

Applause ensued and the show was brought to a conclusion. After that, Winter and everyone else had been shown how to conjure a sort of holographic menu with a simple hand gesture, which they could then use to load simulated environments from a list of hundreds of options. The instant Winter laid her eyes on something called *Lake at Sunset*, her mind was made up. She'd needed somewhere to relax for a few hours.

And now here she was, half asleep, leaning against a lonely tree at the perfect distance from the waterside.

The crunching of grass made her turn. She saw Hayley approaching, staring off towards the horizon.

She was wearing something far more casual now. A long pink floral top and some simple shorts. Her pure white hair looked longer than it had before. Straighter too.

Winter corrected her posture and made an effort to look more awake as Hayley rounded the trunk.

'Hello,' Winter said, trying to keep her eyes open.

'Hi Winter. Just wanted to check you're settling in okay.' She seemed to be making an effort to be more professional. Casual suited her better. 'How are you doing? I know you were in quite a rush to get here.'

'Not so bad now we're moving, I guess. The sooner we arrive, the better.'

'Well, don't you worry about that. We'll be clear of the Tarqis Crater in under an hour. Then we can really start to pick up some speed.'

'A crater?'

Hayley opened her mouth to speak but hesitated. She stepped closer and took a seat beside Winter.

'Before the war started, the Aralians tried to build a series of relays along the length of the superspace corridor called the Tarqis Chain. The idea was to speed up communication with Earth.'

'Right. Fifty years is a long time.'

'Fifty years in normal space, yes, but in superspace it's impossible. Light doesn't travel in straight lines here. It curves randomly and spreads apart. Things start to get blurry when they're about a kilometre away. Much further than that and you'd be lucky to see anything at all.'

This was news to Winter. She had been taught in school how the original Pioneers had spent years carving a safe path through superspace as it would destroy anything that strayed into its natural, untamed expanse. That was enough to convince her that the laws of physics worked differently here, but if she had ever been taught that light travelled in anything other than straight lines, she had long since forgotten.

'I get it,' Winter replied. 'The relays would catch the signals before they could curve too much, then boost them on to the next one.'

'Exactly. Without those relays, raw data could never reach the other end of the corridor. But the war broke out just as the first few relays were being installed. The Conglomerate destroyed them, not realising the explosions would damage superspace.'

'And that made this crater?'

Hayley nodded. 'The curvature of light is even more pronounced here and it's a bit of a rough ride, too. It's not dangerous or anything, but it's best not to go too fast until we're out the other side.'

Her mission made a little more sense now. Without something like the Tarqis Chain to transmit messages, everything would have to be delivered in person. Even if the relays did exist, she doubted her mysterious contact would want to make use of such a public channel.

Winter looked back to the sunset as it lingered on the horizon.

'In any case, you don't need to worry about anything. We'll be there before you know it,' Hayley said. 'In the meantime, just relax. You've certainly picked a good spot for it. That's exactly why I made this place.'

'You did what?' Winter's jaw dropped as she surveyed the landscape in awe. The way the hills rolled out into the distance, the spread of the trees and flowers, the beautiful irregularity of the lake. It was a perfection that only nature could attain, or so she had imagined.

'You can purchase all sorts of environments and install them on to the SSR system, but building them for yourself adds a personal touch that you just can't buy.' She looked down and brushed her fingers through the blades of grass.

After a short silence, Hayley turned to face Winter. 'I don't mean to pry, but how come you're in such a rush? Orson said he booked you on at the last minute because he owed someone a favour.'

Winter tensed up. The relaxation she'd been cultivating abandoned her.

'You don't have to tell me.'

Winter forced herself to relax. She had to say something. 'I have to take a message to Earth.'

Hayley looked a little confused. 'That's it? Must be important.'

'So I'm told.'

Hayley's face screwed up. 'You mean you don't know what it is?'

'Not exactly. It's stored in my–' Winter suddenly realised she hadn't mentioned her implant. She moved her hand to the back of her neck to fidget with it. Only this time it wasn't there.

'Your implant? I noticed it while I was putting your electrodes on. Some kind of spinal modification?'

Winter remembered the look Hayley had given her while they were preparing for the SSR. She had definitely found it.

'I broke my neck on a job a few years ago. The implant bridges the gaps in the nervous system and lets me carry on living.'

'Really?' Hayley exclaimed, a little more awe in her voice than concern.

Winter cast her mind back and remembered the discussion. Then the argument. The fight. The defeat.

'Misunderstanding with a customer.'

'Ouch.' Somehow Hayley's eyes found a way to widen further.

'Yeah. No kidding.'

In an instant, the world changed. The birds and the wind fell silent. The ripples in the lake and the leaves in the trees froze in place. Every element of the world ground to a halt.

Then the alarms blared.

'What?' Hayley sat upright, her gaze darting about in all directions. She leapt to her feet. 'Oh no! No, no, surely not!'

Winter's eyes darted around trying in vain to understand what was happening. 'Hayley, what is it?'

'I have to get to the bridge. Now!'

'You have to tell me what's going on!'

'Winter–'

'Tell me!'

'I don't know, Winter! I don't know, but we haven't had a red alert on this ship before. I have to get to the bridge!'

With a flick of her fingers, Hayley summoned a computer interface that appeared in front of her. She poked at the virtual buttons then vanished into the air.

Winter slumped lower, dropped her head into her hands and screamed.

Everything had been going so well.

CHAPTER 7

Gunfire filled the air. Enemies surrounded the encampment. Ammo supplies dwindled. Magazines ran empty.

It was good to be back.

Orson kept his head down as he moved along the trench, rifle in hand. He retrieved a handful of spare magazines from a fallen soldier, then took a defensive position, hoping to complete the task his dead comrade had left unfinished.

He rested his weapon atop the trench wall, steadying his aim as he stared down the sights.

Three of them, behind cover. He'd seen them run in. Now he could make out two helmets over the terrain. Enough to see where they were, but not enough to take the shot.

They weren't shooting, so they wouldn't stay for long. They'd move soon.

Orson aimed a couple of metres to the left of their refuge and waited.

A blur of motion. He squeezed the trigger.

The gun belched fire. He quickly recovered from the recoil and watched one of the soldiers stumble forward and another buckle at the knees, both collapsing to the ground. The third runner made it safely behind another obstruction.

Orson cursed, then shifted his attention to another group moving up on the right. He could just about discern a leg poking out from behind cover.

In a practiced motion, Orson switched the firing mode to single shot, then lined up the enemy up in his sights. The target wasn't moving. An easy shot.

Orson ducked at the sound of a bullet whizzing past his head. He heard a thud and a yelp. He brought his aim around to the left in time to see an enemy soldier flop into the mud trying to claw his way towards his fallen gun, snivelling pitifully as his fingers raked through the sodden earth.

Orson looked to see where the shot had come from. He lowered his gun when he saw Sam crouched several metres down the trench in the uniform of the Solar Conglomerate.

She scurried towards him. 'Always pay attention to your surroundings, Captain,' she said, echoing one of the first lessons he had taught her.

'I always try to,' Orson replied, turning back to the wounded soldier and firing off a round to end his struggling. 'I thought we had people defending the south?'

'I turned them off. Where's the challenge if we always have people covering our flanks?' Sam rested her weapon on the trench wall and looked out over the battlefield.

'I'm not here for a challenge. I'm here for a bit of escapism.' He watched as Sam executed a pair of advancing soldiers. He decided to keep his eyes on the trench, keen not to be outflanked again.

'You're here to relive the war, Orson. Are you telling me the war wasn't challenging?'

'Of course not.'

'Then I don't see the problem.'

Orson fired a wild shot at a motion at the end of the trench, but he quickly held his fire. It was an arm, waving at him frantically from around the bend.

He waited and watched. The arm retracted and a man moved into view. He ran towards Orson, one hand firmly clasped over his helmet. In the other he held a flagpole.

'Stand down, Lieutenant,' the man ordered. 'We're overrun. I'm calling a ceasefire.'

He stood up tall, waving the white flag over his head.

Orson aimed his rifle up. The traitor's skull exploded and his helmet flew off into the battlefield. His body dropped into the mud with a splat. Orson turned to Sam with a frown. She looked back at him, her mouth agape.

'Was that another one of your challenges?' Orson asked.

'I thought a bit of dissent in the ranks would mix things up a bit, but … Is that how you handled it in the war?'

'Believe what you like,' Orson said, returning his attention to the trench.

'That's pretty dark.'

'You have no idea.'

Sam aimed back out into the approach and opened fire again. 'So you had no tolerance for cowardice?'

'Cowardice and treason are the same thing. You know what the punishment for treason is?'

He fired a few more rounds, bringing down three more Aralians.

'I'm sure I can guess,' Sam responded.

'Disloyalty is a plague. Best to quell it before it spreads.'

'Did you have to … "quell" often?'

'Thankfully not. Once or twice, that was all. Most of my brothers and sisters in arms were as faithful as I could have hoped.' Orson sighed. 'I would have died for them, given the chance.'

He couldn't feel the pain in his leg in this simulation. It was almost enough to convince him he could fight again, but he had to remind himself this wasn't real. He had to support the Conglomerate in a different way. His own way.

His thoughts moved to the smuggler he had welcomed on board and a smile formed on his blood-spattered face. He was finally useful again.

'What do you think of our passengers?' he asked over his shoulder.

'Haven't really spoken to them yet. Same as ever though, I guess. They're just people.'

'Are they?'

Sam hesitated. 'Like I said, I wouldn't know.'

Confident that no-one else was approaching along the trench and far more interested in the conversation, Orson joined Sam in bringing down the soldiers advancing from the west.

'Ah, come on, Sam. What about Winter? Are you telling me you haven't even thought about that?'

She shrugged. 'Aren't we just doing Short a favour?'

'You must have realised it's more than that.' He paused to fire a shot at an advancing Aralian. 'Short said she was in trouble and needed an urgent ride to Earth.'

'She's a smuggler, Captain. They're always getting into trouble. That's what they do.'

'Then why don't we get more jobs like this?'

Sam seemed to ignore the question and swapped out her ammo magazine, which reminded Orson to do the same.

'You know what she told me when she came on board?'

Sam refused to take her eyes off the fight. 'What did she say?' she asked.

Orson turned away from the fight entirely to look at Sam. 'That she was carrying a message,' he told her. 'A highly confidential message.'

Sam's left hand flashed through the air and caught a grenade that had been tossed towards them. She held it up in front of Orson.

'Did you spot this?' She threw it back out and it detonated in the air. 'This is the least interested you've been in this simulation in ages.'

'Maybe that's because I know it isn't real.'

With a swipe of his fingers, a virtual interface appeared between them. He pressed a control and the action that surrounded them froze. The soldiers stopped moving and bullets hung in the air.

Sam lowered her gun and turned to face him properly.

'You're right. I'm here to relive the war, but that's just because it was the only time I ever knew I was making a difference. But now I've been given the chance to be useful again.'

Sam leaned against the trench wall. 'Go on, then. What's with this message she told you about?'

Orson smiled and stood opposite her. 'She told me very little, but she did say it could save lives. Aside from that, it's confidential.'

Sam furrowed her brow. 'That's not much to go on. Still not sure why you're so excited.'

'It's exciting exactly because of how little she can say. Sensitive information like the kind she's carrying can only be for the Solar Conglomerate. We're delivering military intelligence, Sam!'

'All due respect, but you're making huge assumptions. How can you know she's not working with the Aralian Pioneers, hm?'

Orson shrugged. 'She's a smuggler. As far as the Pioneers are concerned, she's a walking middle finger.'

'Then why wouldn't she just tell you what it is? She must know you fought for the Conglomerate.'

'I'm not a soldier anymore, Sam. I have no right to that kind of information. Besides, she's doing this all unofficially. No uniform, no military escort. They've gone through a lot of trouble to keep this a secret, so it's sure to be something big.'

'So much effort to keep it secret and yet you've worked it all out already?' Sam said, tapping her foot in the mud. 'Sounds like they didn't exactly cover all their bases.'

He shrugged again. 'Not my fault she came to me.'

Sam lowered her gaze and shook her head.

She wasn't convinced. Not that she needed to be. If anything, it meant that the cover was working as intended. Orson found some comfort in her disbelief.

'As long as you've got something to believe in, Captain, I won't try and take that away from you. Just try not to be too disappointed if it doesn't turn out quite the way you expect.'

'I just want to do my bit. Is that too much to ask for?'

'Of course not.'

'Well then.' Orson stood up straight, readied his rifle once more and looked out at the horde of Aralians, frozen in their advance. 'Shall we get back to work?'

'Only if you're going to pull your weight this time. I can't keep saving your life, you know.'

Orson smirked, then resumed the simulation.

* * *

Arali's simulated blue sun shone overhead and the now silent battleground glowed in its cool radiance. Starlight shimmered in the craters filled with water and blood.

Orson appreciated the stillness, perched atop a low wall. He never used to have any fondness for the Blue Season of Arali. It made the nights a little too bright for his liking. A pale moon in the sky was enough for him.

Yet his service on the frontlines, and subsequently his time spent in this simulation, had given it a meaning for him. That glowing blue star was his reward for a job well done.

Sam trudged up behind him and rounded the wall. She dropped her gun into the dirt, then pulled herself up next to the captain.

'Not exactly a record time today.'

Orson cast her a sideways glance. 'You think those extra challenges of yours might have had something to do with it?'

'Blame me if you want,' Sam said. 'I think it's fair to say you were a little distracted.'

'Just keeping an eye on your performance, that's all,' Orson said, but thoughts had been on Winter and her message the entire time. 'You've improved a lot over the last few months. I'm impressed.'

'Maybe, but it'll still be a while before I'm ready to take you on.'

'Nonsense. It may seem that way in here, but just remember this isn't the real me. Out in the real world, who knows? You might just have the edge.'

Sam smiled at him. 'Well, I guess we'll have to spar some time, won't we?'

'Alright,' he agreed. 'When we get to Earth and clear out the hold, I'll go a few rounds with you. On one condition.'

'What's that?'

'Go easy on my leg, won't you? I'm not sure how many more times I can get it stitched back together.'

Sam chuckled.

They sat in silence for a time, looking out over dozens of Aralian corpses lying in the dirt. Life seemed so cheap in war, especially virtual war like this when an entire army can be generated and rejuvenated on a whim.

'You really think Winter's going to save lives with that message of hers?' Sam asked, looking out over the carnage. 'You think she'll save many?'

Orson shrugged. 'I couldn't say for sure, but if it's as important as it seems, it could finally start bringing an end to the war. I suppose you could call that saving lives, but there will always be more death before the end. Of that, at least, you can be certain.'

'War will take lives anyway, that's what it's for,' she said. 'I wonder if any end could be worse than letting it continue.'

'Try not to confuse cause and effect.' He gestured to the battlefield before them. The bodies and the blood. 'If you ask me, this will always be better than victory for the wrong side. Conflict just means the future isn't set in stone. Means there's hope.'

'Is that what you see when you look out there? Hope?'

'I see progress, of a sort. You just have to learn to look past its grizzly face and see the good that will come of this.'

'And who's to determine what's good and what's bad?'

'The ones who win.'

They turned and looked at each other.

'That's us, Sam,' he said. 'That's us, if we keep doing what we believe in.' Her gaze shied away from him, but he kept his eyes fixed on her.

'You keep on leading the way, Captain, and I'll follow as far as I can.'

Orson smiled. 'I believe you will.'

Silence fell once more. Orson continued to look out over the landscape, a sense of pride and accomplishment simmering inside him.

Sam instead stared at the mud beneath her feet, soaked by the blood of her enemies that glistened blue in the pale starlight.

A blast of blaring sound shocked their spines upright. The soft blue that had coated the scene flashed with deep red, an alarm echoing through the environment with each pulse of light.

'A red alert!' Orson exclaimed, pushing himself off the wall. 'So soon after the transition to superspace. You think Winter might have been followed?'

'I'd doubt it.' There was a look of scepticism on her face, though it was mixed with an undeniable apprehension.

'This had better not be Julian's fault. If this is just his latest cry for attention I'm going to strangle him.'

'We won't know if we don't get to the bridge,' Sam said, summoning her interface with a flick of her fingers and tapping at the controls. Orson did the same.

A swift gust of wind blew past them and the battlefield faded away.

CHAPTER 8

The ship's central tunnel was dark and loud. Deep vibrations, generated by the powerful forces of the vessel's propulsion drives, echoed off the grates that covered the dark metal bulkheads. Every surface was hard and cold to the touch. The air tasted of oil and steel.

She moved out carefully, keeping a steady grip on the handholds to arrest her motion. She braced her feet against the wall, let go with her hands and kicked hard, launching herself down the length of the corridor like a bullet down the barrel of a sniper rifle.

It was common to add gravity to one's simulated spacecraft, but there would be no gravity on her ship while it was in flight. She found that the need to move in such a deliberate and considered way forced everyone to keep a degree of focus at all times.

She flew in a practised trajectory down the length of the vessel, then grabbed the handles on either side of the doorway at the far end. Her muscular arms quickly suppressed her momentum enough that she could punch a button on the door.

It slid open and the flight deck came into view. A small crew was buckled into seats around a shared panel that curved around the base of the canopy glass. All she could see of each of them was a mess of hair, drifting and waving around in zero-gravity like seaweed. One of them turned to face her.

'Gram, we're coming up on the target now.'

Their job was off to a good start. They'd been in superspace for less than a day by the time their target had shown up. They had kept their distance, hiding in the safety of the Tarqis Crater. But now that the target had left the region and moved into the cavernous transit tunnel, they moved in and stalked the other vessel, slowly and silently drawing nearer.

Both ships were still accelerating, so SSR was necessary for this stage of the operation, but it wouldn't be long until they could stretch their real legs again.

Gram looked out into the dark depths of superspace. Nestled amongst the cloudy wisps of colourful gases was a tiny white speck.

'How far?'

'Five kilometres and closing.'

'ETA?'

'We're matching our acceleration with theirs now, so we'll ease up right alongside them in about fifteen minutes. We'll be within communications range in three.'

Gram smirked. Calling it communications almost made it sound legitimate.

She turned to the SSR technician to her left. 'How's our client?'

'Paul is happily traipsing his way through some god-awful jungle simulation,' he replied. 'I honestly thought no-one would ever touch it, but he's been in there for ages.'

'Has anyone told him our progress?'

'I didn't want to interrupt him. He's having such a nice time, covered in snakes and parasitic wasps and shit. Figured I'd leave him to enjoy what little time he has left in the sim. Let him carry on doing whatever gets him there.'

Fair enough. For Paul, this would be the most enjoyable part of the job. Besides, it kept him off the crew's collective nerves for a little longer while they carried out the intricate procedure that lay ahead of them.

'Good call. Just give him some warning before we turn it off. I don't want to piss him off again. I've barely recovered since last time.'

The technician smiled, then turned back to his computer.

The speck in the distance gradually approached, its fuzzy, indistinct shape resolving into a spacefaring vessel. It was an ugly thing – little more than an engine with a cargo bay slapped on underneath. It could probably achieve some decent speeds, but it wouldn't be winning any races.

Whereas Gram's ship, the *Shameless Renegade*, had been built from the ground up to compete with military interceptors. The habitable area was sandwiched between two enormous engines, each one with a shock-absorbing frame around it to prevent them from shaking the ship apart. Together, they could clear the superspace corridor in under a week, though they were rarely used to their full potential.

After a few minutes of watching and waiting, the engineer announced that they were in range.

'Light curvature has reduced to within tolerance. We should be able to get a solid connection.'

'Well then, do it,' Gram returned. 'Tell me when you're in.'

The engineer started typing commands into his workstation. He paused after each one, but as they approached their target the waits became shorter until there was scarcely a moment that he wasn't occupied.

Everything seemed to be going smoothly for a time, but it wasn't long before his screen began to flash red with almost every input.

Gram watched in anticipation. She knew from past experience that each flash was a security alert. The other ship was fighting back and with each alert, a message would be sent to their system administrator. By now, any crew even half-awake would have detected some kind of intrusion and would be deploying countermeasures.

Watching a digital battle from the sidelines, and having no idea who was winning, made Gram uncomfortable. She found it better to divert her attention and trust in her crew.

'Well, once again I'll leave this part to the nerds.' She turned to the SSR tech again. 'Where's this jungle simulation of yours? I'll go and have a word with our client.'

'Alright, but don't blame me when you hate every second of it and don't you dare say I didn't warn you!' He brought up a list of settings on his console and began searching for Paul's location. 'You're the one who keeps accepting jobs from the weirdos who dig safaris and all that crap.' He hit a few more controls and a floating interface appeared before Gram, inviting her to visit the rainforest.

'Quit your bitching. I can handle a few flies.' She turned from her crew and pressed her hand against the virtual display. In an instant, the world and people around her fell away into a deep black void, leaving her floating alone. Then, rising from the abyss, was an entirely new world. The blackness warmed up into a dazzling blue with smatterings of white clouds. Grass and thick foliage flew up to meet her. With it came the sounds of wind, rustling leaves and the cries of countless different creatures. Shadows large and small darted between the boughs above her head and swarms of insects flitted around in the damp dirt and moss.

Gram's stomach lurched as she felt the sudden pull of gravity. Her legs kicked out as she fell to the ground.

She looked down to find her boots submerged in mud up to the ankle. She yanked one leg out and gave it a shake, hoping to flick some of the thick muck away, but to no avail. It wouldn't have mattered anyway, she thought, as she plunged her foot back into the mud and began trudging through the undergrowth, following what looked to be another trail of footprints, leading deeper into the rainforest.

She was harassed as she travelled, by creatures small and numerous. Colourful insects buzzed around her, despite her tireless attempts to swat them away. Why someone like Paul – anyone, in fact – would consider this to be a form of relaxation, she could only imagine.

Her musings were cut short as the trees thinned out and she nearly stumbled over a fern into a small clearing. A holographic interface hovered in the air in front of a man in a camouflaged coat. Scattered on the ground around him were a variety of containers and instruments.

'I'm going to need to have a word with your technician, Captain,' Paul said, his back to Gram. He continued working with his interface without sparing her a glance.

'Not a captain, Mr. Narn. Just an employer.' It was a good thing she was being paid to put up with this man. She'd started pub brawls after less trouble than he'd given her. Still, she had to play her part. 'Is there a problem?'

This time, he turned to look at her, his face lined with irritation. 'This simulation is extraordinarily inaccurate. This is supposed to be a recreation of Earth's Amazon rainforest, but instead I feel like I've been cast into some kind of fantasy land.'

It would have convinced Gram. At the very least, she would expect a rainforest to be as disgusting as this simulation was proving to be. 'Our technician hasn't built any of these environments. They have all been bought from third-party developers.'

'Then in that case I'd like to know who the developer is. Either this has been designed by a moron, or someone is playing a pathetic joke.'

'I'll talk to the technician. What's wrong with it anyway?' She stepped further into the clearing and had a much more thorough look around.

Paul grabbed his interface and swung it around to show her. 'I've made a list,' he said. 'I'm making a note of everything that needs amending. Suffice it to say, it's exhausting. I've been examining the wildlife specifically. I've caught and analysed a variety of creatures and none of them are a match with the ones in my textbooks.' He pointed to a pile of papers he left lying in the dirt by his tools.

'How can you be sure the books aren't the problem?'

'If I'm honest, I'm sure they're wrong by some measure as well.' He took a step over to his collection of captured bugs and plucked a jar out of the mud. 'But I can be fairly sure that nowhere on Earth can you find these!'

He held the jar up and inside was a winged humanoid creature rather like a pixie, only a few inches in height. Gram stifled a chuckle, agreeing for once with Paul. Someone was probably taking him for a fool. 'As I said, I'll talk with the technician.'

'See that you do. In any case, you came to see me about something?'

'Yes, I did. We're approaching the target. It shouldn't be long now until my engineer has disabled them. The pilot will then bring us in closer and we can board. The ship should be yours in a matter of hours.'

'That's good news, Captain.' Paul's face remained unmoved. He didn't seem to realise how rare it was for a job like this to be performed so quickly.

'Call me Gram.'

'I wonder if the simulations on their system will be any good.'

Gram ignored the passive criticism. 'I hope you understand that it's not truly your ship until every term of our contract has been fulfilled. Namely, the transfer of any and all of their occupants and valuable cargo to me. You're only getting the ship.'

'I know.'

'And I need your payment in full once the job is done. I'm not letting you slink away without coughing up a penny.'

'I know!'

'Just making sure. We're going through a lot of trouble for you. I hope you appreciate what this kind of service is worth.'

'Are you done? I'm paying you good money for this job, which you so readily described as a milk run back on Arali,' he scoffed. 'You're getting the better end of this deal, Gram.'

'This deal is a process. So far, you'll find we're delivering. Until you do the same, I'm calling the shots.'

Paul's glare began to falter, then he gave in and half-turned back to his equipment on the ground. 'What do you need me to do?'

'We'll be coming out of SSR soon, so you won't have to put up with our half-arsed simulations anymore. When that happens, I just want you to keep out of our way. The crew will be moving stuff from ship to ship for a good few hours. While that's happening, just lock yourself away somewhere, okay? Don't offer to help, don't talk to anyone and don't touch anything. Just have fun floating in zero gravity. Breathe occasionally, if you have to. We'll let you know when you can come out. Then you can sit on your brand new spaceship and play around in your own jungles. How about that?'

Paul stared back at her before responding. 'Whatever you say, *Captain*.'

Gram recognised his attempt to reclaim some lost ground, but she refused to take the bait. Instead she just watched as he squelched back through the mud and swatted at some flying insects. He took a seat on a jacket he'd laid down and picked up the jar with the pixie in it again. He stared at it, shaking his head in despair.

'I'm heading back to the bridge. We'll let you know when we're about to shut the system down. It'll only be a few minutes.'

He didn't react.

Gram summoned her interface and prepared to leave the rainforest. She glanced back up at Paul. She rolled her eyes, then punched the button and was whisked away to the flight deck on the *Shameless Renegade*. Gravity faded away and her feet left the ground.

She adjusted herself to face out into space and found herself in good time, watching as the ventral hull of their target gradually slipped by underneath them. She smiled at another job going exactly the way she had planned.

'What did I miss?'

'Well, Gram,' came the hesitant reply from the engineer as he turned slowly in his chair to face her, 'I kind of have good news, bad news, and … good news again.'

The smile dropped from her face. 'What did I miss?' she asked again, more insistent this time.

'Well, it's all fine for the most part. They're not accelerating anymore, so we can dock and board like normal. I have total control of their course and speed, too. That's the good news.'

'Right.' Gram waited for the rest, but it didn't seem to be forthcoming. 'And the bad news?'

'They've shut us out of their SSR system entirely and locked themselves inside it. There's no way to get them out without killing them.'

Gram would have slammed her fist against a wall, if only it were that simple in zero-gravity. Instead, she had to settle for loud cursing.

The payment Paul had agreed to give them wasn't even close to the sum he'd need to buy his own starship. His fee covered the job. The bulk of the profit would be made by taking the crew and passengers from the ship and selling them off as slaves on the black market. If they had managed to seal themselves in their pods, with their minds still in the computer, removing them would mean killing them. Dead bodies make bad servants. One slight hiccup would cost them thousands.

The engineer swallowed deeply, glancing back at his display. 'I did say there was more good news, though.'

Gram looked up, expecting to hear of some solution to the issue at hand. A sudden clunk reverberated through the ship and the compartment shook slightly around the bridge crew.

'We have successfully docked,' he said, his voice wavering. 'All aboard the *Redemptive Veteran*!'

CHAPTER 9

When Winter left the lakeside, the only things that didn't vanish into darkness were the flashing red alert light and the ringing noise that accompanied it.

The flight deck materialised around her, along with all four of the ship's crew. Hayley sat on the left, Julian on the right and Sam at the front. Captain Orson stood leaning over Julian's shoulder.

'What's going on?' Winter asked, her eyes flitting around the room.

Julian spared her a brief glance. 'Oh, for god's sake, who let her in?'

'Not now, Winter!' the captain barked. 'Hayley, lock the bridge. Don't let anyone else in.'

'On it, Captain.'

The tension in the air was almost tangible. Winter stood back and left them to their jobs.

'Just focus, Julian,' Orson said, a bit too loudly.

'They're breaking through defence after defence. How are they doing it so quickly?'

'Just focus,' the captain repeated. 'Do whatever you have to do. Stop them getting any further.'

'You know what would help me focus? Somebody turn off that bloody alarm!'

'Alarm controls are at your station, Julian,' Hayley called.

'This is your simulation, can't you find some way to do it? I'm pretty busy right now!'

'Shut up!' Orson yelled. 'If you don't stop your bickering we're all going to pay the price.'

The crew fell silent. Everyone concentrated on their workstations, panic etched into their faces. Winter bit her tongue. She desperately wanted more information but now was not the time to ask.

'Okay, okay.' Julian forced himself to calm down a little. 'Hayley, I'm giving you access to the main systems. I need you to look for any kind of unauthorised software that could be transmitting our security data.'

'How the hell do you want me to–'

'I don't care, Hayley! All I know is that they have access to information they shouldn't, and that needs to stop right now. Get searching. I'll keep trying to slow them down. Fat lot of good that's doing, anyway. I'll probably only be able to buy us a minute or two. I might as well just get down on my knees and beg them to stop.'

'You're doing fine,' the captain said as he paced uneasily around the small open area in the middle of the cockpit. Julian huffed in response and continued wildly hammering at the controls on his console.

Winter could just about make out clusters of code scrawled across Julian's display, alongside diagrams, like trees made of blocks and wires. Angry red lights bled from the tops of the diagrams and oozed their way down. Occasionally a flicker of triumph would pass over Julian's face as a handful of green indicators flashed up, but were promptly surrounded and engulfed by the advancing wave of red. Before long, the first of the trees was consumed by the crimson tide. Then it blinked and vanished from the screen.

'The unidentified vessel has closed to two kilometres,' Sam reported.

'God damn it!' Julian cursed, the red patches on his screen growing with increasing speed.

'There must be some way to shake them off, Sam,' Orson pleaded. 'Just buy us a little more time.'

'Superspace corridors aren't that wide, sir,' she said, 'and we are travelling at extremely high speed. If we turn even a fraction of a degree too much in any direction, we'll fly straight out of the safe zone and be torn apart.'

'Just give me whatever you can manage.'

'Then you're going to have to settle for nothing. I don't have many options, sir, and each one will either have no effect, or it will kill us.'

Orson continued to pace, a hand on his chin. 'What about decelerating?'

'What would that do?'

'If we slow down, they'll fly right past us. It could give us a little more distance, at least.'

'I think you overestimate this ship, Captain. The rate of deceleration would be far too slow. We'd just let them get closer.'

'It might just give them something else to think about for a moment. Give them something to react to.'

She swivelled around to face her captain. 'That ship is an interceptor. They caught us because they can accelerate a lot faster than we can, forwards and back.'

'We're out of options, Sam. Are you able to tell me conclusively that there is no chance that it could work?'

'Well … no, but–'

'Then do it.'

Sam clapped a hand to her forehead and dug her fingers into her scalp. She clenched her jaw and turned back to her controls.

She reached towards the throttle and eased it down, slowly at first, then she slammed it all the way back. Sam stared at her display, then threw the throttle forward again. She rattled it back and forward furiously before spinning in her chair to face the engineer.

'Julian, what have you done to my engines?'

'*Your* engines?'

'Answer me!'

'I haven't touched *my* fucking engines. Don't know if you've been paying any attention at all, Sam, but I'm trying to reprogram my entire security framework!'

'Well, you've obviously done something. I have no velocity control.'

'Good! That plan was rubbish anyway.'

Sam turned to the front once more, then threw her arms up in frustration. 'I've lost sensors now, too. I have no idea how far away they are.'

'What's going on, Julian?' Orson stepped in.

The engineer slammed his fist into his console. 'Do I have to do everything on this ship?' he bellowed. 'Fine, I'll get you your bloody sensors!'

He discarded the code and diagrams he had been working on and tried to open something else, but the computer had other ideas. A red message covered his display. He cursed and hammered at his controls, but the message remained.

'Oh shit! Hayley, have you found that software yet?'

'I think … yes.'

'Kill it! Kill it now!'

The captain interrupted again. 'What's going on?'

'The intruder's through security. They're locking us out of every single system. We need to stop them before they get to us.'

'What do you mean "us"?'

'Hayley!' Julian rushed her.

'Done!' she reported.

'Good, now cut the interface between the main computer and the SSR pods!'

'Are you mad?'

'Just do it!'

One by one, the workstations around the flight deck began to shut down. Everything died. The sound of the engine shaking through the bulkheads faded into nothing. Even the red alert stopped, leaving the bridge in an eerie silence.

Julian leaned back in his chair with his eyes closed, breathing deeply, but he soon gave up and punched his console again with an angry cry.

Winter looked around. Hayley was biting her knuckles, staring at her offline workstation, her eyes red. Julian sat seething in anger. Sam buried her face in her hands. Orson stood still, his gaze dancing around the room before settling on Julian.

'What did you do?' he demanded.

'Every system on the ship was compromised,' Julian said, turning to face Orson. 'The only thing I'd managed to keep them away from was the simulator. Hayley cut the link between us and the main computer, so they can't reach us. We're safe, for now.'

'They may not be able to reach us, but we can't reach out there either,' Hayley interjected. 'We have no control over the ship anymore. Navigation, power management, everything. It's gone.'

'Can someone tell me what's going on now?' Winter asked. Everyone seemed to have forgotten that she was in the room. Julian looked towards her, then rolled his eyes and turned away. Orson sighed and continued to pace. Sam remained unmoved.

'We were approached by another ship,' Hayley said softly. 'They broke into our computer and now have full control of the *Veteran*.'

'I gathered that. Who are they?'

'Raiders,' Julian said, continuing to stare at his inactive workstation. 'Anyone else would have either opened communications or opened fire. Raiders want to board the ship and take all the valuable crap they can find. Maybe even the ship itself.'

'And you've locked us in this infernal machine?' Orson yelled. 'What the hell are we meant to do from in here?'

Julian spun to face him. 'Woah now, old man–'

'*Captain!*' Orson corrected him at the top of his lungs.

'Okay, Captain,' Julian began again, growling through gritted teeth. 'Let's get one thing perfectly clear: we are not locked in this simulation. All we've done is divorce ourselves from the ship. It just means the raiders can't take us out of our pods. We still have full control. We can still shut it down whenever we like.'

'Then shut it down now!'

'What?' Julian sounded baffled by the suggestion.

'I won't be caught defenceless with a raiding party crawling around inside my ship. We're getting out to take the fight to them!'

'Listen, if we leave our pods now, we'll be splashed across the back wall. We're still accelerating and we're not going to stop accelerating until they decide it's time to board. When they do, they'll do it with body armour and machine guns. We, on the other hand, will be outnumbered, unarmed and practically naked. If we shut down the simulation now, we surrender ourselves to them.'

'I will never surrender to them.'

'Somehow I knew you'd say that, Captain Pride.'

Sam finally lifted her head and swung her chair around. 'What's to stop them just shooting us? I mean, the pods are tough but they're hardly bulletproof.'

'As I said, raiders are going to look for the valuables. We've got a crew of four on this ship and a healthy handful of passengers. If they have any brains at all, they'll want to let us all live so they can sell us as slaves. That's where the real profit is.'

There was a sharp intake of breath from almost everyone on the bridge. Hayley returned to staring at the wall, tears welling in the corners of her eyes. Orson began to pace again, a hand caressing the bald patch on the top of his head.

'You told me to do whatever I had to do,' Julian said. 'What was I supposed to do?'

There were no suggestions. The deck remained silent but for the sound of Orson's footsteps as he walked up and down the limited length of the floor.

'I'm going to have to tell the passengers, aren't I?' he asked.

Winter didn't know where to look or what to say. Orson summoned his interface and scrolled through his list of buttons and submenus. 'I'll do it later,' he said. 'I need a drink.' With that, he touched a control and dissolved into the air.

Winter backed up against the nearest bulkhead and sank to the floor. She hugged her knees in and pushed her face into them. But she refused to cry.

She had done what she'd had to do. She'd found a ship and was on her way to Earth. Her part was done. Didn't she deserve a break?

She had been sure it was all over. All she had to do was wait a couple of weeks and her job was done. Now though, whether she would even make it to Earth was debatable at best, and if she did it would probably be as a product for auction. No way she'd be delivering any messages in that state.

Even if she did somehow manage to complete her task, who would be able to go back to Arali and report the accomplishment of the mission in her stead? Who would free her parents? Who would get her friends off the hook? Who would disarm the bomb on the back of her neck?

She instinctively reached for it to find it absent, just as before. When she could feel it, it was almost comforting. She could feel like she was keeping the message safe. Without it, she felt as if she'd left it behind somewhere and would never find it again.

In a sense, that was true. She'd left it on the real *Redemptive Veteran*, not this virtual clone. Embedded in her real body, not this digital duplicate. As soon as these raiders boarded, it was as good as lost. The only thing protecting it from them was a thin pane of glass and a dollop of gel.

Maybe they weren't even raiders? Maybe they had their own plans for that message and had been following her since Arali.

Had she done something wrong? She tried to recall everything that had happened since that last night at home, searching for her mistake.

'Well, they must have docked by now,' Sam said, breaking the uncomfortable silence. 'We won't know exactly when the acceleration will stop, but it's sure to be soon. Then they'll climb through the airlock and grab what they can. So, Julian, what's our next step?'

Julian shrugged. 'I don't know why you're looking at me. I'm no tactical mastermind, I'm just doing my job.' He paused. 'At the very least I've bought us some time. If I'd done nothing, they could be pulling us out of our pods in less than an hour. Now it could take them days to regain access.'

'No,' Hayley sniffled, stifling her tears. 'They won't do it at all. The SSR won't accept new system connections while it's online. It would have to be reloaded completely for them to link it back to the main computer.'

'Even better. That means we have as much time as we need to come up with a plan.'

'A plan?' Sam laughed. 'We're massively outgunned. What kind of plan could you possibly conceive to get out of this?'

'That right there is exactly why we need time! We can't think our way out of this on the spot. Time is the one thing we have to work with. If we can just put our heads together I'm sure we can come up with something!'

'Right, sure. Let's all come up with an ingenious plan to fight our way through an entire raiding party.' She stood and with a flick of her fingers, conjured her personal interface. 'I'll leave that with you for now. I'm going to join the captain in the bar. Maybe this scheme of yours will all start to make sense when I'm pissed.' And with that, she dematerialised.

'Yeah, yeah, enjoy the hangover,' Julian muttered to himself. He looked over to Hayley and his expression softened. He got out of his seat and moved to her side. He rested a hand on her shoulder. His face turned red and his lip started to tremble.

'It's okay, Hayley,' he whispered to her. 'Everything's going to be alright.'

She refused to lift her face from its cradle in her palms.

'We'll think of something. Just you wait.'

She took a deep uneasy breath. 'You really think so?'

Julian's gaze dropped. He said nothing. Hayley turned slowly in her seat to face him. She wrapped her arms around his waist and nuzzled into his stomach. Julian wrapped his arms gently around her neck and bowed his head, eyes closed.

Winter steadily rose to her feet. She'd only been getting in the way since she arrived and these two needed to be alone. A flick of her fingers, a few taps on the menu and the world around her dissolved into darkness.

She squeezed her eyes tightly shut and wished that she could fade away just as easily.

CHAPTER 10

The remaining suspension gel, thinned to a watery consistency, drained away through the bottom of the tank. Gram opened her eyes.

Time was of the essence now. The *Redemptive Veteran*'s crew was cunning. The raiding party no longer had control over when the other ship's simulator would deactivate. The targets could wait until the perfect moment and let themselves out. For all Gram and her crew knew, that moment could be now.

The ships were physically linked, so their speeds were unified. That meant if it was safe for her crew to leave their simulation, it had to be safe for the *Veteran*'s crew as well. They could be getting out of their pods now, just as she was, to mount some kind of defence.

According to the manifest they had accessed, the *Veteran* carried a cache of small firearms. With no dedicated armoury on board, any weapons would most likely be stored in cargo, but there was no way to be certain. They could be within arm's reach of the SSR pods, for all she knew.

Gram's engineer had assured her that that every system was fully isolated from the simulator, so the crew couldn't know when it would be safe to step outside of the virtual world. As much as she trusted her crew, Gram wouldn't take any part of their situation for granted. Their first objective was to secure the *Redemptive Veteran* and its crew, and make sure there was no way for them to put up any resistance.

She kicked the door of her pod and it swung out with a

metallic screech. It clanged and rattled as it locked itself in the open position. She eased herself from her seat and floated out into the room. She was surrounded by her crew, each of them doing the same thing.

The *Shameless Renegade* boasted a force large enough to tackle most independent vessels. Besides the bridge crew, there were also around twenty mercenaries. As most jobs were uneventful, all they normally had to do was look menacing, so they were pretty cheap and Gram could support a large number of them using only a small percentage of her profits. They had proven to be extremely useful should a situation ever turn ugly, and she had a nagging suspicion that this may turn out to be one such occasion.

Motion was slow. Despite the rush to accomplish their objectives, every step taken in zero gravity must be taken with care. A wrong move could leave someone drifting through an open space, wasting precious time as they waited for another handhold to come within reach.

With this in mind, Gram turned to face the locker beside her pod and drew out her flight suit. Everyone on this ship had seen each other's bodies many times and when they needed to move quickly it was useful not to have to disrobe upon leaving SSR. Instead, they went without the robes that many vessels used and entered the simulator naked.

Keeping a grip on her locker with one hand, she began the tedious process of donning her skin-tight outfit. It wasn't very comfortable, but it was hard for opponents to grab in a brawl. She slipped on her boots, then put on her combat harness with a pistol on her hip and a rifle slung over her back. Slamming the locker shut, she moved forward among her mercenaries as they made their way out of the barracks and filed down the ship's central tunnel towards the airlock.

The armed brutes gathered silently around the aperture. Gram cut through the crowd and made her way towards the opening. She locked eyes with the mercenary nearest to the front and gave a nod. With only the most basic command structure on this ship, leaders were assigned when needed. This man was a leader now.

She turned upside-down and floated through the airlock in the floor. Without changing her orientation, she emerged upright through a hole in the deck of the other ship.

They were surrounded by cases, crates, and all sorts of miscellaneous property. There was even a small ground vehicle. This had to be the cargo bay.

She kept hold of the inside of the airlock and took a note of the handholds on this ship. On the *Renegade*, they just used bare metal grates that covered most decks and bulkheads, or long poles that ran along the lengths of the walls. This ship used rubber holds set into the various surfaces. They were surely more comfortable to use, but Gram didn't care for them being spaced so far apart.

Their numbers grew as the mercenaries made their way through. Gram searched through her small army for the leader she'd assigned. She floated over to him, drew a glass tablet computer from her harness and brought up a rough layout of the ship that her engineer had compiled.

'Assemble a team of eight and advance on this SSR suite,' she told him, indicating its location on her device. 'I'll do the same and head to the other. Anyone left is to stay here and guard this airlock. If there is any resistance, take them alive if you can. Once it's secure, open comms and report to the *Renegade* bridge. Understand?'

'Uh-huh.'

'Remember, take them *alive*.' Some of these mercenaries had proved to be a bit trigger-happy in the past. Firepower had its uses, but not when it left a bullet hole in your pay cheque. She had learned that if you choose to trust a hired gun, you need to really spell their orders out for them. Especially if they were as cheap as these.

Gram wasted no time in rounding up her team, bringing her rifle to bear and leading them out of the cargo bay. Following the map on her device, she found the SSR suites close by.

She split her force to check every corner and guard every access route, still left with four of them by her side when she reached her destination. With no reports of any disturbance, she called them all back to her as they prepared to break into the room.

SSR Suite #1.

This would normally be for the ship's crew, who often proved more dangerous than the passengers. Passengers tended to have numbers on their side, but the crew would have weapons, training and a duty to protect the ship.

She listened through the door to hear any activity on the other side. She heard nothing. She hoped they would still be inside their pods, but she wouldn't risk the possibility that they had set up a defensive formation. They could even have booby-trapped the door.

At that thought, she fell back and let one of the mercenaries take the lead.

Once everyone was in position, waiting motionless in the air, Gram gave the order.

At the press of a button, the door slid open and the gunmen funnelled in. She tried to follow, but their numbers quickly filled the suite and the entrance was blocked.

The fact that no weapons had been fired was encouraging. It seemed her engineer had been right all along.

The mercenaries left the room one by one and most of them went to patrol the rest of the ship. Two remained with Gram as she was finally able to enter the room herself.

Three large white pods were set into the back wall and there were lockers to the left and right. The pods were a lot nicer than the ones on the *Renegade*, with doors made of large, thick windows in metal frames that would slide into the ceiling. Gram almost wished she could justify upgrading her own pods – old, oily and with manual hinged doors.

She floated over to the pods. All three were in use, their occupants encased in thick, transparent gel.

Usually this sight would please Gram. Slaves in their cans, just waiting to be cracked open. This should be the image of a mission accomplished.

Today it was an image of defeat.

If the pods were opened without the simulation being properly deactivated, the occupants would die, or at best they would suffer severe mental trauma. Even cutting power to the system would be catastrophic. The crew would have to shut down the system of their own volition, knowing that they'd be surrendering themselves to a life of slavery.

Gram holstered her weapon with a sigh of dejection. They were at a stalemate.

She drew her tablet again and opened a communication channel to her ship.

'Gram here. Suite One is clear. The crew are still in their pods.'

'Told you so,' the engineer replied. Gram rolled her eyes. 'The other team checked in. The passengers are secure too.'

'Great. So we've avoided one possible disaster and now we're just left with the original problem. Let me congratulate you again on your brilliant cock-up.'

'Don't be too quick to criticise me, Gram. It's not often that I make a mistake like this, but you know me. Every time I do, I make up for it with an equally spectacular solution.'

'Whatever,' she grumbled. 'Let me know when your epiphany strikes.'

'Don't go anywhere just yet! I may already have our golden bullet!'

'What do you mean?'

'While you were busy with your little military exercise, we've been checking the ship's logs. I've found something of interest in the passenger roster.'

'Whatever you're thinking, it won't matter. We can't get to the passengers. You said it yourself.'

'You'd be amazed what an engineer can do with the right tools and a bit of good fortune, and it seems we have both today.'

'Don't beat around the bush. Just tell me what you've found.'

'Can't just tell you. I have to show you. I'm making my way to the second SSR suite. Meet me there.'

He cut the link.

Gram didn't like having information kept from her, especially not when it was so crucial, but the confidence in his voice wasn't usually misleading. Whatever this solution of his was, it had better work.

'Stay here, guard the crew,' she told her squad. 'If the pods open, restrain them. Take them alive and report it to me immediately.' She didn't expect the pods to open any time soon, but they should be ready for it. It's what she wanted, after all.

She left the room and began to follow the hallway around to the second suite. When she arrived, the door hissed out of the way and the full eight-man team Gram had sent was still there. She sent half of them back to the cargo bay and left the others to guard the passengers.

Squeezing through the doorway and the oncoming swarm of muscle was the engineer. He wasn't so graceful in zero-gravity but managed to make his way in regardless.

'Don't leave me waiting,' she demanded. 'What have you found?'

The engineer held up a finger, then made his way to a workstation on the wall to the right. With a little bit of system navigation, he conjured the passenger records he had mentioned.

'I was looking through all sorts of documentation on their system, trying to find anything that might provide a little bit of leverage, when something caught my eye.'

He sifted through the records in turn, before settling on one in particular. One that stood out.

'This one. Odd, right?'

Indeed, there was something missing. 'So there's no picture. Big deal.'

'Yes, it is a big deal. Every transport ship we've ever boarded has had a profile for every single person on board, both crew and passenger alike. Each one should have photographic identification. This ship follows that rule too. Everyone has a portrait, except for this one person.'

'And why should we care?'

'Like I said, this just caught my eye. It got me interested, so I read on.' He began to scroll through the document, but it ended abruptly. 'It turns out this kind of information is normally supplied when the journey is booked. The passengers have to prove they're legit. This one though; she had no booking. I'd guess she just jumped on at the last minute.'

'Where are you going with this? Where's your solution?'

'I'm getting there! As you can see, there's not a whole lot of information on her. We have her name, gender, blah blah blah, and a few notes from the *Redemptive Veteran*'s SSR technician.'

Gram moved to look at the screen over his shoulder. 'What did he say?'

The engineer read directly from the screen. 'I have had to reconfigure the datastream directed to electrode #4 to be compatible with a neural implant affixed to her spine.'

'An implant?'

'Like I said, I can do a lot if I'm given the right tools, and this little widget is one hell of a tool! The crew may have severed the connection between the simulator and the main computer, but the interface between the simulator and this implant is still in place. It has to be to keep her in virtual suspension.'

'So how do we exploit it?'

'Well, we can't use it to shut off the entire simulation, nor can we safely remove everyone from it. What we can do is force her implant to reject any signals from the simulator. There are three other electrodes in play, so it may be a little rough for her, but it should be safe. More or less.'

'You're saying we can bring her out?'

'Precisely.' The engineer looked very pleased with himself.

'Okay, so we have one passenger to sell, assuming she survives. I don't know what you mean by "more or less" safe, but it sounds like she could still be damaged by this. It better not make her any harder to sell.'

'You're not seeing the big picture here, Gram. The first attempt might require a little bit of guesswork, but I reckon we can pull it off. After that, we can put her back in and take her out again as many times as we like! I suggest we pull her out, interrogate her to find out the situation inside the virtual world, give her a message, and put her back in her pod so she can deliver it. Then we can take her out again to get the response from the crew. You wanted an interface with the people in the simulation. She is that interface.'

'And what kind of message do you expect me to give her? We don't have any leverage. We can't just ask them to surrender and expect them to obey.'

'We have their real bodies,' he said. 'That's all the leverage we need. As for the content of the message, I'll leave that with you. You can be incredibly persuasive.'

'You think so?'

'Well, you persuaded me to join your raggedy-ass crew.' The engineer sniggered.

'Fine.' Gram floated over to the pods, looking for their girl. 'Which one is it?'

'The only one who didn't appear on the system, I'd imagine.' He pushed himself across the room and moved from pod to pod. 'Ah-ha! Found her.'

Gram joined him and looked inside. She was a young woman, with long dark hair. Even when asleep, her face was sharp. She'd obviously spent far too much of her life frowning.

'How soon can you get her out?'

'Well, I'll need to formulate some kind of jamming signal. I can't look at the settings the system's using because of the broken link, but if you give me a few hours I reckon I can give you something that works.'

'Good. I want to give them a little more time to surrender themselves willingly first anyway. Plus I need to work out what to tell her when she comes out, and what to get her to tell the crew when she goes back in. Be back here in twenty-four hours. If we're ready to proceed, we'll see if this plan of yours bears any fruit.'

'Perfect,' he said, holding himself to the wall with a firm grip.

'Good. I'll be back on the *Renegade*. Keep me posted.' She looked at the girl in the pod one last time.

'I look forward to meeting you, Miss Starling,' she said, then propelled herself in the direction of the door.

CHAPTER 11

The crew had been very selective in choosing a venue where Orson could address the passengers. Sam's proposal was for it to be done on their simulated spacecraft to help provide the impression that they were still in charge and that they were safe.

Hayley argued that it would be daunting for them, surrounded by an environment that to all of them was still unfamiliar. She'd elected for a garden that she had designed for in-flight wedding services, with bright blue skies, calming green grass and a beautiful white gazebo.

That had struck Julian as something of a cliché. All of these settings were far too formal, he said. What they needed was to simulate ravenous hunger in all of the passengers and seat them at a long table with a buffet, where they could put aside their stress with as much comfort eating as they could endure.

In the end the cliché won out and Hayley took the time to make a duplicate of the garden she had chosen. She removed the floral bouquets and the decorative arch. It was designed to seat a large audience, but with only seven passengers most of the chairs had to go too.

Now, here they were. Winter watched Orson take to the step of the gazebo. His crew were on the grass to the side, hands clasped behind their backs in an effort to look dignified and in control, though there was an uncomfortable lack of pride and determination in their poise.

The other passengers had gathered and were sitting on

wooden chairs on the grass, lined up in a single wide rank. They shifted and fidgeted, their apprehension evident.

Orson stood tall and spoke with authority.

'You are all aware of the red alert we experienced yesterday. First of all, we would like to apologise for it lasting so long. I can assure you it was disabled as soon as the immediate issue was resolved.'

'He's scared.'

Winter sat at the edge of the group, next to the boy she'd met before entering her pod whose name she'd learned was Isaac. Even in the virtual world, he was as insightful as ever. Orson seemed stoic enough to her eyes, but she knew the boy was right.

'Everyone's scared, but him most of all,' he whispered, looking up at Winter. 'What's he so afraid of?'

Isaac's mother, sitting on the other side of him, grabbed his chin and turned his head back to face the captain. 'Quiet, this is important!'

Orson cleared his throat. 'Unfortunately, the alert was no drill. The crew reached the bridge in record time to respond to the emergency and were resourceful in combating it. They put all of their effort into keeping us safe from harm.' His lips parted again but he hesitated. He took a breath, swallowed, then continued. 'Which is why it pains me to tell you that their success was only partial.'

Winter could feel the tension in the air thickening. A few people began to call out their questions to the captain.

Out of the corner of her eye, she saw Isaac tilt his head slightly as he gazed straight at Orson.

'Please,' the captain said softly, raising his hands in front of him. The crowd hushed and he carried on. 'Right now, in the real world, our computer systems have been overridden by another crew. We no longer have any control of the ship. It is our present understanding that we have been boarded by a raiding party, most likely looking for valuable commodities to sell.'

'Excuse me,' came a well-spoken Aralian voice from another seat further along. A man raised his hand to get the captain's attention. 'How could we be boarded in superspace? I thought it was too dangerous to be conscious.'

The captain frowned at the man and passed the question to Hayley.

'The human body can withstand being in superspace; it just can't take the acceleration. They would have brought us to a constant velocity in order to board. That probably means it will take a bit longer to reach Earth. So, uhh, sorry about that.' She looked back to the captain.

'As I was saying, they are most likely looking for any valuable commodities we have on board. Unfortunately, to raiders, people are often considered a commodity. If they got their hands on us, they would take us prisoner and sell us into slavery.'

The crowd exploded into shouts and screams; everything from desperate questions to furious accusations. Winter simply turned her head and watched. Everything they were saying had already crossed her mind hours ago, so she stopped listening. She looked towards Isaac, who was staring at Orson and appeared to be unaware of the commotion.

It took a full minute for the crew to calm the crowd enough for the captain to resume.

'I mentioned that this crew, standing before you now, did manage a partial victory. Just as the intruders have restricted our access to the ship, we have restricted their access to the SSR system. For the time being, we are safe. They do not have the ability to turn off the simulation and remove us from our pods. Only we have that ability.

'This turn of events has blessed us with something very few people in our position have ever had, and that's time. We have weeks, possibly even longer, as Hayley pointed out, to come up with a plan to turn the tables before we reach Earth. Until then, we are beyond their reach. They cannot hurt us. We are safe.'

This was no consolation to the crowd, who once again erupted into an uproar.

'This is your fault!'

'What can you do about it?'

'You've killed us all!'

Amid the bellowing, Isaac stood up and retreated from the gazebo towards the grand manor that overlooked the garden. Winter watched him leave, hands in his pockets, trudging slowly up the grassy hill.

The boy had seemed ill at ease right from the start. She hadn't known him for long, but aside from his persistent curiosity, Winter had only ever seen him express fear. Maybe that's why he was able to identify it so astutely.

She looked over at his mother whose bitter snarl was directed towards the captain. She didn't seem to have noticed her son wandering off. Winter's resentment for the woman grew each time she laid her eyes on her. She knew that it must have been hard for the other passengers to understand the crew's efforts, but no-one wanted this to happen. No-one but the invaders deserved any of this blame.

The only two who had managed not to unload their emotional burden were Isaac and Winter herself, although she was just about at capacity. She was sure it wouldn't be long until she found herself screaming at someone.

Perhaps he was feeling the same way. Seeking solitude might make it easier for him to deal with it all. He was only a young boy, but he had wisdom beyond that of his peers.

Everyone else was far too busy to pay Winter any mind. She took the opportunity to slip away from the madness and made her way briskly up the hill.

Isaac had taken a seat in a plastic chair on the patio, occupying a spot in the shadow cast by a large parasol. It was a good vantage point, overlooking the chaos at the foot of the slope.

'Are you alright?' Winter called up to him, nearing the crest of the hill.

He seemed calm. Perhaps he was even better at tempering his feelings than she'd given him credit for, not that he'd given her any indication of where his boundaries might be. In any case it was impressive that he could remain so unmoved by the news, for better or worse.

Winter helped herself to a chair opposite him, also in the shade. He didn't react immediately, but soon he turned to face her with those piercing eyes of his. He tilted his head again.

'The captain never looked at you while he was speaking. And you're as scared now as you were before he said anything.' His eyes bored into her. He squinted. She could almost feel him probing her thoughts. 'You already knew.'

Winter got the impression this was something she'd need to get used to and that the sooner she started pretending it was normal, the sooner she'd grow accustomed to his insight. 'I was on the bridge with them when it all took place. I saw their struggle. Their desperation. I watched it happen and it terrified me.'

'But now you're okay. That is, you pretend to be okay. Now that everyone else knows what you know, you're no different to them, but you act tough because you need to be better.'

'I just recognise when I have no control,' she said. 'This is the situation we're in. I've come to terms with it.'

Isaac looked away. 'No. You haven't.'

Even Winter didn't see her motives with that kind of clarity. Was it really all written on her face like that?

'You have a need to be stronger than everyone else. You take everything in your stride because no-one else will.'

'Except you.'

Isaac blinked, his concentration broken. He looked into Winter's eyes but this time she stared back into his.

'You take everything you're given and you deal with it, just like I do. You're detached from your feelings, enough to keep yourself from showing them at least, but you're familiar enough with them to recognise them in others.' She was making a lot of assumptions here, but each seemed fair. She wasn't even thinking, really. Just looking at him and letting the words come on their own. Was this his secret? 'You're very good at sensing fear. How come you know it so well?'

Isaac broke eye contact. He leaned forward in his chair and looked down at the ground.

Winter didn't dare to inquire any further. The boy clearly had a lot on his mind and she didn't want to make him any more upset than he already was.

She looked down the hill. The crew was still by the gazebo but some of the other passengers had peeled away from the group, pacing around the lawn.

Winter went to lean back in her chair when she felt something in the back of her neck. Sharp but subtle, like a pin placed tenderly against her flesh. She tried to move a hand to feel where her implant should be, but her arm wouldn't respond. She tried again, to move any part of her body but nothing happened. In her mind she was kicking and flailing, desperate for some part of her body to move. Even just a little. Even her eyes.

Then in an instant, everything she had tried to do happened all at once. Her entire body convulsed in the most violent and inhuman way and she was thrown from the chair on to the ground.

She steadied herself, breathing rapidly as she looked around and saw Isaac. He had recoiled from her and fixed her with a horrified stare.

His voice trembled. 'What was that?'

'I don't know-w-w-w-w.' Winter's voice caught on the last syllable and it reverberated in her mouth like a buzzing insect, then after a few seconds, it abruptly ceased.

She doubled over and started panting. Her presence began to feel less and less physical. She brought her hands up in front of her face, but the motion refused to stop. They passed clean through her head before reappearing where she had meant for them to be.

The sensation in her neck grew into a searing pain, streaking its way down her spine and up into her brain. She roared in agony and clapped her hands over the base of her skull, right where her implant ought to be.

Her eyesight began to blur and darken, then piece by piece, she evaporated.

* * *

Isaac gaped as Winter faded into nothingness. He waved his hands through the air where she once was, but felt nothing. He patted his hands on her seat. It was warm – she'd been no illusion – but beside that there was no sign that she'd been there at all. She had simply melted away.

He looked around desperately for an explanation. His eyes swept over the manor, scanned across the ground and finally settled on the garden. Everyone was still there, some of them still in fits of rage and fear.

Now seemed as good a time as any to break it up. Someone down there would know how to find Winter.

He leapt to his feet and broke into a sprint down the knoll. The steepness of the slope made it feel like he was running on nothing and more than once his balance faltered, but he managed to remain upright.

By the time he reached the bottom, he was travelling with such speed that he cleared the open garden in seconds. He sprinted into the heart of the riot which immediately fell silent.

He tried to speak but his voice would not come. His throat hurt. He bent over, wheezing, and propped his weight up with his hands on his thighs as he gasped for breath.

'Isaac, what are you doing?' His mother spoke with the same tone she had been using to berate the captain.

He looked at her. 'Winter's gone,' he sobbed, feeling the tears finally escape his eyes.

'What the hell's this kid talking about?' one of the others demanded.

'Doesn't matter,' the captain barked. 'She knows what she needs to know. She can go where she likes.'

'No,' Isaac struggled. 'She was sitting normally, then she just … broke.'

'What do you mean "broke"?'

'I don't know. She moved super fast and fell on the floor, then her hand went through her head, and then she screamed and disappeared!'

Everyone who had parted from the group began to return one by one, all eyes on Isaac as he recounted what he'd seen.

'Sounds like a computer glitch to me.' Isaac looked around towards the kind voice and recognised Hayley, the lady who helped him into his pod. 'Not really surprising, after everything the system's been through, the processor's surely having a rough time. I'm honestly kind of surprised we haven't seen anything like this sooner. Don't worry, I can find her.'

She pulled up her holographic interface and tapped and swiped through various menus. Her face quickly turned to one of concern.

'She's not coming up.'

'What do you mean she's not coming up?' Julian took a look at the results over her shoulder, more than a hint of irritation in his voice. 'You must have done the search wrong.'

'I didn't do it wrong.'

'Well then, run it again. If we've got a glitchy system it could just be throwing up negative results.'

A few more seconds of data entry. Isaac fidgeted nervously. He wasn't used to feeling this impatient.

'She's not appearing in any simulation.'

Isaac hesitated then asked, 'Is she still in her pod?'

Hayley's head drooped, but her eyes tried to look him in the face. 'There's no way of knowing.'

Isaac's mother demanded, 'I thought you said we were safe in here!'

The uproar began again. Julian yelled until the ruckus dipped and he could be heard.

'Apparently there is a slight fault with the system. Until we have diagnosed the problem we cannot jump to any conclusions. We will find Winter. For now, all I can do is promise you that it is totally impossible to remove a single person from the SSR alone. The entire simulation would have to be powered down. We will investigate the issue and return to you once we have some new information.'

The passengers appeared to find little comfort in this as their volume increased again to fill the gap he left.

Leaving the crowd to Sam and Orson, Julian guided Hayley around the side of the gazebo. Isaac watched them stop in the shade and speak in hushed voices. He couldn't make out what they were saying, but he knew one thing for certain: they were afraid.

CHAPTER 12

Isaac faded from Winter's vision as everything turned to darkness and the shocking pain coursed its way through her body. She screamed through the torment, her mind addled. She almost didn't notice the feeling of her implant, present on her spine once again.

With a sharp snap like the flick of a switch, the pain ceased. She remained still and silent, trying to steady her breathing, until she felt a liquid oozing down her legs. She opened her eyes and looked down to see the last of a gelatinous substance seeping away through a drain beneath her bare feet. Only now did she realise that she wasn't lying on the ground as she had been, but sitting upright.

Her head whipped from side to side as she assessed her environment. She was back in her pod, stuck down in her slimy chair, gowned in a thin white fabric, though the robe no longer rested upon her knees. It floated freely above her legs.

She looked out through the glass. There were five unfamiliar figures. Two facing away sitting at Hayley's computer terminal, and three suspended in the air around the suite, armed with high-calibre rifles. Winter pushed herself out of her seat and had to bring her hands up to shield her head from the ceiling as she drifted towards it. She floated unhindered in an environment devoid of gravity.

A low hissing noise filled the chamber. With a clunk, the heavy metal door jumped out of its bolts and slid up, out of sight.

The two strangers by the workstation turned to look at her. The first was a woman, tall and brawny with a pale blonde bob and clad in a dark flight suit. Her face bore a thin smile and squinting eyes as she looked Winter up and down, malice oozing from her.

The man hovering above Hayley's stool had nothing more than a thick auburn stubble covering his scalp and a beard of about the same length. He was smaller than the woman and leaner. He had a smile too, though his was more prideful.

The woman kicked at the bulkhead and hurtled towards Winter with alarming speed. She placed her hands on the sides of the pod and stopped inches away from Winter's face.

'What do you know? It worked,' she muttered, apparently to herself despite being nose-to-nose with Winter. 'You and I need to have a little cha–'

Winter slammed a fist hard against the woman's cheek, sending her reeling across the room. In unison the three armed guards trained their weapons on Winter as she rubbed her knuckles.

She didn't care. She knew she was too valuable to kill. Besides, getting the chance to unleash some of the anger she'd been saving up was worth the risk.

The woman brought herself to a stop against the ceiling on the far side of the room. She wiped the fresh wound and glanced at the wet blood on her fingertips. She nudged herself back towards Winter, sparing her a shrug as she drifted slowly across the space. 'I think perhaps we got off on the wrong foot?'

'Speak for yourself,' Winter retorted. 'That felt like the perfect conversation starter.'

'Well, you've certainly got us talking. While we're on the subject though, try to hit with your first and second knuckles next time or you'll end up breaking something.'

'I guess I just got excited.' Winter curled her lip.

'Indeed.' The woman touched down and held herself in position using a grip set into the nearby wall. 'I'm Megan Gram. You can use whichever of those names you prefer. And for the record, the rest of my crew is equally punchable, so feel free to mix things up.'

'Sure.' Winter began removing her electrodes as she stared at Gram. When she popped off the one on her neck, she rubbed the base of her skull which still faintly throbbed. 'How did you manage to get me out of the system? I thought you were locked out.'

'We are. Your lot has really done a number on our productivity.'

'I'm sure they'd be glad to hear that.'

'The other pods are still locked. No-one else has been taken from the simulation. We can't deactivate it from out here.'

Relief swept through Winter like a wave. It was good to know for sure that the crew's plan had worked. However, for the second time in recent days, she found herself wondering what set her apart from the others. Her captor could have chosen anyone on the ship. Why her?

'You haven't answered my question. How did you get me out?'

Gram laughed. 'I don't have to answer to you! But I guess I might tell you if you cooperate. Let's just say you're going to help me get your friends out of their pods.'

'I doubt I'll be much use to you,' she said. 'I'm not even on the crew.'

'That won't be an issue, Winter, don't worry.'

'What do you mean?'

Gram keyed open the door. 'I'll explain. Follow me.' She gestured through the opening and waited.

Winter wasn't in the mood to be patient, but whether she was promised answers or not, it seemed she had no choice but to go with the raider.

She took hold of the edge of her pod's opening and slowly pulled herself out, already struggling to keep control and nearly drifting into the middle of the room. She was glad now that she'd chosen the pod nearest the wall. She found herself able to reach a rubber handhold.

'First time in zero-G, huh?' Gram looked amused. 'It's fine, we have time, but don't take too long, hm?'

Winter scowled at her, continuing to grapple her way along the bulkhead towards the door. It was hard to stay dignified when she couldn't control her movement.

Gram slipped through the opening as she neared. 'Stay close,' she instructed and propelled herself down the corridor.

The route wasn't that long but became a little more tedious each time Winter misjudged her trajectory or missed a handhold. Despite the initial difficulty, Winter was able to pick up a few simple tricks along the way and she began to gain some much-needed control.

They travelled into the cargo hold and down through the airlock in the centre of the deck. She found it a little disorienting to emerge in a new environment upside-down, with the two spacecraft joined as they were.

The ambience of the new vessel was forbidding, with bulkheads comprised of exposed cabling and electrical components, covered over by dark metal grates. They were cold to the touch with patches of oil, which formed dark stains on Winter's gown as she wiped it from her hands.

As she was led along the ship she was able to piece together a good mental map of the structure. This central tunnel appeared to run the length of the ship, with all the various rooms tacked on to the sides. One exception was their SSR room. As they passed through, Winter took her brief chance to look around. It acted as part of the tunnel itself, expanding out to the left and right to form a large circular chamber. The pods were arranged in rows parallel with the length of the ship, with tall lockers squeezed in between them. They were bunched tightly together. There must have been at least thirty, built of a dark rugged metal.

Gram showed her through to the other side where the tunnel continued as before. She then braced herself against a section of the wall. She grabbed the protruding handle of a door and yanked it open. It juddered along its rails and stopped with a clunk.

She pushed herself through and Winter peered in as Gram drifted towards a wide desk that stretched out from the wall on the right. She gripped the near edge and pushed against it to somersault over the top and land in a chair on the other side. She strapped herself in and beckoned Winter with a finger.

Winter took a similar chair on the closer side, fastening herself to it as her captor had. In addition to keeping her from floating away, it also did a good job of stopping her gown from moving about too freely.

There was a square glass pane, just over a foot wide, embedded in the surface of the desk and flush with the grey plastic panelling that spanned its length. Gram slid a tablet computer into a port, then tapped at it until the panel on the desk came to life with various displays. She held down a control and leaned in towards it.

'Send Paul to my office. We need to talk.'

She released the button and the screen faded grey and dormant. The smile Gram once bore had left no trace. Now her brow furrowed as she leaned back in her chair.

'The *Veteran*'s crew,' she said, straight down to business. 'What's their plan?'

Winter tilted her head quizzically. 'What?'

'The crew of your ship. They must have a plan. What is it?'

'I've already told you I'm not a part of the crew,' she replied, rolling her eyes. 'How the hell should I know?'

'You already knew we were on board when we pulled you out, and probably so do the other passengers. The crew would have every reason to discuss their plans with you, to keep you calm, to get you involved, whatever. You know what they're planning, so tell me.'

'That's it? That's what you're going on?' Winter faked a chuckle in a display of false confidence. 'You're not making any sense. Why not get the crew themselves to spill the beans? In fact, why not get everyone out right now? You've clearly found a way.'

'Answer the question.'

'You first.'

'I don't think you understand how this works, Miss Starling.' Gram drew a pistol from her combat harness, held it above her shoulder and let go, leaving it to stay suspended in the air, acting as a constant threat.

'You're going to kill me?' Winter looked from the floating gun to Gram. 'You can go right ahead. You have a lot more to lose than I do.' With her friends and family on the line in the event of Winter's mission failure, that was almost certainly untrue. Even so, she hoped she might be able to call Gram's bluff.

Gram pondered, a finger on her chin. 'An answer for an answer. Deal?'

'Deal. You start.'

'Fine. We have found a way to break you out of SSR, and you alone. No-one else on your ship has what we need.'

'And what's that?'

Gram silently tapped a finger against the back of her neck. Winter imitated the gesture and found herself once again fidgeting with the shape of the implant beneath her skin.

'One of the electrodes used to keep you in suspension has to be placed directly on top of it. My engineer found a way to make it reject the system input and remove you from the simulation. No-one else on the *Veteran* has one, so we used you.'

Winter felt the urge to punch her again. It had been less than two days since someone else had commandeered the same device for their own purposes and she had felt violated beyond words. Now it was happening for a second time and her anger bubbled its way back to the front of her mind. To retain control and an appearance of confidence took all of the willpower she could conjure.

'In other words, I'm irreplaceable.' She managed to convince one side of her mouth to curl into a sneer.

'Perhaps, but we don't need to kill you to get what we need from you.'

'What does that mean?'

'Hold it there! My turn.' Gram leaned in closer as she asked again. 'What is your crew planning?'

Winter would have been more than willing to lie, if only she could come up with any useful deceptions. For now, the truth would have to do. 'They have no plan.'

'Bullshit.'

'I'm sorry?'

'Your crew methodically severed our access to one of our most crucial assets. There must be some intention behind it.'

'Are you a complete idiot? They weren't methodical, they were desperate! If they had a plan they would have done more to stop you. All they did was to keep themselves safe from you, for all it was worth. They are trapped in there, no more free to get out than you are to get in. What kind of plan could they possibly concoct?'

Gram offered no response.

The door rattled open behind Winter and a man floating in the corridor clawed his way across the threshold from the side. He was smartly dressed, his pale creaseless shirt tucked into his dark trousers.

'Paul, what took you so long? My ship isn't that big.'

'My apologies,' he said mockingly. 'Naturally I came as soon as I received your urgent call, but your ship is just so beautiful, I couldn't help but get distracted.' His eyes flicked over to Winter. 'Well then, who's this? I didn't realise you were ready to replace me after only a short delay.'

'Don't be ridiculous. Get over here.' Gram snatched her floating pistol from the air and Paul drifted carefully around the desk, apparently still getting used to moving in zero-gravity himself.

'Winter, I'd like to introduce to you my client, Paul Narn. Paul has commissioned my crew and I to repossess the *Redemptive Veteran* for him.'

That meant this whole situation could be traced back to him.

'Paul, this is Winter, one of the passengers from the *Veteran*. She's going to help us.'

'Not if I have anything to say about it!' Winter sneered.

'You don't.'

'Hang on a moment,' Paul interjected. 'You got one out?'

'Just the one for now.' Gram turned to Winter. 'We have a job for you, Winter, and you're the only one who can do it. As such, we're prepared to offer you something in return, so long as it doesn't interfere with our end of the agreement. What can we do for you, Winter? What do you want?'

'I want to get off this fucking ship.'

'Careful what you wish for, Miss Starling.'

'Okay, then. First, tell me what you want me to do. I don't negotiate payment before I know the job.'

'No. Question time is over. Now we're coming to an agreement, and this time I go first. Name your price.'

Winter carefully considered her options. Her immediate thought was to free everyone on the *Veteran* once they reached Earth. Of course, that would be a massive hit to the raiders' profits. She'd never agree to it. Another problem was that she didn't know for sure that they were even going to Earth. They were just as likely to be heading back to Arali.

Her own situation came to mind. If they were going to Earth, she might be able to convince them that setting her free would be a worthy trade. If not, perhaps she would have time to get another transport on Arali. They were only a day or so away.

'Have we turned around?'

'Once we're done here our business is on Earth. That's where we're going.'

'When we get there, I want you to set me free. Let me go my own way.'

'I said don't interfere with our end. Everyone we take from that ship has the potential to make us a lot of money, including you.'

'Which is why I'm only asking for me, you can keep everyone else. Only it sounds to me like you need my help to get them out in the first place. If you decline, you have one slave to sell, and a ship filled with ten useless SSR pods. That might affect its value a little, am I right?' She aimed the question towards Paul, who shifted uncomfortably under Winter's scrutiny. 'But let me go and you could walk away with ten potential slaves and your client gets his ship exactly as it was promised to him. Sounds like a no-brainer to me.'

Gram sat back in her seat. She suspended her handgun in the air before her and fidgeted with it, prodding it into a spin and catching it again. 'You strike a hard bargain.'

'Years of practice.' Winter's eyes were fixed on Gram's. 'What do you say?'

Gram hesitated a little longer, then swiped the gun back up. 'Deal.'

'No it isn't.' Winter leaned forward, tugging on her seatbelt. 'It's not a deal until I know what I'm signing up for. Tell me what the job is.'

Gram frowned, but her face soon relaxed a little. Winter began to suspect she might actually be enjoying this. 'I need you to be a messenger for me. A conduit for this exchange between realities. I give you a message, you go back into the simulation and give that message to Captain Orson. We'll have no way of knowing when you will have delivered it and it may take him some time to figure out what to say next, so we'll give you an allotted time until we pull you back out again. When we do, you'll tell us what he said. Chances are this won't be a one-time task. We'll probably have to send you in several times if we're going to resolve this stalemate.'

Once again, her implant was being manipulated beyond its design just so that she could run an errand for someone she didn't know. At least in this case she was allowed to know what the messages were and who they were for. That was far more than the other guy had given her.

Still, it didn't require actively working against the *Veteran*'s crew and passengers. It wasn't even that much effort. It almost certainly meant enduring the agony of being ripped out of the simulation again, but she could deal with the pain as long as it meant she would get to see her family again. Even that was far from a guarantee. She didn't imagine raiders cared much for honest deals and she shouldn't be surprised if she ended up being double-crossed. But what choice did she have?

She saw nowhere left for this negotiation to go. All cards were on the table. It was deal or no deal now.

'How could I possibly refuse?' Winter leaned back in her chair. 'What's the message?'

CHAPTER 13

Fear. It was everywhere. It was visible in every eye, pungent in the air, audible in the subtle twangs in every voice. Fear polluted every environment. It was inescapable, insufferable and invincible.

And how could it not be? But it was the wrong kind of fear. An egocentric fear. One that worked only for self-preservation.

Isaac was afraid too, but he didn't broadcast it like everyone else. His fear was the right kind. Justifiable. More a concern than anything else. Concern for others; for Winter.

She was the only one anyone knew to be in immediate danger. The only person anyone needed to worry about. She wouldn't be afraid for herself, after all. She was too stubborn for that.

If anyone else was in danger, contrary to the guarantees of the crew, there was no sign of it. It had been five hours since Winter had disappeared and everyone else was still here. If the raiders had some way of prising people out of their pods alive, they were taking a long time to deploy their solution. At the very least, they could surmise that these raiders were experienced professionals who should know that there would be no benefit to pulling someone from their pod unless they had some way to keep them alive.

The obvious conclusion was that they had chosen Winter for a purpose.

But no-one cared to listen to him. They would cover their ears and continue to scream. 'We're next!' they would cry. 'It's all over!' No-one could say anything that would convince them to stop and listen. If anyone cared at all for Winter, they did very well to hide it. Even Isaac saw no such concern in their faces.

After a full hour of dealing with the terrified passengers, the crew had fled to their simulated flight deck and locked everyone else out of it. Maybe they thought that by giving everyone some time alone, they might calm down a little.

So far they'd been wrong. In fact, two of the men had tried to commit suicide before realising that death was impossible in SSR. They didn't give up easily though. They had refused to deploy their parachutes in a skydiving simulation and walked away intact. They had sat underwater for ten minutes trying to drown themselves, to no avail. The sense of futility made everything worse for them.

With no authority to complain to, or to seek consolation from, everyone had retreated into their own private simulations. Isaac had done the same, hoping to find some comfort in solitude. With Winter gone, there was no-one else he wanted to talk to. Everyone else seemed to find his presence worsened the situation. He could tell they felt uncomfortable around him. Even his own mother did sometimes.

He stood at the edge of a tall precipice, looking out from his vantage point over a sprawling canyon that disappeared off into the distance. The pale grey of the rock provided the perfect boundary between the pastel-blue of the sky and the lush greens of the grass and leaves below.

He kept his interface open, hovering beside him, using it to conjure objects that he could cast over the cliff. Clothes, food, utensils, sporting equipment, the list went on and he selected and threw each one in turn.

He reached into the interface and drew out a small china

cup. He inspected it briefly, then tossed it out into the breeze. There was some primal satisfaction that came from watching as it tumbled through the air and shattered against a rocky outcrop, scattering shards of china to be lost in the trees at the foot of the rock face.

He continued to watch long after it had vanished. Then from behind him, his ears caught the familiar sound of a brisk gust of wind. He spun around to see the ship's SSR technician fading in. The blades of grass scattered and flattened, making way for her feet as they materialised. As her form solidified, the cool clifftop air swept her hair out to the side, then abated and allowed it to settle. She surveyed the surroundings and smiled as her eyes found Isaac, then she began to walk in his direction.

'Meeting's over. For now, at least. I just wanted to check that you're okay.'

He turned back around to face the canyon. Hayley stood beside him and followed his gaze.

'Have you got a plan?' Isaac asked.

'Not yet,' Hayley spoke sadly. 'I'm sure we'll think of something though.' He didn't even need to look at her to know she doubted her own words.

'Why did you come to see me? Everyone else is alone too, and they're more scared than I am.'

'Because you're quieter than they are. I already know what they're feeling; they won't stop telling me. But you never say a word.'

She was just like Winter, placing his feelings above her own. Why did she care? No-one else did. Maybe she didn't and it was all just a job.

They stood in silence for some time. In any other situation it would have felt awkward, but right now just having her company seemed to help, though he couldn't think why.

After a time though, he had to speak.

'Do you think Winter's still alive?'

She didn't answer immediately. Her head tilted downwards. 'We don't know.'

'We?'

Hayley nodded. 'We discussed it for quite some time, and we honestly can't say with any kind of certainty.'

'You must have some ideas though, right? About what might have happened to her?'

'Well, we have two leading theories. The first is that they found some way to force her out of the simulation. It would probably have meant brute-forcing their way past certain systems, which explains the glitches you saw when she disappeared. If so, she'll most likely have been taken into custody to be sold as a slave whenever we make planetfall. That would at least mean she's alive. That doesn't tell us why we're still here though. We'd have expected them to have taken us too by now, so I don't think that's what happened.'

She chewed her lip before she continued. 'The alternative is that they pried her pod open and pulled her out while she was still plugged in. It would explain the glitches, and it would also tell us why she was … screaming.' She hesitated. 'It would also mean she's dead. The brain needs to be eased back into control of the body and it wouldn't have had that time. I hate to admit it, but it's the most likely of the two. It's the only one to tick all the boxes.'

They fell into silence once again. A light breeze played with Isaac's long fringe and tickled his brow.

'But like I said, we can't be sure,' Hayley added.

Isaac had already considered both theories. The raiders would have to be stupid to try yanking someone free of the system like that, but Hayley was right. It was the most likely of those theories. But despite every reason to believe that

Winter was dead, he'd discounted that possibility. It made no sense to cling to the hope that she was still alive, yet he did. He couldn't give up on her yet.

'You're a lot like her, you know,' Hayley said.

That made Isaac turn to look at her. 'What do you mean?'

'Right after you came on board, I found her on her own, sitting by a lake, just staring out towards the horizon. She would ask me questions just like you, but she never told me why she was asking them. She kept her feelings all to herself, so that it wouldn't be anyone's problem but her own. It seems to me you're the same.'

'I knew what she was feeling,' he said, turning his head back to the rocky ridges in the distance. 'I knew right from the beginning. She was afraid, like everyone else is now. Afraid for herself. She was running from something.'

'She told you?'

'I just knew. I could read it on her face.'

Isaac watched her carefully. He hadn't paid much attention to Hayley's expression since she'd come, but now he was surprised to see that she showed the same concern he did. She was worried for Winter.

He looked out over the canyon again.

'She's still alive. She's still running.' His voice remained still and unwavering as he spoke. 'She wouldn't die without seeing it coming. That would be the worst way to go. To die screaming the way she was. She deserves better than that.'

'We won't die by their hands,' Hayley said softly. 'We'll die when the world is ready to be without us. And if it were up to me, it would be with a view like this.' She raised her arms out wide to behold the splendour of the landscape and breathed deeply, inhaling the fresh air through her nostrils. 'If I die with a view like this, I'll die happy.'

Isaac briefly entertained the thought but shook it from his head. 'I don't want to die at all. Life may not be all it's made out to be, but it's all we have. Everything we are and everything we were is here, in this reality. Life gives us everything, and death just steals it away again. It's a thing we tolerate because we must, but there's no point in glorifying it. The comfort we take from that will only be wiped away like everything else.'

She gave him a sideways glance. 'Sounds like you've thought about it a lot.'

'Lots of time to myself.'

Silence fell between them again. The steady breeze wafted past their ears. It was almost calming enough to allow Isaac to forget about the troubles of the real world. His mind drifted like the clouds, far away …

BEEP BEEP

… and was immediately brought back to the present.

He followed the sound and found himself looking up at Hayley again. She scowled and conjured her interface panel with a flick of her fingers.

'What was that?'

'I created an alert that should go off whenever the number of simulation occupants changes. That was it, just then.'

'You mean someone else was taken?'

Hayley's face was grim and unresponsive as she produced a list of everyone currently occupying a space in system memory. Then her eyes widened. A double take and a few steps back, then her expression softened as she cupped a hand over her mouth.

'What is it?' Isaac demanded. 'Who have we lost?'

'Wrong question,' she replied. The corners of her mouth formed a smile as she turned the hovering display towards him. 'Winter's back.'

Isaac staggered from the relief he felt hearing those words. He felt a peculiar tingling sensation in his stomach. Despite his unwillingness to accept her death, he found himself quite unprepared for her return so soon. Something dissuaded him from believing she could be capable of coming back at all.

'Are – are you sure?' He took a closer look at the list and it did indeed report that she was back. 'This isn't … I don't know … an old report, maybe?'

'No, this is current. She's definitely back.' Her voice grew in excitement. She swiped the screen back to face her and with a few more taps she announced, 'She's in the garden where we held the meeting. I'll bring her here.'

'Shouldn't we go to her?'

'She's probably about to move to a different sim anyway, since there's no-one in the garden. If we go to her we might miss her. No, I'll bring her to us.'

A little more tapping and then a sharp gust of wind blew around them. They turned away from the precipice and watched.

Clad in sand-coloured fibres and thick black boots, the strong, slender form of Winter Starling resolved, looking a little surprised by her surroundings. When her eyes fell upon Hayley and Isaac, she began to jog in their direction. Hayley waved to her vigorously and Isaac stood staring wide-eyed in disbelief.

'Hayley!' she called, coming to a stop in front of them.

'What happened? We thought you might have been …' Hayley trailed off.

'Killed? Oh, no, it's just like Julian said. They don't want to kill any of us.'

'You met them?' Isaac asked. 'So they managed to get you out?'

'How did they manage that?' Hayley joined in again, then she shook her head slightly and looked Winter up and down. 'And why did they put you back in?'

Winter hesitated. 'They did pull me out, yes, using the implant in my spine.'

This was the first Isaac had heard of any implant, but Hayley's expression flashed with familiarity. Then she pushed her hands into her face and stamped a foot into the dry soil with frustration.

'Dammit! The implant, of course! Why didn't I think of that?'

'What implant?'

'That's a story for another time, Isaac,' Winter said. 'Right now I need to see Captain Orson. That's why they sent me back. They want me to deliver messages between him and them. I have twelve hours to get a response from him, then they pull me out again.'

'Messages?' Isaac parroted.

Recovering from her fit of annoyance, Hayley was upbeat. 'This is good though! It's better than any of the theories we had. After all, you're still alive and no-one else is in danger of being extracted from the system. We're still holding all the cards.'

'They've made some pretty substantial progress, Hayley. With me they at least have some leverage. We hardly have all the cards.'

'Still, you have to admit it could be a whole lot worse.'

'Well, that's a given.'

'The messages!' Isaac interrupted. Winter and Hayley both turned their heads around to face him. 'You said you have messages for the captain. What are they?'

Winter's tone turned to one of scepticism. 'Nothing

particularly interesting. They want to ask him to shut down the SSR, assuring him that no-one will be harmed.'

Hayley screwed her face up. 'He already knows that. We all know that.'

'I know. I already told them that.'

'So why bother?'

'I think it's their attempt to open up some kind of dialogue. They're willing to bargain.'

'Bargain? How? It seems like a pretty all-or-nothing arrangement to me.'

'They didn't say. They just told me to deliver it to him and respond within twelve hours.'

'Well I think we all know what he's going to say. Do we really need twelve hours?'

'Trying to demonstrate their leniency, perhaps? I don't know. In any case, I need to take it to him. I can at least use the time to tell him what I learned from my time on their ship. Where is he?'

Hayley turned her attention back to her interface and searched for Orson's location. 'It's a safe bet he's either getting drunk, or he's … Oh, yes, there he is. He's in his combat sim. He's restricted access to it, but I can get us in.'

'Okay then, do it.'

As Hayley worked on sending them to the correct simulation, Winter turned to Isaac. 'We can catch up later, okay?'

Winter faded away once again, the faintest remaining traces of her encouraging smile swept away on the breeze. He watched the spot where she had stood, then turned back to the cliff edge and looked out.

He lowered himself to a sitting position, dangling his legs over the edge. With no-one left to see, he allowed a smile to tug at the corners of his mouth.

CHAPTER 14

Winter breathed deeply, the pain subsiding. She had been yanked from the SSR six times now. After the first time, the extractions had become less painful. But now they were getting progressively worse again. Each time the jolts to her neck grew sharper.

She had to push these concerns to the back of her mind. As much as she hated it, helping Gram had to be her priority.

To trade the lives of these strangers for her friends and family. It wasn't a fair choice, but it was one she had to make. At least this way, everyone could live.

But her mission was failing. Every time she had gone back in, she had been given a different way of asking Captain Orson to surrender. By now she was having to explicitly ask him to name his price. But Orson was proud and stubborn. The raiders wanted his ship and his freedom. He wouldn't give those up even if there was no-one else at stake. No-one was surprised with the response he gave, every single time.

'Get the fuck off my ship.'

The stalemate hadn't shifted an iota. Gram had only the option of convincing the captain to turn the simulation off and Orson couldn't find any terms he would agree to in order to make that happen.

Fortunately, Gram had no way to look into the simulation. She just had to take Winter at her word that she was doing what she was told. She'd had no reason to lie yet, but if she did Gram would have no choice but to believe her.

At the very least, Winter thought, it was buying the crew time. The raiders had to give the captain enough time to consider his response and try to find some middle ground. With that time, however, the captain could give his simple answer in seconds and spend the rest of the time working out a plan.

However, the plan was slow to form. Resources were too limited to do anything elaborate. In fact, their meetings appeared to be conducted more out of courtesy now, rather than any sense that they could mastermind an escape.

Hayley and Julian spent their time poring over screens filled with code, trying to see if there was a way to get a technological edge from inside the computer. They'd played with the idea of forcing an incredibly slow data link through the ship's power grid – the one system that remained linking every system on the *Redemptive Veteran*. But such a link, they insisted, would take days to establish, and they refused to give an estimate on how many.

Everyone had their role to play now. Hayley and Julian worked on the data hardline they had proposed, Orson and Sam considered what to do with it once it was serviceable, the passengers continued to chip away at the crew's patience with their insufferable, albeit understandable anxiety and Winter delivered each side of the bickering argument to its rightful recipient.

The gel thinned and leaked away through the drain in the floor again, leaving a sticky residue soaked into Winter's robe. She had been given her old clothes back so that she could wear them when she was awake, but they were no good for her in the pod. Initial concerns about the harm of wearing them in SSR were no longer relevant, seeing as the acceleration had ceased. But she didn't like moving around for hours at a time in clothes slick with suspension gel, so she kept the garb on standby, ready to slip into when she awoke.

The same people were always there. Three guards, an engineer at the workstation, and Gram. Today she was in the doorway, her back pressed to one side and her feet braced against the other. She raised her head at the hiss of the pod door sliding open and fixed Winter with an expectant stare.

'Get the fuck off my ship.' Winter didn't need to deliver the precise message, but doing so gave her a free pass to swear at her captor. She took what she was given.

Gram flung her head back against the edge of the bulkhead she rested against, impacting with an audible thump. 'Son of a bitch!' she cursed loudly.

'Don't know what you were expecting.' Winter pulled herself out of her seat. Getting quite used to certain movements in zero-gravity now, she expertly swung herself out and helped herself to her clothes.

'I'm just doing what I can,' Gram said defensively. 'Can't he see I want this to end just as much as he does?'

Winter pulled her trousers on before taking the robe off to help preserve her decency. 'That's not the problem and you know it.'

'Yeah, I know. Sometimes I just like to think the problem is simpler than it is. It's tough coming up with complex solutions. Helps to streamline it a bit.'

'Let me know how that works out for you.' She peeled the gown from her skin and flung it into the middle of the room. Gram looked at one of the guards and made a sharp gesture with her head. He rolled his eyes, then pushed himself towards the garment and snatched it up before returning to his post.

Winter pulled on her boots and, while they didn't serve the same practical purpose as usual, she clipped her various belts and straps over the top of her thick padded jacket. Her weapon holster was empty, as was every pocket and pouch.

'Come.' Gram beckoned from the doorway. 'My office.'

'Surprise, surprise,' Winter muttered through her exasperation. She kicked away from the wall towards the door, meaning to catch it on the way past and swing herself through.

But it didn't work out that way. When her arms should have reached out, they refused to move. In fact, her entire body failed to respond to her instructions. She sailed past the door, limbs drifting freely like a ragdoll. She managed to make a panicked squeak as she flinched, rapidly approaching the computer terminal on the far side of the suite.

The engineer cried out at the sudden impact between her and his desk. All three guards raised their rifles, training them on her head. The engineer batted her away with a backhand to the face. She grunted with the blow as it cast her back across the room in a spin.

'Freeze!' one of the guards screamed at her. 'Or we open fire!'

'What?' With no power from her lungs, her voice was pitifully weak. 'No, don't shoot.' Her numb arms and legs continued to drift uncontrollably.

Gram poked her head back through the door at the ruckus. 'Winter, what the hell are you doing?'

One of the guards fired a shot. Winter yelped and squeezed her eyes shut as it went wide and smashed against the bulkhead. 'Don't shoot!' Gram commanded and the guards held their fire.

A sharp click in the back of her neck and Winter had full motor control again. On her approach to another wall, she wedged the toe of her boot into one of the rubber wall grips to hold herself in place, then held her hands above her head.

She curled her body in to bring it to a complete stop. Then she waited.

Silence fell upon the room. The soldiers kept their weapons trained on her until Gram gave them a hand signal to lower them. She moved fully into the room and floated her way over to Winter, staring her in the eye.

'What did you do?'

'I didn't do anything!' she retorted, wiping blood away from her nostrils.

Gram's expression hardened, pressing her for a deeper response.

'I completely lost control of my body. It was just like–' She stopped herself before revealing any details about the night she had been held captive on her kitchen table, although the similarities were undeniable. 'This was your fault.'

'What?'

'You! Do you even know what my implant does? Do you know what it's for?'

Gram raised an eyebrow, then turned to look at her engineer. Winter followed her gaze and glared at the man, who promptly broke eye contact and began to fidget with his ear lobe.

Winter nudged herself away from the corner and drifted towards him. 'I don't have a machine in my spine for no reason, you know. It's vital. It's the only reason I have any control over my body at all. Without it I'd be dead! But when you lot need a new toy, you just take what you can get. You didn't even stop to think about the kind of damage you might be doing!'

'Explain,' Gram demanded. Winter cast her a glance, to find she too was glaring at her engineer.

He hesitated, biting his lip. A bead of sweat formed on his forehead.

'Speak!'

'It was always a possibility,' he stammered, losing the impressive confidence he usually displayed. 'After all, we are hijacking a piece of technology and making it do something it was never designed to do. We have to tell it that the signals it's receiving are dangerous and force it to reject them. It also has to quickly prepare the neurons that haven't been exercised recently. Overall, it's quite a technically … violent procedure. It could cause minor electrical damage to the device itself.'

'It was fine before. Why's it only beginning to misbehave now?' Gram demanded.

'Any damage the device has sustained is most likely compounding. It'll get worse with time.' He looked up at Winter, his face red. 'I thought we could continue a while longer before this started to happen.'

Winter glowered at him, making no effort to hide the infernos raging in her eyes.

She thought they'd already crossed the final boundary and yet they continued to find ways to step even further. Not only had they manipulated the machine that kept her alive for their own purposes, they had been progressively destroying it. She wondered how long it would be before it failed completely, and she was left to float in zero-gravity as she slowly asphyxiated. That voice had threatened her with the very same death, back at home on Arali.

The raiders understood their mistake at this point, but they had no comprehension of how far the implications of her death spread. If she died, her mission failed. The lives of her friends and family would be forfeit.

The more she thought about it, the more she worried it may already be too late. The message she was carrying; it was embedded in her implant. There was no way to be sure it was undamaged. It may have even been completely wiped after all the device had been through.

After a brief silence, Winter looked over to Gram, whose head was hung low. It snapped up again and her eyes shot a deathly glare at her engineer. With a quick hand motion, the soldiers raised their weapons once more. Winter backed up out of the line of fire.

The engineer's back jerked upright, as if he were tied to a post. His eyes darted around the room, staring down the barrel of one gun, then quickly flitting over to the next. Sweat poured from his skin.

'Tell me now,' Gram spoke flatly. 'Can you repair the implant?'

He was about to open his mouth when she cut him off.

'It's very important that you answer me truthfully.'

He glanced around the room again, at each of the three rifles aimed at his head. He gulped. 'There's a good chance I can do something about it,' he said. 'I can't make any promises though.'

Gram glanced to the guards on her left, then over to Winter on the right, before focussing again on her engineer. Winter wondered if she might actually order his execution, or whether this was just a show of power and authority.

'Tell me how. And this time, don't leave out any crucial details that could jeopardise the rest of the job.'

He held up a finger, then looked down into his lap, squeezed his eyes shut and muttered to himself. After a moment he looked up again, his face red.

'Okay, I'll need some kind of surface. Just a table will do, but I'll need to be able to fasten her to it. We can't have her floating off in the middle of surgery …'

'Surgery?' Gram exclaimed. Winter wasn't filled with confidence.

'I have to get to her implant. Don't worry, there's nothing too complicated about it, I'll just need to put her under an anaesthetic and make an incision in the skin on the back of her neck.'

The words sent shivers down Winter's spine.

'Once I have access to the device it should be fairly straightforward. I guess it depends on the extent of the damage.'

'Right,' Gram said. 'Do we have any anaesthetic?'

'We have some basic medical supplies on board, but nothing like that as far as I know. But I could try to use her implant to numb her body, like what happened just now. She wouldn't feel a thing.'

'Now, hang on a sec,' Winter interrupted. 'Are we seriously going to let this moron try to fix the damage he caused by messing around with my implant, by letting him mess around *more* with my implant?'

A quick look seemed to confirm that Gram shared her scepticism.

'This doesn't involve anywhere near the kind of intrusion that the SSR extraction does. This won't cause any damage, I can assure you.' He hesitated before adding, 'And even if it did, I'd be going in to fix it anyway.'

Winter turned to Gram. 'Is there anyone else we could get to do this?'

She ignored the question and asked the engineer her own. 'You said you couldn't guarantee success. What do we stand to lose?'

'Oh, nothing! Nothing can go strictly wrong, it's just that things won't necessarily go right. I don't know how damaged it is, so I don't know if I can fix it or not. It certainly won't get any worse.'

Winter almost screamed at him. He had done so much damage already, she couldn't stomach the idea of letting him touch her again. But she held back. He seemed to be the only one with any chance of fixing it, and the consequences of leaving the implant unrepaired were too awful to contemplate.

Gram released a sharp sigh of resignation. Despite Winter's doubts, she waved her hand and the guards lowered their guns. The engineer allowed himself to relax, measuring his breathing until it returned to a regular pace.

'What's the first step?' Gram asked.

'I'll need to scan the implant. If I can construct a model of it, I may be able to work out where the fault is before she goes under the knife.'

Winter shuddered at the prospect of being paralysed again, strapped to a table and entirely at the mercy of a man whose competence had just been called into question.

'I have the tools I'll need to perform the scan,' he continued. 'I use them to perform maintenance on our own ship whenever we–'

'Shut up,' Gram commanded. 'I've heard enough of your voice. Just do it. Take Miss Starling wherever you need her to be, then send her up to my office when you're done.'

'Uhh, right, yes Gram.' He unclipped the harness that held him in his seat and floated towards the door. 'This way, young miss,' he said, gesturing for Winter to take the lead. She paused to shoot a glare at Gram, then swung around the doorframe, out into the corridor.

'Keep a close eye on her!' Gram called after them. 'We don't want her floating away from you if her implant has another tantrum!' The engineer didn't respond.

Winter began to wonder if Gram's patience was nearing its limits. Maybe if she and the *Veteran*'s crew continued to make life difficult for her, she'd eventually just give up?

Unlikely, but it was one of the few comforting thoughts she had left.

CHAPTER 15

'Silence, everyone. Silence. Let's get started.'

The chairs in the garden had all been moved back to make some room in front of the gazebo, where Julian paced left and right. Everyone else, passengers and crew, with the exception of Winter, sat in an arc around him. The rabble gradually fell to a reluctant silence.

News of Winter's survival had spread, as had her intention to assist the captain in negotiating a deal with the raiders. This had helped to reassure just about everyone in the simulation, particularly the passengers. However, they still doubted the crew's competence and would no longer accept being left out of important decisions.

Julian understood their unease and had suggested to the rest of the crew that the passengers might feel more involved and content if they were allowed to discuss their predicament and agree on the best way to proceed. He said that breaking down the wall they'd erected between themselves and their passengers might make their side stronger.

Orson disagreed. He trusted that his crew was capable enough to explore all possible options without having to consult the ignorant masses. Bringing the passengers in would not only be a slow and painful experience, it would in fact be a slow and painful regurgitation of a discussion they had already concluded days ago.

Despite the captain's aversion, Julian had Hayley and Sam on his side and before long they managed to twist Orson's arm.

Julian marched to the far left of his makeshift stage, conjuring his system interface as he walked. He froze it in the air, then stretched it across as he strode back the other way, forming a broad blank panel that hovered before the assembly.

He turned to his audience and brought his hands together with a loud clap. 'Okay,' he began, ensuring he had everyone's attention before continuing. 'We're all here to talk about our situation, and to figure out how to resolve it. The crew and I have been working tirelessly to come up with a solution and we thought it was time to get you all involved. Quite simply, we have two options on the table, each with their own merits and … drawbacks.'

There were mixed expressions across the faces he saw. Some of the passengers seemed to be paying close and considered attention, while others looked anxious and uncomfortable.

The kid seemed far more interested in the people around him than the discussion. His mother sat beside him, arms crossed, looking as unimpressed as ever.

Julian tried to ignore her and scrawled a heading at the top of the panel with his finger before turning back to look at the passengers. 'The first option is to surrender. Given the information that Winter has been able to provide, they do appear to fit the description of a typical raiding crew, as we suspected. This means that by surrendering, we would be giving ourselves up to be auctioned off to the highest bidders.'

Murmuring began to grow as they were all reminded of the raiders' intentions, but Julian hushed them down again and wrote another heading beside the first.

'The other option is simply to *not* surrender. By doing this we wouldn't just hand ourselves over, but there's no way of knowing what might happen in the long run. Our situation could get better or it could get worse. There's much less certainty with this option.'

The crowd stayed quiet this time, as if waiting for Julian to elaborate, but instead he moved on.

'Uh, let's start gathering some opinions then, starting with our first option. Would anyone like to offer anything?' People began to call out, so Julian hurriedly added, 'Raised hands only, please!'

The adult passengers all raised their hands. Some level of order had to be maintained and it would be far too easy to let the situation get out of control. They'd been very vocal about their feelings up until now, but it seemed they still had a lot left to say.

Julian selected a woman who sat near the middle, plump and fair-haired. Hands dropped back down as she spoke.

'Well, none of us want to be sold,' she said, finding her confidence in speaking with all the attention on her. 'We all want to be our own people and, you know, live our own lives and all that. We won't get that if we give ourselves up.'

Julian caught Orson rolling his eyes at the woman and her mundane insight. He started to wonder whether the captain had been right about this being a waste of time.

'Good.' Julian made a note of her point beneath the *Surrender* heading. It was an obvious point, of course, but at least it was somewhere to start. He turned back to his audience. 'Anything else?'

Hands darted back into the air, but this time his eyes were drawn to two middle-aged men sitting to his right. They were both dressed smartly, one in a grey shirt, and one in a light blue. Both sat the same way too, mimicking each other, consciously or otherwise. They leaned back with their legs crossed; one ankle resting atop the opposite knee. They looked so similar it was difficult to tell them apart. At random, Julian gestured towards the man in the blue shirt, who lowered his leg to the ground and leaned forward in his seat.

'It seems to me that surrender guarantees survival and the other doesn't.' His voice was deep and confident. His nearly identical partner bobbed his head steadily as he continued to speak. 'They have promised us our lives at the very least. Sure, it'll suck, but over time we might find ourselves in a position to break free of whatever life we're living. The alternative doesn't give us any protection. They could decide that killing us is more profitable than leaving us alone to plot against them.'

A murmur of agreement rippled through the crowd and heads turned towards Julian again, who considered the response. 'Right, yes, okay,' he said, about to turn towards his notes again, but a lone raised hand caught his eye.

'Um, actually–' Isaac began, but his mother fixed him with a stare. He lowered his hand slowly back into his lap.

'Go on,' Julian said. 'It's okay.'

The boy looked at his mother who had dropped her gaze to the floor. He took a deep breath and continued.

'There is no guarantee. By now we've caused them a lot more trouble than they expected. It wouldn't surprise me if they sought some kind of revenge once we're at their mercy. While that doesn't necessarily mean killing anyone, it's also probable that not all of us would fetch much of a price as slaves. I doubt it would affect their profit much to execute some of us.'

'Isaac!' the boy's mother hissed. 'That's enough of that!'

'Mrs Vince, do you have something to say?' Julian said.

The woman squirmed in her seat. 'He is clearly far too young to understand what's going on. The point is ludicrous.'

Everyone watched as she discredited her son, who shrunk back into his seat, offering no objection.

'It might not be what we want to hear, but it's still valid. I think perhaps you underestimate your son. He could be quite valuable in this discussion.' Julian stepped back and addressed the wider audience. 'Does anyone have any response to Isaac before we continue?'

A large man, the husband of the fair-haired woman who had spoken earlier, raised his voice.

'Don't criminal organisations usually have codes of honour? The raiders may have a rule against needless killing, or at least some kind of honesty policy.' There was a level of uncertainty in his tone. Perhaps he wasn't entirely convinced by his own argument, or maybe he was just aware that such speculation wasn't likely to sway anyone. Whatever the case, Julian responded with a smile and a gracious nod.

'That may be true, and it's certainly worth taking into account. Thank you.' He turned back to Mrs Vince. 'That's how we discuss matters. If we shut people down, we might miss something important. We'll be happy to hear anything you want to add, as soon as you've finished trying to take information away.'

The woman simply sneered.

Julian's gaze darted sideways to catch Hayley looking at him with an amused smirk. He smiled back as he turned to make further notes on his interface.

'One last point on surrender.'

Noticeably fewer hands were raised this time. It seemed that most concerns were about their chances of survival. But this time, Julian was surprised to see Orson lift his hand.

'Let's hear what our captain has to say on this one.'

The crowd groaned, but Orson spoke anyway.

'Surrender is just a fancy word for giving up. We haven't been able to explore all of the options yet, and we could still discover a better solution. If we continue negotiating with them through Winter, we can buy ourselves more time to explore every option. Giving up now not only brings our resourcefulness into disrepute, but it is also, at its heart, humiliating.'

Isaac's mother lifted her arm into the air. 'I'll counter that. I have new information to bring to the table,' she said mockingly.

A wave of exasperation swept over Julian, but he saw no reason to stop her.

'You say our time comes from negotiating through Winter, yes? Well then, where is she? She's been out there for nearly a full day. She isn't supposed to be out there for anywhere near this long! You have dismissed every single offer they've made. By now they're probably tired of arguing with a brick wall. You've pushed them to the end of their tether, Captain, and now we have no time left. I say that a decision must be made here and now.'

Orson rolled his eyes and folded his arms as he leaned back in his seat. 'My decision has already been made. We are not giving ourselves up until we are certain that every other option is a dead end.'

'I wasn't talking about your decision, I was talking about ours.' She rose and stood in the open space beside Julian. 'We don't need to discuss this anymore. Frankly, this whole meeting is incredibly condescending. We all know what's going on, and we have just as much right to a decision as the captain or any of his crew. I call for a vote, right now!'

'Hang on a minute, Mrs Vince, just sit back down and we'll talk it through a bit longer.' Julian stepped forward and laid a hand on her shoulder.

'Back off!' She batted his hand away. 'The time for talking is over. We are taking a vote now! All those in favour of surrender, raise your hands.'

Her hand was immediately in the air. Four more could be seen: the two men in shirts and, somewhat hesitantly, the couple near the middle.

Isaac was the only passenger who hadn't moved. He sat silently, watching the other passengers. His mother stared at him coldly and Julian could almost feel the ice in the air. Isaac's gaze fell and he cast his vote.

'That's six,' she announced. Despite an unquestionable majority, she continued to press the issue. 'All those against?'

Hayley and Sam voted. Orson scowled, his eyes fixed on Julian.

This was a nightmare. He wished he had listened to the captain's earlier objections. He was right; the crew had everything in hand until now.

'Captain?' Hayley said.

'I won't participate in this farce.'

'Not that it matters anyway!' Mrs Vince chirped. 'Either way, you've been outvoted. The decision has been made, Captain Orson. Shut down this simulation.'

Julian spotted Hayley shifting uneasily. As the administrator of the system, she would have to be the one to turn the SSR off, but she wouldn't do that without the captain's order.

Orson reached over to his right and placed a steady hand on her knee. 'We'll talk about this later,' he said. 'Until then, do nothing.' Then he stood and marched to the front. 'This ship is not a democracy,' he barked. 'There is a reason why we have a captain, not a government. On this ship, we do not vote. The information is given to me and I make the call. That is it.'

His outburst elicited nothing besides fierce glares from his audience, but he was not swayed. He continued.

'I will not be cowed into defeat so easily. I have faith in my crew. They have never let me down before and they will deliver again. We will not be the ones to wave the white flag. I am fighting for your freedom! I have always been fighting for your freedom. Why do you refuse to do the same?'

He stood his ground, apparently unaware of the spiteful stares of the passengers. Hayley and Sam averted their eyes. Julian licked his dry lips and shuffled backwards.

'So that's it? There's no changing your mind at all?' asked the man in the grey shirt.

'None. Surrender without exploring every available alternative is a sure sign of weakness. I would never have allowed it in the Conglomerate forces, and I won't start now.'

'I don't care if you were a soldier before, Captain, you're not anymore,' Mrs Vince sneered.

'I still have a duty to protect you all.'

The big man in the middle stirred. 'So, why are we even here if we don't get a say?' The rest of the crowd joined his voice in uproar. Chaos resumed.

Orson released an exasperated breath. His posture loosened and he turned to walk away. He shrugged. 'Ask him.' He gestured towards Julian. Suddenly, the passengers' collective vitriol was turned on him.

Julian ignored them and followed Orson, who summoned his interface. 'Give me a shout if Winter turns up,' he called back with a tone of disinterest, then with a tap of a few buttons, he vanished from the garden.

CHAPTER 16

The scan was long and tedious in equal measure but the engineer, though obviously unpractised in medicine, had managed to cobble together a crude yet serviceable map of Winter's neural implant.

The process involved a metal implement pressed against the skin of her neck. After it emitted a rhythm of clicks and a brief hum, he adjusted its position and performed the process again. Once he had gone all the way around Winter's neck, he made some notes on his computer before beginning the process again.

He gave her no indication of how long the process would take and she wasn't permitted to talk or move in case her motions interfered with the scan. It was tempting to hurry him up, but the last thing she wanted was for him to do a sloppy job. She simply had to swallow her impatience and wait for him to finish.

After what felt like an hour, he seemed satisfied with his scans. He packed up his tools and set about analysing the results. He had said that determining the source of the issue could take some time and that devising a means of correcting it safely would likely take even longer.

Frustrated by the wait, but with no intention to hurry his progress, Winter allowed herself to be escorted to Gram's office. She fastened herself into her usual seat while Gram busied herself on the far side.

The raider was facing away, operating some kind of mechanical appliance. 'Can I get you a drink?'

'I'll take some water.'

'You'd be making a mistake. The tea won't last much longer at the rate we're guzzling it.'

'Alright, I suppose a warm drink would be nice. After all, there's always a distinct chill on this ship. You cold-blooded bastards suck up all the heat.'

'As fun as this has been, I won't miss you when this is over,' Gram said above the hissing sound of the machine she was operating.

'I'm amazed you've put up with me for this long.'

Gram made a short grunt as the machine fell silent and she turned around to face Winter. In her hands were two identical grey cups with domed lids and thick straws.

She gently pushed on the wall and drifted over to the desk. She let go of one cup, letting it float into Winter's waiting grip. She placed the other one on the table, a magnet on the base holding it in place.

Winter set her drink down too. 'You're not putting me back in that pod again, are you?' she asked. That was what being called into the office normally meant. 'If you think I'm going to let you put me back in there with my implant misbehaving like this, you've got another think coming.'

'No need to panic. I'm not giving you another message yet. You'll have nothing to deliver until I'm assured it's safe to put you back in again.'

'It's not the "going in" part that scares me. It's coming out again.'

'Touché.'

'So what do you need me for? It's hard to believe you'd call me in just for the company.'

'Ah, well, I have a different mission for you.' She slurped her tea through the straw. It must have been boiling hot, but she didn't wince. 'No implants or SSRs, you'll be pleased to hear, but I'm afraid this one isn't going to be very fun. I don't envy you in the slightest.'

Another one? She wasn't even angry about being used at this point. She was just fed up. How many times would she be made to do someone's dirty work for them before she could finally stop and rest?

'What is it this time?' she grumbled.

Gram sipped her tea. Without looking up at Winter, she moved the straw away from her mouth and said, 'Dinner.'

Winter shook her head, unsure if she'd heard her correctly. 'I'm sorry?'

'Our mutual acquaintance, Mr. Narn, is feeling a bit sidelined. On any other job he'd have the ship by now, but with the trouble your crew is causing us he's not got a lot to do. He wants to be more involved, so he's asked that I send you to have dinner with him.'

'Narn?' Winter racked her memory, trying to put a face to the name. 'Paul Narn? That prick who's paying you to steal the *Veteran*?'

'I prefer to think of him as a spoilt, mind-numbing snob.'

'Like most of your clientele, I'd guess.'

'Right.'

'And you want me to have dinner with him?'

'No, *he* wants you to have dinner with him. And before you ask, no, I have no idea what he expects to gain from it. As far as I'm concerned, you have both been a pain in my arse since this job began, and I think it's about time you two spent some quality time together, with me far away from the both of you. What's that old saying? A problem shared is a problem halved?'

Winter had only met Paul briefly before and had managed

to avoid further contact with him since. Despite his unquestionable involvement in the capture of her and everyone on the *Redemptive Veteran*, he had seemed nice enough, if a little snooty. His dry humour was on about the same level as hers. Perhaps it wouldn't be as painful as Gram made it out to be.

'As long as you can guarantee we won't be doing anything other than talking.'

'I wouldn't worry about that,' Gram said, her lips curling at the sides. 'None of the bedrolls on this ship are big enough for more than one. Besides, he doesn't strike me as the rapey sort.' She winked slyly and Winter nearly retched. 'In any case, if you do decide to punch him I might look the other way for you. I'd have pummelled him a few times myself if I didn't have a professional reputation to maintain. Just try not to make too much noise, would you?'

* * *

The door rattled as she knocked. It was sealed and she couldn't hear anything from the other side.

Winter looked back along the *Shameless Renegade*'s central tunnel. She could hear rather than see the rabble that was the crew, strapping themselves into their seats around a pair of long tables that pulled up out of the deck in their SSR suite.

She'd been eating there ever since she first came aboard. It was a relief to finally have a chance to escape the mess hall, and all the muscle and testosterone they had somehow managed to squeeze into one chamber.

She would normally sit alone at the periphery of the group, which made it much easier to ignore any comments cast her way. Sometimes she had hoped her silence wouldn't be so readily accepted. She wouldn't mind an excuse to smash one or two of them against a bulkhead and she would have her chance if ever they decided to instigate the brawl.

She found herself hoping Narn might start something over dinner, though her first impression of him wasn't one of a fighter. She just hoped that, if it came to it, he would be able to offer some resistance. It wouldn't be so satisfying otherwise.

She knocked again, keeping a grip on the wall. She could hear a quiet shuffling noise from inside. Someone was in there.

At last the door ground along its rails as it slid open and presented her host. He had dressed smartly, his medium-grey jacket pressed smooth, sitting tidily on top of a white shirt. His trousers were a similar shade to the jacket, creased in perfect vertical lines that led right the way down to his immaculately polished black shoes. He'd swept his hair over and trimmed his pale stubble.

He was dressed to impress, but it wasn't working. He looked like a pushover. Like he'd spent too much of his life indoors, with soft clothes and every comfort. He certainly wasn't dressed for zero-gravity either.

'Miss Starling. Do come in,' he greeted her. He raised his arm to guide her into the room.

She took a moment longer to examine him, squinting as she watched his face, before sliding past him.

His room was nearly identical to Gram's. There was a desk near the middle and a selection of appliances against the back wall. A smaller room was sectioned off in the corner. He had added a lit candle to each end of the desk. They certainly brightened the room which, like the rest of the ship, was mainly comprised of dark metal grates and steely surfaces. Even so, Winter found them troubling. She could guess why he would want to insist on a candlelit dinner.

Paul offered her the nearest seat, which she took. Then he rounded the desk and made for the small room in the corner.

Winter inspected the flames burning on the candle wicks. This was her first time seeing fire in zero-gravity. The flames didn't rise and tail away from the waxy column. Instead, they twisted into a sphere of bright blue plasma.

Paul re-entered the room, this time struggling to hold a pair of glass balls, each nearly a foot in diameter, to his chest with one arm. Using his other arm, he braced himself against his seat and his momentum dissipated. He then placed one of the balls on the desk in front of Winter and one in his own spot. He took his seat and strapped in.

Winter examined the object, its thick, flat base held against the desk by magnets. Inside, a strange orb floated, rotating slowly. It was yellow and brown, with a wet sheen to its surface. Upon closer inspection, it appeared to be food. Potato for the most part, with small chunks of a red meat steak pressed into its surface. Carrots and various green vegetables were visible and the entire meal was coated in a thin layer of gravy.

Paul pulled a small device from the base of the glass globe. It was a black cylinder that tapered away to one end and curved into an elegant handle. Then he opened a round window in the side of the ball.

'Go ahead,' he said. 'Do enjoy it.'

She looked at the object in his hand with uncertainty, then attempted to copy what he had done. She opened the window in the side as he had, then found and extracted the instrument in the base. Upon closer inspection she managed to identify a small button on its polished shell, just below the point where its shape sloped towards the handle.

She wasn't sure whether or not to press it.

She glanced up at Paul again, hoping to figure out how it

worked based on his example. Instead, he sat quietly watching her, apparently waiting for her to take the first bite. All she could learn from him was how to hold the tool. She gripped it the way one might hold a pencil, with her index finger resting on the button.

From here she had to figure it out herself. She refused to be caught asking him for help.

The instrument was some kind of eating implement, Winter surmised, but not like any she had seen before. It seemed this ball was made to contain food in zero-gravity, so it made sense that the device in her hand would have been made for the same purpose.

She drummed her fingers on its surface, perfecting her grip, then began to reach it through the circular hole left by the open hatch. She pressed the tool against the food and the end sunk into the soft mass.

The contact affected the food's gentle rotation and nudged it slightly away from her. Nothing was brought away with the instrument as she pulled it back out. It seemed she had done little more than dent the revolving lump.

'You've never used a korde before, have you?'

Winter shot Paul a glance. A smirk played at the corner of his mouth as he watched her.

'What was your first clue?' Winter growled back.

He loosened his harness. 'Allow me,' he said as he began to drift around the table. He took a position behind Winter, leaned over her shoulder and gently took her right hand in his, holding the device – the korde, as he called it – and allowing his head to hover beside hers.

She shook him off and snatched her hand away. He grabbed at the back of her seat to stop himself from spinning off into the open space behind. Winter turned to face him in her restraints and held the korde out to him. 'If you must show me, do it yourself.'

He eased himself towards her again and took the device. He held it the same way he had before, with his finger on the button.

'It's really very simple,' he explained. He reached his arm in front of her, positioning the end of the implement in the threshold of the hatch. 'You hold it here, then press the button.' It clicked down under his finger, then he began to move his wrist so that the flat end of the korde made small circular motions.

Winter watched his hand so closely that she barely noticed as a chunk of potato split away from the main body and began to move towards the opening. Paul stopped rotating his wrist but kept the button held. The gravy-soaked lump floated right up to the korde, then stuck itself to the end.

He turned his smile to face Winter and said, 'That's how it's done.' He then moved it up in front of her mouth and an expectant stare fell over his face.

Winter glared back. 'What are you playing at?'

Paul looked hurt. 'It's simply an attempt to break the ice.'

'Something else is going to break if you don't back off.'

He retreated. With a flicking motion he expertly tossed the food into his waiting mouth. He left the korde floating beside Winter to be reclaimed, then drifted back around to his seat. He began to carve a small chunk out of his own meal. Winter tried her hand at the korde, making circular movements with her wrist.

'Smaller,' he said after swallowing another mouthful.

His advice was unwelcome, but useful nevertheless. Before long she found herself able to take small mouthfuls of meat and potato using the new instrument. It was better than the dried, vacuum-packed morsels the rest of the crew was devouring, but it still left a lot to be desired. Paul was surely not a practised chef.

'I brought these on board with me. They aren't often used in spacefaring vessels. I've only ever used them on space stations before. I can quite enjoy a spell on board one of those orbital resorts,' he said, then took another bite. 'Have you ever been up on one?'

The answer would have been no, if only Winter had been inclined to grace that question with a response. Space resorts were a holiday destination for the rich. She had never struggled for money, but never had she been wealthy enough to afford even a brief period of zero-gravity luxury.

After a short silence, Paul returned to his food. Apparently discontented with the lack of conversation, he spoke again.

'You're a very intriguing woman, Miss Starling. May I call you Winter?'

She shrugged and chewed her steak, glaring at him under the shadow of her brow.

'You're very brave. That you're doing this job so willingly, without a fight, without reward–'

'Stop right there. No-one said I'm doing this willingly. I'm not. I'm doing it because I have no choice, which is also why I'm not resisting. As for my reward, your good friend Gram has promised me my freedom when we reach Earth.'

'Is that right? A promise from Gram?' He furrowed his brow. 'And you expect her to deliver?'

'Seems she's made you a few promises too. What makes my deals any less credible than yours?'

'I have something she wants. We've made a mutually beneficial agreement. She acquires a ship for me, and she gets paid. We both win. Your deal, on the other hand, means she has to give something up for you. She's a businesswoman, Winter. I don't think she's going to accept that so readily.'

'What choice do I have? I either take her word for it, or she locks me up and carries on without me. At least there's a chance this way.'

'Not quite. You're not alone, you know. There is a third option.'

Winter raised an eyebrow.

'The *Redemptive Veteran* is being sold to me. I already have Gram's ear when it comes to negotiation. I have a few people interested in crewing the vessel under me, but it would be terribly lonely if it were just us. I'll buy you from her. Join me on my ship.'

'You want me to agree to be your slave? How is that any different to being sold to the highest black market bidder on Earth? All I know about you is that you like to flaunt your riches, even though they apparently aren't enough to get you your own starship legitimately.'

Paul's expression hardened. 'Be careful, Winter. I may be your only friend on this ship.'

'My friend?' She forced a laugh. 'All I wanted was a quick, peaceful trip to Earth, and you are the reason why that hasn't happened. Every problem to arise since the *Veteran* launched can be traced back to you. Why would I trust you?'

'Tell me, why are you going to Earth in the first place?'

He paused long enough for Winter's unwillingness to respond to become evident.

'These raiders are a gossipy lot. It didn't take them long to reveal that you booked on to your ship within hours of its departure. You must have been in an awful rush to leave. Either you really need to get away from Arali, or you really need to get to Earth. If it's the former, it seems that travelling the stars is the perfect escape. If it's the latter, then you need the best guarantee you can get that you'll be free when we reach the other side. Either way, my deal will profit you far more than Gram's will.'

He left his korde in the air to the side, then leaned forward and reached for Winter's hand. She withdrew.

'What do you say, Winter?' he asked softly.

She'd never considered that he would want to help her. Every move he'd made so far had made things worse for her. But it had all been indirect, done for the ship and not for her. She wondered if perhaps there was a sliver of decency in him, or whether he had just taken a liking to her. He showed no desire to want to save anyone else. It seemed that whatever she chose, the fates of the crew and passengers of the *Redemptive Veteran* would remain the same. She just had to look out for herself now.

The door suddenly rattled open. Paul jerked back into his seat. Winter swivelled in her chair to see Gram hovering in the doorway.

'We're in the middle of dinner, Gram. Why are you interrupting us?' Paul said.

'Business,' she replied. 'Winter, you're going back into SSR now.'

'What? But my implant is still faulty! You can't put me back in there until it's been repaired!' Winter cried.

'I've just been given the results of the scan. Another quick message or two won't kill you, and it'll keep you occupied while my crew finishes the work they need to complete before it can be fixed. Now hurry along. We've left your friends waiting long enough.'

'What's the rush?'

'We've discussed the situation. Your captain has constantly

disregarded our negotiations and I've run out of patience. I'd considered giving him one more chance, but my mind has changed. We've wasted far too much time appealing to him. Now it's time we shake the tree a little, and see what we can get to fall out.'

CHAPTER 17

The gel crept up her body, engulfing her lower legs before all sensation began to fade away. Her eyelids, red and raw, squeezed shut.

She had always known it was only a matter of time.

Her mind left the body in the pod and began to take hold of her virtual form. Piece by piece she felt the presence of her returning physicality.

The system loaded her in gradually as it always did. She looked down to find her bare body visible, yet surrounded by nothing but darkness. She felt herself being lowered gently on to an invisible surface. Besides the contact she felt against her skin, there was no true sensation underfoot. No temperature or texture; only the illusion of a presence. It felt empty. Ethereal.

As warmth spread throughout her body, pulsing out from her brain, Winter was greeted by peace and quiet once more. She had time to think, but the idea of being alone with her thoughts right now frightened her.

She fell to her hands and knees, threw her head down to the ground and screamed.

Gram's attempts at negotiation had been her one redeeming quality, even if they were always laughably one-sided. But at least she'd tried. Or perhaps she knew all along it would never work and had simply been doing it to gain Winter's trust?

She must have known it would come to this. Had it been a deception all this time?

Winter squeezed her eyes shut, trying to push that thought aside. She couldn't believe after all she'd been through that she was still being manipulated; a puppet beneath Gram's dancing fingers.

She bellowed one last time, thumping her fist against the floor. This time however, the ground crunched softly and the impact felt cushioned. She peeked out and saw the sunlit grass that had materialised beneath her. She lifted her head slowly and found herself in the middle of the simulated garden, surrounded by the crew and passengers of the *Redemptive Veteran*.

Winter quickly picked herself off the floor and brushed herself down, finding that her smuggling apparel had been constructed around her body once more. She turned away from the passengers and towards Captain Orson.

His expression was softer than usual and lined with concern. 'What happened?'

Winter shivered as she opened her mouth to respond. 'Gram … the raiders have changed their tactics. They're not negotiating anymore.'

'They were hardly negotiating in the first place. What's changed?'

Sam nudged the captain hard with her elbow. 'What happened, Winter?' she asked.

'They kept me out while they figured out how to repair my implant–'

'Repair?' Hayley interjected.

'I'll explain later. Anyway, Gram told me she couldn't put it off anymore. That they'd wasted too much time trying to make things work …' She gulped. Her weakness in dealing with them lingered in her mind and pulled her thoughts on a diverging path. 'This was bound to happen. There was nothing

I could do to stop it. It's been out of my hands from the start! We didn't cooperate at all. Of course they were going to break eventually!' Her head fell into her hands.

Julian moved to her side. He put his hands on her shoulders. 'Slow down. Come on, take it easy,' he said. He gave her time to measure her breathing and bring her face out of hiding. 'What exactly did she tell you?'

Winter managed to calm herself a little, but the tears that had already escaped from her eyes were left to roll down her cheeks and tumble into the grass. 'Since we refused to talk to them, they would have to … go to plan B.'

Orson grew impatient. 'Hurry up, girl! What is she planning to do?'

She looked up at him, standing with an exhausted slouch. 'We're not as safe as we'd like to think we are. Three of us are going to die.'

A tense silence fell over the crowd. Despite the crew's promises of safety, Winter guessed they'd been expecting this. but no-one wanted to believe it.

The fair-haired woman stammered. 'But … but we're safe in our pods. We're safe in here, you told us we were!'

'The pods aren't protecting us from them. They have our bodies,' Julian corrected her. 'What's protecting us is that our minds aren't in them right now. They can't enslave an empty shell.'

'No! We were protected by the profit they could make by selling us.' Isaac's mother spoke up. She turned to Orson. 'But you had to go and make everything so hard for them, didn't you? Clearly their earnings are hardly worth the effort it takes to get through to you!'

'I had to make a decision. Making the right one is never easy,' the captain shouted back. 'What would you have done?

What plan could you possibly have conceived that would be so infallible?'

'Anything that would have kept us alive! In case you forgot, I voted to surrender. We all did! It may not be as noble as your decision, but at least we all would have lived. That's all I want, Captain. I just want to get to Earth alive!' She hesitated, then turned her burning stare to Winter. 'Three people will die?'

Winter nodded.

'Who?'

Winter avoided eye contact, keeping her eyes fixed on her feet. 'She didn't say exactly, but she did say–'

'Spit it out!' the woman screamed.

'She told me it would be one man, one woman and … one child.'

She lifted her head and looked at Isaac. He was wide-eyed with fear.

Even Gram must have thought this was excessive, but apparently she wanted to prove that no-one was safe anymore. She said that they would start with the ones worth the least so they could retain their most valuable commodities.

'But … but that means …' Mrs Vince's head darted between Winter, the captain and her son. She whispered to herself. 'Isaac?'

Tears welled in the corners of his eyes. His fate was sealed.

'They're going to kill my son!' she cried, fixing Orson with a furious glare. 'This is all your fault!'

A sharp intake of breath. Everyone spun to face the sound and saw the grey-shirted man. He stood stiffly with his arms wrapped tightly around his chest and he shivered between irregular breaths.

His blue-shirted friend wore a look of confusion and concern. 'What is it?' he asked.

'It suddenly got very cold,' he said. His teeth began to chatter.

'What do you mean cold?'

'Something's not right. I feel … I don't know what I feel.'

Winter's eyes dropped away from him, unable to watch as the truth settled in.

'No way,' said the blue-shirted man. 'You can't die. Not you!' He began to look around in desperation, trying to find something that might miraculously save his friend's life. 'Why are you all just standing there?' he shrieked at the other passengers. 'Help me! Help me, please!'

He turned back to his shivering friend, then wrapped his arms tightly around him and buried his head into his friend's neck. He sobbed openly as they shared their last moments together in a strong embrace.

All in an instant, the grey-shirted man jolted upright and he gasped sharply. Then he froze. Everything, even the slightest of movements, ceased. He breathed no more.

The colour started to drain out of him. Every facet of his appearance, from his clothes to his skin to his eyes, faded into a stony grey. A small holographic panel popped up in front of him.

Connection interrupted. Attempting to re-establish …

Isaac gasped. As Winter turned to him she saw a kind of terror she'd never seen before. She wanted to go to him, to help him, but she had already failed. She had betrayed him and now she couldn't stand to look him in the eye.

Winter turned away from Isaac, somehow finding it easier to look at the man who was already gone. She had hardly known him, in fact she didn't even know his name, but his blood was on her hands. His final expression was one of fear and disbelief, now permanently etched on to his features.

She turned away, her gaze falling towards the floor. She couldn't take another look at his face. There must have been something she could have done to save him. Maybe she should have delivered her own messages to Gram instead of passing along Orson's dismissive cursing? She could have negotiated on their behalf. If she'd done that, perhaps diplomacy would have stood more of a chance? At least she would be able to tell herself she'd tried.

But that opportunity was long past now and she hated herself for it. Why couldn't she have acted sooner?

'He might still be okay, right?' the fair-haired woman asked, clinging tightly to her husband. 'It might still reconnect.'

Hayley's mouth opened slightly, but she hesitated before responding. 'The system is being hopeful, but I'm afraid not. If the connection drops unexpectedly at all, his mind won't survive. I'm sorry.' She trailed off.

The woman's lip quivered, then she buried her face in her husband's chest. He winced a little as she tightened her hold on him.

'It's alright,' he said, gently pulling her in further. 'It's okay, you're fine.'

'No, I'm not,' she whimpered. 'It just got very cold.'

Winter's head swivelled in her direction. Her husband loosened his hold on her and looked down at her face.

He stared at her for what felt like ages, his mouth agape. Lost for any words, he took her in his arms and squeezed her tightly. He sobbed openly.

'I love you,' his wife blubbered, muffled by his tear-soaked shirt.

'I love you too.'

She wasn't shaking anymore. Colour seeped away from her leaving her grey and cold in her husband's embrace.

The crowd's attention settled upon Isaac. His eyes were wide, and his skin was pale. His eyes were glossy, yet not a single tear had touched his cheeks.

Hayley stepped over to him. She reached out her trembling hand and placed it on his shoulder. He didn't react. He stared unblinkingly at the woman who had been the last to go.

Hayley knelt down and took a hold of his hand, squeezing it gently.

'We talked about this, didn't we? You remember?'

He nodded silently, still refusing to avert his gaze.

'This happens to us all in time, when the world is finally ready to be without us.'

'Why would it be ready so soon?' He spoke with a tone that might have made him seem composed if his body weren't shaking so violently. 'What have I done wrong?'

'I don't think anyone can say why the world works the way it does, but I don't believe it's because you did anything wrong. Things might only get worse here. Maybe you're just being spared what's left to come? You're a wonderful young man, Isaac.'

'You don't have to say that. I know I'm not.'

'I think you do a lot more good than you know. You tell truths no-one else can see. You bring out the best in everyone you talk to. You're an angel, Isaac.'

His eyes moved slowly to meet hers. 'You really believe that?'

She managed a smile. 'Yes. I really believe it,' she whispered.

Winter's tears continued unabated. She wanted to say something too. Something to comfort him, or to ease her conscience. But something held her back. She couldn't bring herself to say anything.

Isaac sniffled once and a flood of tears cascaded from his eyes. Suddenly he tensed up and wrapped his arms around his shivering chest. 'I don't want to die.'

'I know.'

'I wish I had that view again. The cliffside.'

'We don't need that,' she said, wiping her eyes. 'We have everything right here, look. Beautiful nature, people who love you … What else could you need?'

He paused, squinting at her, trying to read her face. 'People who love me?'

'Yes, of course!'

His gaze lifted and passed over the crowd. He stayed silent as he surveyed them. He looked back to Hayley.

'Who?' he asked.

Then he froze. Every motion stopped and his lifeless avatar stood rooted to the spot, a look of confusion on his face as the colour drained away. Isaac was gone.

Hayley made no attempt to hide her tears now. She stood, turned away from his body and was met by Isaac's mother, hatred rising from her like smoke from a flame.

'Why?' the woman demanded. 'He was on death's door, and you filled his mind with lies! Why?'

'What lies?' Hayley spat back. 'That there was someone here who loved him? I thought it was the truth at the time!'

'Shut your mouth!'

'Just take a good look at that face. That is the face he made when I told him he was loved.'

Winter allowed herself one more look. His confusion was all too obvious. It was almost too much for her to handle, but she kept looking. Maybe the idea that he was loved had left him with some hope in his final moments. Maybe there was still room for a happy ending, of sorts.

But all she could see was the only thing she had ever seen in his eyes. The same fear he carried with him through life.

'I'm done with you now,' Hayley spat. 'He's all yours.'

She stalked past the bereaved mother, who slowly stepped towards Isaac's empty body. She knelt beside him and touched him gently.

His body refused to move.

Winter stepped back, trying to distance herself a little from the group. She had caused them enough trouble. But as Hayley was making her own exit, Orson took her arm and led her towards Winter.

'How close are you to a solution, Hayley? They're going to use this against me as some pro-surrender propaganda and I need something to hit back with.'

'We're having to construct a whole new interface with systems that weren't designed to have one. It's slow progress, and it's going to be very flimsy once it's established.'

'I need an answer. How close are you?'

Hayley screwed up her face as if trying to work something out in her head. 'I think we can start running the first tests in two or three days if we work flat out.'

'Do it.' He softened his grip. 'We'll get them back for this. This won't go unpunished, understand?'

Determination burned in Hayley's eyes. Orson let her go and she strode off. Then he turned to Winter.

'Gram is going to want our reaction to these murders, I'm sure.'

'I know what reaction she wants. But if I know you like I think I do, she's going to be disappointed.'

'Tell her we're completely unfazed, and that we remain resolute. We will not surrender to them.'

'Okay, but ...' She hesitated. 'Are you sure that's the best thing to do? Maybe we should make her think she has changed your mind a bit. Use this to make her think we are willing to negotiate now, even if it just buys us a little more time.'

'They've shown us the carrot and the stick now. They won't kill any more of us. They'd lose too much profit.'

'That's what you said last time.'

'My decision stands.'

Winter frowned at him. He didn't understand Gram at all, but he was still so certain he could call her bluff. He was playing a very dangerous game, but Winter already knew there was nothing she could say to convince him to stop.

'Whatever you say.'

Immediately after she spoke, a crippling pain erupted in her neck and she collapsed to the floor.

'Why so soon?' she screamed towards the sky. 'You always give me hours in here. Why not now?' She fell on to her side, grasping her neck and writhing in pain.

'One more thing before you go, Winter.' Orson knelt down and leaned over her. Darkness filled her vision as she became less and less physical. The captain shrank into the distance and his words echoed around her. 'Give that bitch a punch from me, would you?'

CHAPTER 18

'I'm going to kill you!' Winter flung herself from her pod and tackled Gram out of the air. They slammed into the wall. Beneath the thud of the impact was the sound of the guards around the room raising their weapons and disabling the safeties.

Winter didn't care. She swung wildly, landing two solid hits on Gram's cheek and jaw before being shocked by a painful jolt in her neck. Her body went limp. Gram made a gesture for her guards to stand down, then kicked Winter hard in the stomach.

The strike launched her across the room, but she felt nothing from the blow. Then her implant returned to its normal behaviour and the pain flashed through her. She clutched at it as she impacted against the wall.

Gram lashed out. She took a hold of Winter's wrist, twisting it up and around behind her back. Her other arm held Winter in close.

'Don't test me further,' the raider whispered in her ear. 'This crew seems intent on causing us as much trouble as they can. It's tiresome, and a waste of all of our time.'

'Can you blame them after all you've done to them?'

Gram ignored her. 'I spent just shy of a week trying to come to a diplomatic solution but they refused to cooperate. I didn't want it to come to this but you made it necessary.'

'Killing innocent people is never necessary!'

Winter's fury flared as she saw the corpses around the room.

Three pods had been forced open. The gel that filled them and surrounded the bodies inside still mostly held its cylindrical shape, but had been gouged out around their faces to create a channel to their foreheads.

Her eyes fixed upon Isaac. He was almost as pale as his gown, which was covered so densely in the thick suspension gel that it remained unstained by the river of blood pouring from the gaping bullet hole between his eyes.

'It was never my intention to shed any blood. Death profits no-one in this business, but I had to make a strong statement. Something your friends will finally have to acknowledge.'

'Well then, you're out of luck,' Winter growled. 'You may have shaken the passengers, but the captain is the one calling the shots. He's ex-military. He's used to losing people for his cause, and he's totally unfazed by your show of power.'

With her back to Gram she couldn't properly gauge her reaction, but she thought she could feel the raider's face contort into a snarl. 'In that case, I know who'll be next to go. I think the *Veteran*'s crew needs a change in leadership.'

Gram's strategy appeared to be working. Winter might have called her bluff on a threat like that before, but now there was no reason to think she wouldn't deliver.

It was difficult to tell if Orson had everyone's best interests in mind given his recent decisions, but he had certainly not proved himself to be an enemy. He had done Winter a serious favour by letting her on board and so despite his abrasive and occasionally unpredictable behaviour, she felt compelled to consider him a friend, or an ally at the very least. Either way, his death would be no more acceptable than Isaac's, or anyone else's.

Killing Orson might not change much though. The title of captain would carry on down the crew, none of whom would want to surrender themselves any time soon. Then again, his death could change their minds. The raiders would be making a loss on Orson, but it could still work out in their favour. Not that she would admit that to Gram.

'You think his replacement would bow any more easily? You're kidding yourself. Killing him won't damage their morale. The only thing it will damage is your profit,' she spat. 'Imagine how much an ex-soldier would sell for. Far more than the others, I'd guess. I don't know much about your little slave trade but that's a given.'

'Let me worry about the merits of my actions. I don't need you throwing me off.' Gram released her. 'I'll call for you when I need you. Until then, I'll have you escorted back to the *Renegade*. I won't send you back into that simulation with your implant in such a state. Go get it repaired. My engineer's waiting for you, scalpel in hand.'

She had almost managed to forget the gory details of the procedure that awaited her, but at least they were finally doing something about the malfunctions. Every time she lost control she was terrified it would never return.

'I guess I should be thanking you,' Winter quipped as she drifted towards the door, an armed guard following closely. She reached the threshold and turned back to Gram. She pointed at the bodies in the pods and told her, 'You will suffer for this. I promise you that.'

'If I had a penny for every time someone said that to me, I could buy a dozen Captain Orsons. Get the hell out.'

* * *

'Get on the table,' the engineer ordered.

This was it. Winter kept telling herself it was for the best, but it didn't seem to help much. With all anyone had done with her implant so far, the thought of handing it over again left a bad taste in her mouth. Aside from that, this would be the first thing any of the raiders had ever done for her benefit.

She positioned herself on the table in the middle of the makeshift operating theatre. Instruments were kept in plastic containers propped on the bulkheads and a large computer terminal produced various displays, each one a different view of the implant and the surrounding anatomy. Her surgeon hovered in front of it with a glass tablet in his hand. When he faced Winter a look of irritation swept over him.

'On your front,' he said.

Winter used the edges of the table to manoeuvre herself and face down towards its surface.

'That's better. Honestly, how do you expect me to get at the device if you're lying on top of it?'

'Well, Doctor,' she mocked, 'your bedside manner could do with some work.'

'I'm no doctor and being nice to you is not my job.' He placed a palm on her back and pushed her down. Her chin slammed painfully against the table, but her attempt to soothe it with her hand was halted as a leather strap tightened around her wrist.

'I hope you know what you're doing. There are a lot of people I need to get back at, but if you fuck this up I'm going to haunt you first.'

'Try not to worry about it too much. Machines are my specialty,' he said, buckling down her ankles. 'Besides, I can't have you moving about under the knife, or I'm bound to make a mistake or two. I'd strap your neck down if I could, but then I couldn't get at that flimsy little device of yours.'

'Flimsy? And whose fault is that?'

He said nothing.

'What's the plan then? You know what's wrong and how to fix it?'

'What do you think I've been doing flat out for the last day? Yes, I know how to fix you.'

'Then tell me. I don't want you messing around inside my body if I don't know what you're up to.'

He pulled the strap around her remaining wrist even tighter than the straps that came before. Out of spite, perhaps. 'Forcing you out of SSR causes very minor short circuits in your implant. It seems that over time, the jolts have been weakening one connection in particular. When you lose control of your body it means that connection has dropped, but it can fall back into place. Basically I just have to go in there and stick it down properly. It won't take long.'

'Is it a permanent fix?'

'If we keep using the device as we are it's only a matter of time before it weakens again. But if I were you, I'd be more concerned about some of the other connections in there.'

'What do you mean?'

'Almost every component in there is at risk. Honestly, we're lucky it's been this minor. Next time it could shut off your lungs or send a power surge through your brain.'

'And you thought this was a good idea?'

'I didn't have all the facts when we started and I certainly didn't expect we'd still be doing this. I won't lie to you, we're playing with fire here. But it's not like you've left us any other choice.'

'There's another reason to haunt you when I'm dead and buried.'

'Look forward to it. You probably won't have long to wait.'

'You don't seem to have much faith in your captain's plan.'

'She's not my captain, she's our leader. And for the record, no, I don't, but that doesn't matter. I do my job and she does hers.' One final strap fixed Winter's waist to the table's surface. 'Now, are we done talking? I'm ready.'

Winter tensed up and forced herself to take a single long, deep breath. 'Fine. Go for it.'

Her anxiety rose. She felt the engineer push himself upwards. His body blotted out the light from above as he positioned himself over the table.

'You'll probably feel some discomfort and tugging. Whatever you do, try not to move. And for god's sake, keep your mouth shut. I work best in silence.'

Winter decided the best way to respond was to simply say nothing. After a brief pause he grunted. Then she felt a cold broad surface press down directly on to her implant. It clicked loudly and juddered slightly, then Winter could no longer feel her body below her neck. The sensation of the cool metal against her skin vanished. She had no control of any part of her body beside her head.

The engineer got to work right away. As he had said, she could feel him working, her skin stretching down from her scalp towards the pointed pressure of his blade as he cut through the flesh, followed by sharp tugs left and right as he performed his craft.

After a few minutes he stopped. Winter couldn't see what he was doing, but felt a little concerned by the lack of movement. She resisted the urge to ask if everything was okay.

'This wasn't in my scans.' he muttered. 'What the hell is this?'

She remained silent, hoping that he would tell her exactly what he'd found. Something had evaded his scans?

She grew worried as the realisation dawned on her that it

must have been one of the attachments added by that drone. Technology like that would never be in a medical device as standard. If it had been damaged along with the rest of the implant, her mission could fail even if she made it to Earth alive. Gram's carelessness was putting a lot on the line.

'You can talk now,' the engineer said. 'There's something in here designed to avoid active scans. Tell me what it is.'

Even if she was at liberty to talk about it, she didn't want to give the raiders any more leverage over her. 'I don't know what you mean,' she lied. 'It's just an ordinary implant. Anything in there should only be there to keep me alive.'

He grumbled. 'Fine. Go back to staying silent then, if you're not going to be useful. I'll take a look myself.'

She nearly screamed out for him to stop, but he was already tinkering with it again. It took all her effort to remain still. It was even more dangerous for her to make any sudden moves now.

She cast her mind back to what the stranger's disembodied voice had told her that night.

... if you attempt to disrupt this assignment, well, let's just say that I'm no stranger to bloodshed.

She wasn't trying to disrupt her assignment, but she couldn't help the feeling that he would find out if anyone began tampering with his additions. Just letting this guy touch it could spell disaster for her.

'Well, this doesn't look like it should be there,' he said. 'Whoever did this is extremely cunning, hiding it the way they did. I'd better not touch it, I have no idea what it will do. But some of it seems to be completely separate from the main circuitry. At least that much isn't likely to get damaged by this SSR stuff.'

Winter relaxed a little.

'It's definitely not standard medical equipment though. What does it do? Tell me.'

'I really don't know what you're talking about.'

He snorted. 'Alright then. I'll leave it for now.' A series of metallic clicks began right behind her head, likely from one of his tools. 'Don't think this'll just be forgotten though. There are far too many things that don't make sense about you, Starling.'

Winter gulped. She was relieved by the end of his questions, but now that they had something that was both suspicious and tangible, she feared he was right. They wouldn't just let this go.

The pressures and tugs of the engineer's work faded into the back of her mind as she tried to process her rampant thoughts. She was almost surprised when she suddenly became aware of her body again.

'We're done here,' the engineer said. 'Go easy on your neck; I've had to stitch it up. It'll heal up in due course.'

'So it's all fixed? I won't lose control of my body again?' Winter asked as her straps were loosened one by one.

'Can you think of any other reason why we'd be done? Of course it's fixed, but like I said it may well get damaged again through continued use. So, you know, the sooner your crew surrenders …'

'Yeah, yeah, I get it.' Winter pushed herself free of the table and rubbed her wrists. Now that she could feel again, her hands and feet ached from the constriction of the straps. She felt certain he could have done them looser.

The engineer floated over to his computer. The displays had changed since she'd arrived. 'I'm writing my report now. All of the results, and everything I've found …' He paused, giving Winter a significant stare. '… will be forwarded to Megan Gram. She will be made aware of every last detail.'

She tried to maintain a poker face, and threw in a shrug for good measure.

He squinted at her, then simply shook his head. 'Go get some rest, I guess. I'm sure you'll be back to work soon enough.'

Without another word, Winter took her leave, off to seek the refuge of her hauler in the *Redemptive Veteran*'s cargo bay. She would make the most of her solitude, certain that it would be short-lived.

CHAPTER 19

Winter found herself being summoned to Gram's office in record time, a mere half hour after the completion of her surgery. Quite unusually this time, a pair of armed guards was positioned just outside the door.

If she didn't already know how Gram would react to the news, she did now.

One of the guards opened the door for her and shot her an inquisitive glance. She responded with a curt nod and slid on past.

It seemed gloomier than normal. The shadows felt far more foreboding and the rumbling sound of the ship's systems and mechanisms faded into the background. Across the room, out from the darkness, a pair of scowling eyes were fixed on hers and followed her as she entered.

'Take a seat, Miss Starling,' Gram instructed, gesturing to the desk, as if this was the first time they'd met.

Without a word, Winter gingerly approached the chair and buckled herself in. Gram continued to loom, floating in the distance, near the ceiling.

Winter fidgeted with the stitches on her neck as she waited for Gram to say something further, but instead her unblinking gaze continued to bore into her.

'So,' Winter broke the silence. 'What's with the guards?'

Her question was brushed aside. 'I hear your operation went well.'

'I'm still alive.'

'Despite all the odds.' Gram didn't visibly push away from anything, yet she began to drift closer. Her fingers wrapped around her chair's headrest and she slowed to a halt. She pushed herself more upright and towered even taller over Winter. 'What are you doing here?'

Winter glanced around, then back up. 'I don't know wha–'

'Enough. You've been keeping a lot of secrets from us. There are lots of little things that don't quite add up about you. I was happy enough to overlook them before, but now they've begun to concern me. No more games, Winter. What are you doing here? Why are you going to Earth?'

'Why are you so interested?'

Gram rolled her eyes. She unbuttoned her handgun holster and twitched her leg, sending the weapon floating upwards. Then she snatched it from the air and expertly flipped it around towards Winter's head. 'I said no games. I am asking the questions and you are answering them. I can subject you to some excruciating pain, enough to fry that little implant of yours if you force me. Or perhaps I'll turn my attention to another of your friends in their pods.'

'You wouldn't kill another one, no way. You've wasted enough money as it is.'

'At this rate I won't be getting a penny.' Gram's voice grew louder and more impatient. 'A small profit is far better than a total loss. Now stop dodging the issue and answer my simple fucking question.'

Winter's mouth began to dry as she tried to think of a suitable lie to get her off the hook. Perhaps simplicity would work best?

'I have family on Earth. I'm going to visit for a couple of months.'

Gram disabled the safety with a loud click and Winter's eyes flicked back to the weapon trained on her. 'Don't make me hurt you,' Gram hissed. 'I've got far too much blood on my hands for one job. I'd hate to spill any more.'

'It's the truth.' Winter had never acted desperate in front of her before. If she did so now, Gram would know something was wrong, so she remained calm and composed, with her usual hint of anger.

'Then why did you book on to this flight in such a rush? God only knows how many ships would be willing to take you to Earth, so why this one? And why do you have no baggage? The only thing in the manifest marked as yours is that shitty little hauler.'

The simplicity plan didn't seem to be working so far. There might still be a chance to recover though.

'The captain is an old friend of ours, so he lets me ride for free. That should be on their system if you want to check.' Lies hidden behind small truths tended to be more convincing. She should be the only passenger to have not yet paid for her spot. 'And I didn't book on in a rush, it's just my papers took ages to get officially processed. You have no idea how tedious it can be to chase them up about that kind of thing.'

Gram's expression didn't change. 'And your bags?'

Winter thought, then lowered her gaze in mock shame. 'Stolen at the port.'

'Lies!' Gram rounded the desk, then she lowered her handgun, placing the barrel against Winter's left kneecap. Her tone rose as her anger boiled hotter. 'I will shoot your leg clean off unless you start telling me what I want to hear. You have one more chance. The truth, now.'

Her mind was racing. She couldn't decide whether to stick with the half-formed lie, or to give in to Gram's threats and tell the truth.

She focused on her mission briefing with the mysterious voice in her ransacked home. She tried to recall what she had been told. Some of the particulars had faded, but she had no recollection of being told not to reveal what she knew. That was not the kind of detail she would be likely to forget.

If he had meant for her to keep quiet he would have said so. The whole encounter had been planned down to the final detail and he wouldn't have overlooked that. In fact, the reason he had told her so little about her assignment, he had claimed, was to avoid valuable information falling into the wrong hands. If the meeting itself was confidential he would have said so.

The thought was strangely comforting. She had no desire to tell Gram about her mission, but it seemed that no harm would come of it.

'Well?' the raider insisted, pressing the gun barrel harder into her leg. 'Don't make me count to three.'

'Fine, I'll tell you,' Winter said, squeezing her eyes shut and praying that this was the right choice. 'I've been given a job to take a message to Earth. I was given it the night before we left, and the lives of a lot of people I care about are on the line.'

Gram's grip on the gun loosened slightly. Apparently she was a little more convinced this time. 'Who's the message for?'

Winter tensed up. Her credibility would suffer for this.

'I don't know.'

Gram spat out a brief laugh, then straightened her face and renewed the pressure of her gun against Winter's knee. 'Bullshit.'

'I swear, I was never told,' Winter insisted, trying hard to avoid sounding desperate. As ever she was determined to maintain some level of control over the situation.

'Alright then, sure. Then just what is the message?'

Winter winced. 'I don't know that either.'

Gram groaned loudly. She backed off and hovered cross-legged above the desk. 'Can you see why I'm having trouble believing you?' she asked, carelessly shaking the weapon around with her hand gestures. 'Convince me you're telling me the full and honest truth, Starling. If you backtrack one iota you can wave goodbye to your leg.'

It didn't help that the story was an unbelievable one. Anyone carrying a message should at least know where it needs to go. The best Winter could do was name the planet. How could Gram believe she was delivering a message if she couldn't tell her any more than that?

However, it was the only story she had and she'd already started telling it. It would have to do.

'A lot of details were kept from me intentionally, but I know all I need to. Your engineer found some weird components in my implant, I'm sure you know. Things he couldn't see in his scans, things that he dared not touch because even he didn't know what would happen if he did. I didn't get to see them being installed, but I'm as sure as I can be that the message is in there. I was only told that it had to go to Earth, and that it would do the rest once I get there.'

'What does that mean?'

'He never explained.'

'Who's "he"?'

'I was told all this remotely. He spoke through a robot that broke into my house so I never saw the guy.'

'A robot that broke into your house? Are you even trying anymore?'

'I'd never tell such a bad lie. This time it's true.'

Gram lowered the gun and stroked her chin. 'How many people die if you fail?'

Winter gulped. Sweat began to form on her forehead. Gram had found her leverage. 'My parents and I.'

'You said a lot of people. Three isn't a lot.'

'It's a lot to me.'

'Who else?' Gram insisted.

Winter cursed silently to herself. She'd sprung her own trap. 'Some friends of mine were threatened, but they won't be killed. They'll be thrown in jail.'

'And that's it?'

Winter nodded. It was also true that there was supposedly a lot of lives depending on the delivery of the message besides those she'd mentioned, but in this case the less said the better. The more lives that were threatened, the more power Gram had over her.

'Let us go through the evidence piece by piece. You made a last-minute booking on to the *Redemptive Veteran* …'

'… because I was in a rush to get on with the mission, no time to waste.'

'You brought no luggage with you.'

'Again, I was in a rush.'

'And your implant had been modified to carry this message of yours.'

'Correct. Are you satisfied?'

Gram went silent for a while, seeming to scrutinise Winter's face. She was sure to be thinking how best to spin this to her benefit. While nothing overt presented itself, Winter believed she saw a hint of a smile on the foul woman's mouth.

'You swear by this truth?'

'It's the only truth I have.'

Gram pointed her handgun loosely towards Winter once more. 'If I find out you've lied again, I am holding you personally responsible for whoever ends up dead.'

This shouldn't have made her as anxious as it did, seeing as it was true down to the last detail. It must have been the suggestion that there was blood yet to be spilt.

'I've told you everything,' Winter said, re-summoning her courage. 'Now will you tell me why it's so important to you?'

'Amid lies and deception there's always a tale worth telling. Nothing about you added up until now, and I'm sure it goes without saying I could never have guessed what you'd tell me on my own. I figured that your story must be pretty damn special, what with all these little snippets of fact popping up here and there. I couldn't help but wonder whether your secrets might hold the key to solving our little predicament.' She spread her arms wide triumphantly and kicked her legs out in front. 'I'm starting to think I was right!'

'What are you talking about? How does this help you at all?'

'Once again, Winter, the big picture eludes you.' She rolled back, placing her hands on the desk and flipping herself around to stand upright behind her chair. 'It all comes down to dear Captain Orson; ex-soldier, stubborn git and massive thorn in my side.'

'Right, so what's it got to do with him?'

'As I said, he's an ex-soldier. He has no problem in sacrificing his squad, or in this case his crew, to stand up for what he believes in. He may think that everyone on board is beyond saving, but what if we were to tell him there are others at stake too? People he might still be able to save.'

'What, my parents and my friends? Somehow I doubt he'll give himself up for just them.'

'Then we stretch the truth a bit. Let's say there are a few more lives at stake. Why not tell him that the message itself could save lives?'

Somehow she'd hit the nail on the head without knowing it. Was she about to tell the truth in an effort to pretend to lie?

'I still don't think he's going to go for this, you know.'

'I disagree. I think this is the kind of story that will finally force him to surrender. Besides, you can be quite convincing. If you can get me to sort-of believe that story of yours I'm sure he'll go for it. He'll give in. Tell him all about the robot. I bet he'll love that part.'

'That's not what I mean. He's a very proud man, and he's not a soldier anymore. That kind of behaviour could have been forgotten a long time ago.'

'Then you'd better remind him. The longer this goes on, the itchier my trigger finger gets. I'm prepared for my profits to suffer if it will bring this nightmare to a close, Winter. I will kill again. We've been playing this ridiculous game for far too long. We are getting close to Earth now. It must now come to an end.'

She was right. It was starting to look like game over. The odds had been stacked against them from the beginning, but Gram was holding a mighty hand now.

'That's my next task, I take it?'

'Use the story you just told me. Make Orson surrender.'

'How long will you give me this time?'

'As long as you need, but for every twelve hours the crew remain in their pods, someone else will die, so you'd better be quick about it.'

'Killing the squad won't convince him, Gram. You said it yourself.'

'That's not his incentive, it's yours.' She drifted over to the door like a spectre and opened it wide. The guards outside pushed themselves to the other side of the tunnel and turned. Gram's eyes narrowed and a sinister grin spread from ear to ear. 'Let's get to work, shall we?'

CHAPTER 20

The rays of the white sunlight shone far too brightly for a day as dark as this. The gentle breeze carried a chill despite the sun and picked out goosebumps on Orson's bare arms. He watched from his lookout, the patio behind the manor, as the passengers and remaining crew made their way into the garden and took their seats.

He had suggested removing the seats of those who had died, but Sam told him to keep them. Leave them empty. A testament to their memory. Sure, he could be cold, but the dead deserved no dishonour. He'd agreed and so the chairs stood in place of tombstones. But they wouldn't stay for long.

Winter was by Orson's side. Her tale had been told and she had managed to do something no-one else could. She had changed his mind.

He took another swig of his whisky. 'I wish it hadn't come to this,' he said.

'It's not your fault, you know.'

'Of all the things that could have finished us off …' He looked down at his flask and swilling around what little remained at the bottom. 'I've got to admit, I didn't see this coming.'

She was still leaving a lot of blanks to be filled. Luckily it seemed rather obvious to him. A top-secret message to Earth, that much he already knew. If he'd known how valuable it was he'd probably have surrendered a lot sooner.

Winter had told him that there was only one chance to

deliver it and that the loss of life would be catastrophic should she fail. He had guessed before that it was military intelligence on its way to the Solar Conglomerate. Now he was even more convinced. Perhaps it was news of a large-scale attack? That would explain why there were so many lives at stake and an imminent attack wouldn't leave any time to redeliver it.

Maybe not though. Maybe the Pioneers had a temporary weakness that needed to be exploited. Again, time sensitive information could explain some of the story and if there was a chance it could bring the war to its long-awaited end, who knew how many lives would be saved?

Of course, the exact message could not be guessed and Winter refused to spill the beans. 'I don't know what the message is,' she would say. As a way of keeping classified information secret, it wasn't the most airtight strategy. After all, how could she not know the contents of the message she was carrying?

In the end though, it didn't matter. She had to keep it to herself until she arrived. If she didn't trust him, despite the fact he once fought under the colours of the Conglomerate, that was her call. Probably a sensible one, too. All Orson needed to know was what he had been told. That a message needed to be delivered and that the raiders would only allow it if they surrendered. Working for the scum of Earth, Arali and the space in-between would be a small price for peace.

He brought the flask to his lips and took another glug. He was willing to make some sacrifices for his people. The passengers had been trying to convince him to give up ever since this whole thing started, so they'd be on his side already.

The crew would be different. He had no idea how well they'd take it. He hoped Sam might accept, even if only reluctantly. That was the best-case scenario with her. Julian would be sure to kick up a fuss and Hayley could easily have a mental breakdown. Out of all of them, he found trying to imagine her living the slave's life the hardest.

He felt a pang of guilt as he watched her materialise into the garden and join the gathering crowd. Telling her the news could prove to be the hardest part of the entire flight.

He swallowed the last of his drink, then took one long final look over the lawn. Then he dropped the flask to the concrete slabs with a clang. 'Let's get this over with,' he grumbled and began strolling down the hill with Winter close behind.

The simulated alcohol burned his throat. The eyes that watched his descent stretched the seconds into hours. As he drew closer, the quiet mutterings turned to solemn silence. They cleared an avenue through which he walked. Then he took a seat and invited everyone else to do the same.

He regarded the three empty chairs to the side and honoured them with a slow silent bow of his head. Then he returned his attention to his crew.

'Before I begin, I must ask … Hayley, have you made any progress with your makeshift computer interface?'

'Some pretty important progress, actually. The bulk of the main framework is in place. We're not ready to run any tests yet, but I'm pretty confident it'll work. We just need a little more time before we can start the first trials. See if we can control some minor ship functions. Nothing major to begin with, nothing that might attract any attention. Just enough to see if we have the control we need.'

'How much more time?'

'Probably another day or two. I've got to say though, I'm optimistic.' She beamed at him. She hadn't looked this happy in days. It crushed him.

'I'm afraid we can't wait that long.'

Her smile faded. Curious faces turned to ones of concern.

'Our situation has changed,' he said, trying his best not to allow himself to drop his gaze. 'Up until now, I've been convinced that the best thing we could do would be to wait until a solution presented itself. Now though, I'm afraid time is running short.

'Since the very start of our journey, Winter has been carrying a message. I was made aware of it the moment she arrived. What I didn't know was how sensitive its contents were, or how crucial it is that she deliver it. Now the raiders have been made aware of it and they're using it against us. If we don't surrender, they will ensure that it never reaches its destination.'

Julian raised his hand, but didn't wait for acknowledgement before speaking. 'I hate to say it, but does anyone really care? I mean, everyone here has a reason to go to Earth, that's why they're going. What makes this message of yours so special?'

Winter looked like she was going to respond, but Orson quickly showed her his palm. She retreated to her seat and stayed quiet.

'My decision before now had been based on the assumption that the only lives at stake were our own. If we were to mount a resistance, the only people at risk would be ourselves. That is no longer the case. This is a classified message that concerns the lives of many more.'

'How many?'

'There's no way to know for sure, but it'll be more than just a handful. We shouldn't ignore the possibility that hundreds, or perhaps even thousands could be dependent upon its safe delivery.'

'But we could still give our plan a go, right?' Hayley asked, her voice beginning to shake.

'I'm sorry but we can't. Even if we didn't have to wait, there's no guarantee that we'd be successful in retaking the ship, and if we fail the message won't be delivered. The delay before we can put it into action makes it even worse for us, I'm afraid. The raiders are refusing to give us any more time. For every twelve hours we remain here they threaten that another of us will be killed. In two days our remaining numbers will be halved, and the only two people who can work the system could be among the first to go. I'm sorry Hayley, we can't risk it.'

Her expression fell. The last hint of hope on her face drained away and her lip began to quiver. Orson couldn't look anymore. He lowered his gaze and propped his head up on his knuckles. He squeezed his eyes closed.

'What are you telling us, Captain?'

He lifted his head, following the sound of the voice, to find himself looking at the man in the blue shirt. Rather he used to wear a blue shirt. Now however he had swapped it for a grey one.

'Are we giving ourselves up?'

Orson hesitated, then forced himself to nod. 'We will surrender to the raiders before they spill another drop of blood.'

'Why now?' The large man stood. He had tears in his eyes. 'Why did you have to wait until they had killed my wife? She could still be alive if you'd only changed your mind sooner!'

'Please calm down.' Orson spoke softly, for once unwilling to raise his voice in response. 'I'm sorry for your loss. I wish I'd had some warning before. I had no idea anyone would die, and I didn't believe they'd be willing to kill anyone else until now. I'm changing my mind now to save everyone I haven't wronged yet.'

'You're too late. Your damage has been done.'

'Nevertheless, my mind is made up. Now please, take your seat.'

The man sat back down, but he didn't look any less angry.

Only one person had yet to speak and it was the one Orson had expected to be the most vocal. Mrs Vince sat silently at the edge of the group. Her head hung low and one hand rested upon one of the empty seats. She showed no sign that she might speak up. In fact, she hadn't even left the garden following her son's death.

Julian rose to his feet and walked around Orson, patting him roughly on the shoulder on the way past. 'Mind if we have a quick chat, Captain?'

Orson stood, then turned his attention briefly towards Hayley. 'Make whatever preparations you need to in order to shut down the SSR.'

'But Captain …'

'This isn't an easy decision, Hayley. Please don't make it any harder than it already is,' he said softly.

She opened her mouth again to speak, but hesitated. She lowered her head.

'The rest of you have five minutes. I don't know exactly what will happen when we wake up, so use your time wisely. Make your last farewells to the dead, and it wouldn't hurt to say goodbye to each other as well. We may not see much of one another on the other side.' He lingered in case anyone else spoke up. When he was met only with silence, he turned and followed Julian behind the gazebo.

The structure provided them with a cool shade that felt more fitting under the circumstances. It also helped Orson to feel like he'd escaped the blame from his audience, though he wondered if most of it was coming from inside his own head.

Then he saw the look on Julian's face and considered that he'd just followed the bulk of the vitriol into a dead-end.

'All due respect, Captain, but what the hell are you doing? I've never seen you make a U-turn like this before!'

'Did you hear nothing I said? We have no other choice now. Not unless you want more innocent people to die.'

'Your decision was final. You insisted that you had made the right call. Three people died before our very eyes and you were completely unmoved. Now this girl tells you she has a super important message to be delivered, and all of a sudden we've been wrong the whole time?'

'You don't believe Winter?'

'Of course I don't believe her! She's the raiders' puppet now. They have a gun to her head and she will say anything to get us out and keep them from pulling the trigger. This is a trick, I have no doubts.'

'I've already told you, I knew about the message before the raiders showed their ugly faces.'

'Doesn't sound like she told you much.' Julian took a step back and folded his arms. 'Truthfully, what did you know about it before we took off?'

Orson cast his mind back, recalling exactly what Winter had told him and how he'd extrapolated that information into something useful.

'I knew that it was going to Earth. To the Solar Conglomerate.'

Julian's expression became quizzical. 'Really? Why would she be carrying messages for the Con–' Then his face changed again, and he stared at his captain, head tilted to one side. 'I see. You just want to serve your planet one last time.'

Orson covered his face with his hands, letting out his frustration with a deep growl. 'This is far bigger than that, Julian. I don't know exactly what the message says, and frankly

I don't care. I don't even care if this is a ruse by the raiders or not at this stage. She swears to us that a great number of innocent civilians could lose their lives if it's not delivered successfully. If there's even a chance that she's telling the truth, and I believe she is, then it's our duty to lay down our lives for the good of the many.'

'You've been blind to the truth ever since it became about your precious Conglomerate. You've made a terrible mistake by making it personal.'

'Watch it, boy. You're very close to crossing the line of insubordination here.'

Julian raised his hands in front of him. 'Hang on, I'm not telling you what to do. I'm just making sure you've got a clear head when you make these kinds of big decisions.'

'Well, just you be careful. I've had a hard enough time coming to this conclusion. I don't need you questioning me at every turn.'

He went to head back to the garden, but Julian caught his ear again. 'If you're sure you want to go through with this, just do me one favour, would you?'

Orson looked at Julian over his shoulder.

'Don't make Hayley do it. It's not fair to put her behind the controls. You can't let her live with that kind of guilt behind her. She doesn't need that.'

Orson turned to face him properly. 'What would you suggest?'

'Someone else does it, obviously! I'll do it if I have to.'

'Hayley's the only one with administrative control of the SSR system. Only she can shut it down, and her interface won't respond to your input. It has to be her.'

'Then let her transfer authority to me.'

'A waste of time. We have to shut down immediately. No more delays.'

'But Hayley …'

'I'll have a word with her.'

'It wouldn't take a minute. All she has to do is alter the system permissions.'

'That's enough!' Orson growled. Julian fell silent. 'I said no more delays. Hayley will do it, and she will be completely fine.'

Julian glared at Orson. His hands, held stiffly by his sides, clenched tightly into fists. 'I've been on this ship for a long time, Captain,' he said. 'I've come to think of you as a father to me.'

'That would certainly explain your rebellious nature,' Orson replied. 'Say no more. Let's end this now.' He didn't wait for Julian. He walked away, emerging from the shadows on to the sunny lawn. He approached Hayley, still sitting in her chair, staring at the interface that floated in front of her. He stopped a few strides away. 'Are we ready?'

She nodded, then looked up at him. 'I don't want to do this.'

'I know.' Orson closed the distance, knelt down and laid a hand softly on her arm. 'This is my decision, not yours. Okay? I want you to remember that. You've done nothing wrong.'

She lowered her head. The captain stood and turned to the passengers who had gathered around the small graveyard of chairs. Out of the corner of his eye he saw Julian walk out from the other side of the gazebo, but didn't acknowledge him.

'Time to wrap it up,' the captain announced. 'We're leaving now.' One by one everyone stood, some still wiping the tears from their eyes. Orson stood behind Winter and whispered into her ear, 'I don't know what they promised you to get you to do this, but if I find out you lied to me at all, I'll kill you myself.'

'They promised us our lives. Nothing more,' she insisted.

'Very well.' He stepped away and raised his voice again, speaking to everyone. 'If we're all prepared?'

Some nodded, but other than that there was no motion. No sound. Even the birds seemed to stop singing and the leaves of the surrounding trees fell silent. The world watched them, as if saying one final farewell.

'In that case …' He trailed off, unable to bring himself to say the order out loud. Instead he turned to face Hayley, closed his eyes and bowed his head.

The world began to crumble away around him, leaving Orson suspended in an endless black expanse. Sensation began to seep away from his body. He faded, vanishing from the void that was once the world.

CHAPTER 21

For the first time, Winter woke up gradually in her pod. She could be thankful that there was nothing to shock her awake this time, but she would have gladly endured that pain again if it would give her a chance to fix everything.

But the battle was over. As the gel seeped its way out through the drains, she brought her hands up to cover her face and released a breath through her fingers.

She kept her hands fixed over her eyes, unwilling to confront the others as they were pulled from their pods. Over the whir of the capsule doors was a cacophony of terrible sounds; guns being cocked and deep voices bellowing orders.

She could hear terrified screams moving towards the door. One voice stood out. 'Isaac!' Mrs Vince shrieked. The shrill cries made Winter wince. They hadn't even moved the bodies.

She remained, cringing through the terror and guilt, until the door slid shut and the chamber was plunged into silence.

'Quick work, Winter. I'm impressed.'

Her hands fell away from her face and she opened her eyes. Gram, who floated before her, was flanked by a pair of armed mercenaries and looking as smug as ever.

'It seems you can work wonders, given the right incentive.'

Winter's usual wit had abandoned her and now all she could do was stare at the floor.

'What's this? An unexpected second victory? You've finally learned to shut your mouth! Oh, today is a good day.' She rubbed her hands together vigorously and an enormous grin spread across her face.

Winter forced herself to look up and stare straight into Gram's eyes. She spoke in little more than a gruff whisper. 'Don't you dare forget, you have the blood of three innocent people on your hands. Your victory was not without sacrifice.'

'It never is. I'm always on jobs just like this one. No doubt this one will blur with all the rest. Within a month or two I doubt I'll even remember your face.' She glanced briefly towards Isaac's corpse. 'In fact I can hardly picture the kid without that bullet hole now.'

Winter's anger got the better of her and with a roar she launched herself from her pod at lightning speed, her hands aimed at Gram's throat.

Gram reacted quickly, twirling off to the side to dodge the attack. With one hand she grabbed Winter's wrist. The other took a hold of one of the nearby guards. They circled around him, then Gram's leg kicked against something to halt the spin. Winter felt one of her arms get wrenched up behind her back. Gram held her tightly around the neck and leaned in close.

'I knew it was too good to be true. You'll never learn your place, will you?' Gram hissed into Winter's ear. 'You do realise you're just another passenger to me now, don't you? There's nothing special about you anymore, so if you cause me any trouble you will end up just as dead as them.'

Gram twisted her body and Winter's eyeline was drawn across the array of pods lining the walls, finally settling on Isaac's. His body remained inside, cold and pale. By now the gel engulfing him and securing him to his seat had drained away. His corpse was floating freely inside its capsule, orbited slowly by blood and pieces of brain that had escaped from the fragmented remains of his skull.

Winter couldn't look for long before she felt herself gagging. She forced her eyes shut and tried to turn away.

'And then there's your message,' Gram continued. 'You don't want to get yourself killed before you get that little matter sorted out, do you?' She tightened her grip around Winter's neck.

Finally she relented, freeing Winter from her crippling hold and shoving her hard towards the door. Winter impacted with a heavy thud, but managed to grab the frame. She straightened herself out and rubbed her neck with her fingers, trying to take long deep breaths despite her uncontrollable coughing.

When the spluttering ceased, leaving her throat dry and raw, she cast her venomous glare back at Gram.

'Your friends are being assembled in the cargo bay as we speak for their … debriefing,' Gram said. 'We'll move them on to the *Shameless Renegade* right after, but we can't start without you. Let's not keep them waiting.'

She drew the pistol from its holster and raised it lazily in front of her.

'Get changed and move out. Quickly now.'

Winter had no choice but to swallow her pride and do as instructed. She slipped out of her white robe, slick with gelatinous residue, and piece-by-piece she pulled on her smuggling garb. As she tightened her various belts she noticed now more than ever how light they were, with many empty pockets and holsters.

Once changed, she led the way out of the SSR suite, towards the *Redemptive Veteran*'s cargo bay. When they arrived, she noted how much emptier it was than when she first saw it. Its white bulkheads, more scuffed and beaten than those in the corridors, were exposed now that the stacks of crates and cases had been hauled through the airlock. Winter's old vehicle remained bolted down, either unwanted by the raiders, or more likely too cumbersome to move through the airlock. They'd probably try to move it once planetside, she thought.

Near the middle of the floorspace, floating a few feet from the deck, the passengers and crew of the *Redemptive Veteran* were assembled. Many of them, unused to movement in zero-gravity, had to be held in place physically by members of their armed escort.

'Join them,' Gram ordered as she flattened herself against the ground and propelled herself towards the gathering. Winter fell into line, the two guards hot on her heels. Using the grips set into the deck, they slowed to a stop at the other prisoners' feet, then pulled themselves upright.

Gram positioned herself between the main crowd and the airlock, digging her toes into one of the indents on the floor to keep herself firmly placed.

Seconds later, Paul poked his head out from the airlock tunnel, then pulled himself up alongside the raider leader.

Winter's skin crawled. That man, whose interest was only piqued now that the ship was as good as his. Or perhaps he was just as disinterested as ever, only making an appearance because Gram had called him up to celebrate their long-awaited victory.

Gram swept her eyes over the crowd, each still sticky with suspension gel and each, aside from Winter, wearing their thin loose gown. Her smile returned and she clasped her hands behind her straightened back.

'Well, then!' she announced loudly, her cheery tone echoing around the bare metal bulkheads. 'We've been on the same little ship for the better part of two weeks now, so I think it's about time we were properly introduced. My name's Megan Gram. I'm the leader of the crew who have now successfully commandeered the *Redemptive Veteran*.' Orson squirmed as she said this. Gram mocked him with a pouty face before continuing. 'I'm also the one who has had to suffer through day after day of your defiance, which we can all see now was pointless.'

She raised an arm to the side and gestured with an upturned palm, drawing everyone's attention to the smartly-dressed, well-groomed man hovering at the periphery of the gathering. 'This young man is Paul Narn,' she continued. 'Paul is our client, the man who commissioned us to capture this ship. We can all thank him for the pleasure of this journey.' Her face turned to a scowl for just long enough for her to say to his face, 'It has certainly been an adventure.'

Her stern expression vanished and her mocking smile returned. Sweeping across her audience again, her gaze finally settled on the captain.

'Edward Orson, I presume.'

'Captain,' he corrected her.

She chuckled. 'Not anymore, Edward. Captains have ships. You don't.'

Orson grumbled in response. Winter knew he was resisting the urge to lash out.

Gram's eyes moved to the next in the line-up. 'Let's see. Mature steely face, standing loyally beside your superior officer. Second in command, yes? Tell me, how do you manage to put up with the grumpy baldie?' She gestured in Orson's direction. His face grew redder by the second.

'With patience,' Sam replied. 'Far more than you're capable of. I don't think you two would get along.'

'I'm sure that's true. Luckily it doesn't matter. He'll be locked up in a cell until we get to Earth, like the rest of you. He won't need to worry about socialising from in there.'

'Cells?' Julian remarked. 'If we're not in SSR how do you expect us to survive the rest of the trip?'

'Ah, you must be the brains of the operation!' Gram's attention was drawn to him now. 'Yet for all your brains you don't seem to realise we've done this before. Many times.' She cocked her head. 'I'm going to take a stab in the dark and say that cutting the SSR system away from the main computer was your idea, wasn't it?'

Julian fidgeted awkwardly with his hands.

'A clever plan. You're not the first to try it, but this was the first time we weren't able to prevent it. Some crews are a bit less competent than yours. I've seen people fry the entire system from the inside and force themselves out, which of course means they have nowhere to stay for that deceleration thing you do. We only have a system like that so we can get up to speed. After that, we just blast our way back into normal space at full speed and bleed it off slowly in planetary orbit.'

'You'd do that so close to a planet? You could get us all killed!'

'I've already told you, we do it all the time. No need to worry about how we do it, just accept it. For now, just know that you will be sitting in a cell until we land.'

Julian fell silent. He didn't look convinced, but at least Gram was satisfied now that he'd stopped talking. She moved on.

'Oh, look at you. You seem to be missing something!' she exclaimed as she noticed the stump where Hayley's right leg ought to be. 'I imagine you're Hayley, the last member of the crew? Well, most of her anyway.'

Hayley's face was wet with tears. A fresh crimson cut lanced across her jaw. She managed to meet Gram's gaze and give a quick nod in reply.

'Don't use those big sad eyes of yours on me, young lady; it won't change anything. In any case, I'm sure you came prepared to use that leg, so let me do something for you. I'm not a monster, after all.'

'I beg to differ,' she said, shaking in fear but clearly trying to be as strong as her comrades.

Gram smiled, a slightly kinder smile than her last one, but it quickly disappeared as she turned to one of her mercenaries and barked, 'Fetch her crutches or whatever it is she uses. She must have something.' The man drifted along the floor towards the exit.

Gram's attention returned to her captives, but before she continued down the line she threw her head back and groaned loudly with annoyance. 'I'm already bored of you lot. I've done the whole crew, so you must be the passengers, right?'

The passengers shifted uncomfortably.

'Well, I already know Winter and I just can't be bothered with the rest of you, so I'm just going to call you Harry, Larry and … the mopey one. Seriously, what's wrong with her?'

The man who she'd dubbed 'Larry' fixed her with a stern glare. 'You killed her son.'

Gram was briefly taken aback. Then a look of realisation struck. 'Oh, him? Of course, I see the resemblance. You two look very much alike. By which I obviously mean you both look basically dead. Pale, unmoving, unreactive …'

'Shut your mouth!'

The man yelped as a gun jabbed against his back.

'Shut yours, Larry,' Gram said. After staring him down for several long seconds, she turned her attention elsewhere. 'Take them to their cells,' she instructed the guards. 'One cell for crew, another for passengers.'

Winter's guard shoved her forward and the other mercenaries began nudging their captives towards the airlock.

Gram moved aside for them and caught Paul's attention as she approached him.

'Now that the job's pretty much done, we need to talk business,' she said. Paul simply raised his chin as he watched the crowd making their way over the airlock's rim and disappearing from view.

'Gram,' Winter called. 'I hope you still intend to honour our agreement. You'll let me deliver my message as promised, yes?'

Gram smirked. 'Oh, Winter. That doesn't interest me in the slightest. As I said, you're just another passenger to me now. You'll have to beg your new owner to help you once you've been auctioned off.'

Winter clenched her fists. Paul had been right the whole time. She never meant to honour her agreement. 'You bitch!' she screamed.

Gram didn't react and instead continued to watch with an amused smile as Winter followed everyone else towards the airlock. As Winter neared the threshold, she shot Paul a glance, widening her eyes and nodding her head, hoping to agree to the proposal he had made before. She prayed that he would remember.

'Wait!' Paul called out.

The remaining guards turned to look at him. Gram's attention was drawn too, and her expression turned to one of irritation.

'If you won't honour your side of the deal, I'll have to honour it for you.' He locked his eyes with Gram's. 'Forget the auction. I'll buy Winter myself.'

'Is that so? And what makes you think that you wouldn't be outbid if we went ahead with it? What's in it for me?'

'I guarantee I would beat any price one might offer. In any

case if we do it here and now you can negotiate the price for yourself.'

She narrowed her eyes. She seemed to be scanning him for some hint of deceit.

'Take the girl to his cabin,' she ordered. Winter breathed a sigh of relief and made her way far less reluctantly through the airlock. She was still able to hear the next few sentences of their conversation, echoing around the bare walls of the cargo bay. 'It seems we have even more business to discuss then.'

'Indeed. I think my new command deck would be the perfect place.'

CHAPTER 22

The steel door ground along its rails and fixed itself open with a clang. The *Redemptive Veteran*'s crew were thrown into their cell, thundering into the metal bulkhead on the far side of the shallow room. Hayley's crutches followed and the door slammed shut behind them.

The room was a simple cube. It might have been a decent size for a lone occupant, but for four it was crowded. The walls were flat and featureless, composed of a dark dull metal. The only features were a single dim light in the ceiling and the bars that separated them from the armed guards outside.

One of them, bald-headed with a wide stubbled jaw, leered through, watching as the prisoners recovered and reoriented themselves in zero-gravity.

Julian rubbed his head as it pounded from the hard impact, then glared at the guard. 'The hell are you looking at?' he yelled. The mercenary slid away from the door then turned, beckoning his comrade to follow him out of the room.

Orson tried to stabilise himself, bracing his hands and feet against adjacent bulkheads, but couldn't manage to bring himself to a complete stop. He growled at his failure but didn't give up.

'This is no good,' he said after accidentally knocking himself into a spin. 'We're going to be in here for ages. It's torture.'

Sam decided to join him in giving it a try, but enjoyed no more success. 'How are we meant to sleep if we're going to keep bumping into things?'

'We're not,' Julian grumbled. 'We're supposed to go without. We get slow and clumsy. The longer we go without sleep, the less capable we are of staging any kind of escape.'

'That hardly matters, seeing as we're not going to escape,' Orson said.

Julian shot him a glance. 'What are you talking about, old man? Of course we are.'

Orson's fury returned in a flash. 'How many times must I remind you? You will call me Captain!'

'No, *old man*, I will not! I hate to say it, but Gram has a point. You don't have a ship anymore. You're not a captain so I won't be calling you one. And I won't be obeying any of your orders either.'

'This is the final straw, boy. We may not have a ship anymore, but we are still a crew and you are still a vital part of it. Act as though you deserve the responsibility I've been generous enough to give you.'

'We're still a crew, are we?' Julian forced a wheezy laugh. 'Sure, I'll go with that, but for how long? We're going to be sold off as slaves in just a couple of short days. Even if by some miracle we're bought by the same person and manage to stay together, we won't be a crew. We'll just be the bloody cleaning staff!'

'If we break out, Gram will never allow Winter to deliver her message. The condition was that we surrender.'

'We did surrender! And anyway, do you really think she gives a damn about Winter's package? She doesn't.'

'What are you talking about?'

Julian rolled his eyes. 'This message may mean everything to you, but to Gram it was only ever leverage. She only wanted to use it as a way to coax us out of SSR and it worked. Now it means nothing to her.'

'It will if we break out. She'll use it against us again.'

'How? If we're successful we leave her in the dust. She won't hunt us down, it's too much work for too little reward. Even if she did, it wouldn't be to destroy Winter's message. Revenge won't interest her. As I've said time and time again, she's only interested in profit.'

'And if we were to fail? She could have a gun to Winter's head, just waiting for us to try.'

'Then we get thrown back in here! The moment she destroys that message she has no more leverage, so there'd be no point in killing her. And of course she'll want to keep us all alive, including Winter. Even you should understand she can't sell a corpse!'

The shouting abated and a silence washed over them. Both men boiled with rage, but the stillness brought a slight chill to the coppery air.

Orson shook his head, sneering at Julian. 'I won't let you do this. I forbid you.'

'You can't forbid me,' he retorted. 'Not on your own.'

Orson fixed him with a quizzical stare.

'I can't fight my way through an entire spaceship and retake another without support. I may be good but I'm no super soldier.' He turned to Hayley, who'd been silent ever since they'd been brought on board. Her face was still red but the tears had stopped.

'Me?' she asked. 'You want me? I'm not a fighter, what can I do?'

'Any extra manpower will help. I'm not insisting that you join me, I'm just asking if you will. It's your choice.'

Hayley lowered her head and contemplated silently. She didn't seem desperate to be free, which didn't fill Julian with confidence that she might join him. Perhaps it would be for the best if she didn't. She was right; she wasn't a fighter. Even if she was, he didn't want to put her in harm's way. He had to push that thought aside though, if he wanted their chances of success to be at their highest.

He left her to think for a bit. 'Sam? What about you?'

Sam cast an inquisitive glance towards Orson. He looked back pleadingly, something Julian had never seen him do before. Orson shook his head gently and mouthed the word, 'No.' She turned away and fixed her eyes on Julian's. After a short pause she announced, 'I'm in.'

'Sam …' Orson whispered. The betrayal he felt was all over his face, but she ignored him.

'I can tell nothing's going to stop you from trying,' she said. 'At least if I go with you the chances are a little higher. Besides, you're going to need someone at the helm once it's all over.'

Julian smiled and nodded. 'Can't argue with that.'

'She's right,' Hayley spoke up. 'You'll need all the help you can get. I'm coming with you.' As she spoke her posture became taller and straighter. Something fuelled her confidence. Julian smiled. He had never been more proud of her.

'You all realise this is suicide, right?'

All eyes turned on Orson.

'You have three untrained, inexperienced fighters up against an entire crew of thugs and mercenaries. Even if Gram wants you alive, they won't hesitate to shoot down a bunch of escaped prisoners.'

'So we'll be quiet,' Sam said. 'If you don't mind, Julian, let me take charge. I think I might have a plan.'

'Of course. Makes sense.' Julian smiled. He was glad to have her on board. With the exception of Orson she was packing the most muscle, and she had at least some experience in the *Veteran*'s war simulations. She would prove invaluable.

'Are you sure you won't join us?' she asked Orson. 'You must be the best fighter among us by far. You could be the difference between success or failure.'

'Absolutely not. I'm quite content to enjoy a much roomier cell, getting ready to pick up the pieces after you all get killed.'

Julian waved a hand dismissively. 'Forget him. We'll make do without him.' He ignored Orson's rolling eyes, turning his attention to Sam. 'Tell me about this plan of yours.'

* * *

They'd been waiting sleeplessly for a little over twenty-four hours when the screech of metal on metal echoed through the chamber, and two armed guards returned to check on their prisoners.

Julian watched the mercenaries push their way through the door and unsling their rifles. One stayed back while the other approached the cell bars and slammed the butt of his rifle loudly against the door. 'Wake up, you lot!' he taunted. 'My, my, don't you look hungry.'

Julian looked down at his stomach. 'Actually I'm not so bad,' he said candidly. 'Would you do us a favour though?'

The guard sneered, but before he could respond, something bumped lightly against his head. One of Hayley's crutches. It was drifting freely in the room beyond the cell bars.

'Yeah, that's it. See, my friends here got into a bit of an argument and … well, Sam likes to throw things when she's angry and there wasn't much to hand. Pass it back, would you?'

The hulking man snatched it from the air and considered it before glancing back to Julian. 'Maybe I don't want to. Might keep it for myself.'

'Your boss said she should keep it. I don't think she'd be

happy if she found out one of her guards had decided to take it for himself, against her orders.'

The mercenary looked down at the crutch in his hand.

'Save yourself the trouble, buddy. Just hand it back.'

He remained still for a little longer before reconsidering. He moved his grip up to the crutch's handle, drifted closer to the door and began to pass it lengthways through the bars.

Quick as a flash, Julian yanked it through, along with the guard's arm which he twisted hard. The mercenary yelped and turned with the pain to keep his arm from snapping. Then Sam grabbed him by the elbow of his other arm and pulled it up against the door. The guard was restrained now, facing out towards his partner who had readied his weapon. Being flat against the door, however, he was acting as a human shield for the prisoners.

Julian allowed Hayley to take hold of one arm while he passed a belt around the other side of the bars and looped it around the man's neck. He tugged sharply to make sure he had the man's attention.

'Drop the gun,' Julian growled into his ear through the bars, maintaining some pressure on the guard's windpipe. 'Now.'

He tossed his rifle out into the room towards his partner, with what little movement he could get from his wrist.

'Good boy. Now open the door.'

'If you open that door, I'll kill you,' said the guard on the other side of the room.

The restrained man turned his head towards the fingerprint lock. Sam had been very careful to trap his hand within reach of the mechanism.

The guard flexed his fingers, then pressed his thumb against the pad and the door unlocked with a dull clank, but otherwise remained still.

His partner across the room stared down the iron sights of his rifle. His forehead shone with sweat.

'There we are,' Julian whispered, loosening his grip on the guard's neck ever so slightly. Just enough to let him relax a little. 'That wasn't so bad, was it?'

The mercenary took some long and deep breaths, but Julian cut his inhalations short, tightening the belt once again, harder this time. Sam released her grip and allowed him to use his hand to pull at the belt. Loud gagging noises escaped his mouth as he tried to free himself, to no avail.

His partner rushed forward, gun in hand. At that moment the door lurched along its rails and Sam slipped deftly through the narrow gap, the second crutch in hand. She brought it over her head in a wide arc and launched it with all of her might into the incoming guard's face. He screamed as the impact sent him hurtling back the way he had come. Sam followed him, swiping the crutch out of the air again and thrusting it hard into his stomach. When he doubled over with the pain she brought the handle up and cracked his already bloody nose. His head swung back and smashed against the bulkhead. She caught him by the hair and slammed his head back again, then she let go and watched his unconscious body drift slowly through the open space.

She turned around as the first guard's struggles began to weaken. His eyes fluttered closed and his body went limp.

Julian pulled the belt back through the bars and Hayley released her grip on the guard's wrist. He floated gently out into the middle of the room to join his friend, allowing the prison door to open the rest of the way.

'Good plan, Sam!' Julian said before turning to Hayley and handing the belt to her. 'Thanks for that.' She quickly took it from him and tied it back around her waist.

'I was really hoping he'd stick that gun through the bars,' Sam said. 'Would've loved to wrench it from his hands myself, but I guess this was fun too.'

She checked the crutch for damage, then nudged it gently in Hayley's direction before scavenging one of the floating firearms. Julian followed her lead and helped himself to the other.

'In any case, we may be out, but that was only the first step,' Sam said. 'We are still massively outnumbered, so we'll take every advantage we can get. Julian, take some of their armour. Don't bother stripping them down to the skin, just the padding will do. You and I take point. We'll swipe some gear for Hayley on the way to our first stop.'

'You're sure we shouldn't free the passengers first?' Julian asked. 'Can't go wrong with a few more people.'

'You saw how quickly they broke under pressure in the sim. They'll be even worse in a firefight, trust me.'

She joined Julian in unstrapping some of the crucial components of the guards' armour. She pulled a thick vest over her robe and tightened it to fit a little more comfortably. There were several pads for her arms and legs that were snug enough, though the boots were far too big. A helmet would have been ideal, but it seemed these guards had gone without. Apparently they hadn't expected a fight.

'Keep in mind, we only have one advantage: they don't know we're out. The name of the game is stealth, which won't be easy on this ship. The central tunnel is unbroken along the entire length of the ship, so we could be spotted from a long way off. It also means loud noises will travel and with the open airlock we might even be heard on the *Veteran*. In short, don't fire your guns unless absolutely necessary. No firing unless someone else takes the first shot or you simply have no other choice. Is that clear?'

Julian nodded, trying to match Sam's courage. Hayley looked slightly more apprehensive, holding her crutches close. She, too, acknowledged Sam's orders.

'Last chance, Orson,' she called. 'We don't want to have to leave you behind.'

He remained silent, floating in the cell with his back to them.

'One last chance to bring the fight to the enemies of the Solar Conglomerate?'

'I'm doing my part for the Conglomerate by staying here,' he said wearily. 'Try not to do too much damage.'

Sam bowed her head. 'We'll keep the captain's seat warm for you,' she promised. Then she brought her rifle to bear, grasping it tightly in both hands and turned towards the door. 'Let's go, team.'

CHAPTER 23

Julian peered out cautiously, taking a long hard look first to the left, towards the nearby engine room, then to the right, down the long tunnel that terminated at the bridge.

The coast seemed clear, though there were sure to be adversaries lurking in the shadows. There were many rooms branching off to the sides, each one could be occupied by any number of armed assailants. As long as they stayed out of the way there would be no need to engage them. Seeking extra trouble could only make the mission harder than it was already going to be.

The tunnel was far more open than they would have liked. A well-placed shot could hit them from the other end of the vessel. They would have to stick close to what little cover was available. The doorways to each room were set into wide alcoves. They would serve as light cover, making their approach a little easier, but they weren't deep enough to completely conceal their robes, bright white in stark contrast to the dark, steely grey of the ship's interior.

He slipped quietly through the door, drifting to the alcove on the other side and gently cushioning his momentum. He hugged the wall and watched Sam swing through the doorway into the same position on her side. Hayley followed timidly, hiding behind Sam's larger frame.

They laid in wait, gauging all of the various noises that filled the air. The rumble of the engines, the creaking of overhead pipes, the mysterious metallic ticks beneath the deck plates.

Sam had suggested that doing so would help them to recognise and identify anomalous sounds along the way, allowing them to avoid unnecessary enemy contact. It sounded great in theory. In practice, however, Julian doubted it would be as easy as that.

After a minute or so, he glanced over to his team against the opposite wall. While Hayley was still nervously peering down the length of the tunnel, Sam had closed her eyes and was breathing deeply. Julian flexed and unflexed his muscles and drummed his fingers on the grip of his rifle.

A few moments later, Sam opened her eyes and fixed her gaze ahead. Without another look at her comrades she raised her left hand and made a sharp gesture to move up.

She and Julian rolled around the wall section into the next alcove up and slid back into cover. They paused, then moved up again. Hayley followed, staying one alcove behind them at all times.

Ahead, they began to see where the tunnel expanded to form a large open chamber. They had passed through this room before. Julian recalled its layout as it loomed closer.

It was circular, with several rows of SSR pods on either side, parallel with the central tunnel which remained open and unobstructed. The pods were separated only by narrow lockers. Though it would still be undesirable to be caught up in a fight, this would be the best place for one. Loads of cover and no excuse for being seen.

Only a few alcoves away, Sam was startled by a thud behind her. Julian watched as she spun to face the source of the sound. A door, mere feet away from her, slid open to reveal a big man floating out into the corridor. He lifted his head and the blood drained from Julian's face as he realised he'd been spotted.

With one hand firmly gripping the doorframe, the

enormous mercenary raised his free arm to point at Julian. He opened his mouth wide, but before he could make a sound Sam had dropped her gun, darted across, slapped her hands around his head and twisted his neck past breaking point. In the end, the only noises that came from him were a whine and a snap that blended in with the ambient sound of the vessel.

Julian forced himself to relax. He was already glad to have Sam to back him up. He gave her a thumbs up and mouthed the words, 'Thank you.' She pushed the corpse gently back into its room and sealed the door behind it.

Julian took a second to adjust to the sudden surge of adrenaline before pushing forward.

Right next to the SSR chamber now, they stayed put and listened closely for any early warnings of activity beyond their field of vision.

While it initially seemed quiet, the longer they waited the more Julian heard. Lockers squeaking open and shut. The gruff sound of a man clearing his raw throat. Sweaty flesh slapping on to bare metal and peeling away again. There were definitely people here; perhaps two or three on each side. With the lack of conversation fewer seemed more likely, which was a relief.

Sam had heard it too. She gave Julian a sharp look, then pointed into the room and drew her hand slowly across her throat. He acknowledged and braced himself to enter. Sam did the same and pointed three fingers towards the ceiling.

At least he could be confident that no-one was hiding behind the corner he was about to leap around. He could see the other side of the corner Sam hid behind. She was in the clear and with the ship's symmetrical design she would have told him if he had anyone to worry about. They still had time on their side.

Sam lowered one finger.

Julian pressed his stolen boot against the bulkhead, ready to swing himself into the room. Into danger. Now was a bad time for a realisation to creep into his head, that he could be dead in just a few minutes. His arms began to shake. He'd managed to keep it together until now, but he finally had to admit to himself that he was scared.

One finger remained.

He pushed that thought to the back of his mind. They only had one shot at this and he refused to be the reason for their failure. He swallowed deeply, tightened his grip on the edge of the alcove and watched for Sam's signal out of the corner of his eye.

Her hand fell forward and the last standing finger became a forward-pointing order to charge. Julian obeyed.

He kicked away from the wall, swung around the corner and let go, travelling in a straight line towards the end of the nearest row of SSR pods. Across the room, Sam had done the same, but he forced himself to look away. He was on his own now. She would handle her side of the chamber alone. It was up to him to do the same.

He peered out from behind cover and spied a single man, large and muscular, hovering near the floor doing something with his locker near the far end. Even with his attention diverted he would still catch any movement in his peripheral vision. Could he create a distraction?

No, that wouldn't help. People were free to move around in here. This guy would be used to it. Even if he was spotted out of the corner of the mercenary's eye, his identity wouldn't be compromised. Not if he was quick enough.

With a little preparation, making sure he had the right angle, he threw himself across to the next rank of pods. He cushioned his impact and brought himself to a halt behind his new cover. Looking out again, the raider didn't seem to have noticed, or if he had, he didn't care.

Julian turned his attention to the next zone. Only one short row of three pods stood between him and the wall now, but right around this corner was another mercenary. He wasn't wearing any armour, but that didn't mean this was going to be easy. He still had to take him out without arousing suspicion.

Options were limited. He wasn't confident enough in his own hand-to-hand skills to break the target's neck the way Sam had. He would have to improvise until he had a better weapon.

Another quick peek. This target was much closer than the other, also with his head buried in his locker. If he was fast enough, the mercenary would never know what hit him.

Julian made sure his rifle's firing mode was set to single shot, which, he mused, aptly described his situation.

He gripped the corner with his right hand, ready to swing himself into the open. It meant he had to hold the weapon in his inferior left hand, but at this range he was confident he could make the shot.

Without giving himself any longer to think about how many ways this could possibly go wrong, he jumped out of cover.

He swung his body around nimbly, clasped his right hand across the mercenary's forehead and brought the barrel of the gun perfectly into contact with the base of his skull. He squeezed the trigger.

A gunshot sounded, followed closely by a loud clang as the bullet slammed into the metal surface after tearing through the mercenary's neck. Blood spurted from the fresh wound, but was all funnelled perfectly into the locker. In an effort to mask the kill he loudly cursed, 'Ah, shit.'

'What the hell was that?' someone barked from across the room.

'Don't worry, it's all fine,' Julian reassured them, deepening his voice to approximate what he imagined this man would have sounded like. 'I thought the safety was on.' He kept his head down and crossed his fingers, hoping that no-one would suspect an unrecognised voice.

'Well be more careful, yeah? You'll have the whole bloody ship up in arms, the rate you're going.'

He released the breath he'd been holding. 'Honest mistake. Won't happen again, boss.'

'I'm not your boss, mate, just sayin'. Scared the life outta me.'

Pleased with his progress, he looked around for somewhere to hide the body. Conveniently, it seemed they'd outfitted their pods with sleeping bags so that they doubled as beds. He took a minute to stow the body away in the nearest one.

The adrenaline pumping through him now was causing his sweaty hands to shake. He'd never taken a life before and he'd certainly never considered that it would be so easy. It gave him a strange sense of confidence.

Amid the crimson mess inside the locker, there was some useful equipment. There were plenty of armour pads for Hayley to use, though they were now covered in gore. Julian's attention was caught by a combat knife, polished and glinting in the light, with only a few drops of blood along its blade. For now.

He wrapped his fingers around the hilt and yanked it from its sheath. As he drew it before his eyes he closely examined its form. A bright silver blade, curving elegantly towards the tip before turning sharply down again towards the straight serrated edge. This would be the perfect instrument for racking up a few silent kills.

A locker slammed shut on the other side of the pods. Julian raised his head above the obstruction to see the man he'd slipped past earlier, having now finished whatever he'd been doing, lifting himself away from the deck and pushing himself along the row of pods in the direction of the bridge.

After a quick look to either side, Julian squeezed through the gap between two pods, knife in hand. He looked left, following the raider on his way out and was surprised to see him turning away from the exit, towards the site of Julian's first kill. He could be about to check on his late comrade. That was a risk he couldn't take.

As the man rounded the corner Julian propelled himself down the ranks of pods. As he approached the final pod his left hand shot out and found purchase on a small feature of its casing. His momentum carried him around the corner and he laid his eyes on the raiders back. He brought his knife up.

He slammed into his target with considerable force and plunged the blade deep into his neck. After a few moments of muscle spasms they both collided with an SSR pod. Julian slammed the raider's forehead into one of the machine's many angular edges. The body went limp.

This time the gore was not so well contained. A patch of blood remained on the pod's sharp angles and several globules had escaped into the air. Hopefully they would disperse and be less noticeable, but the fact was that they were leaving a trail behind them anyway. The mere passage of time brought with it an ever-increasing likelihood of discovery. They would have to leave soon.

Julian had begun bundling the second corpse into a pod when a deep yell startled him.

'Oi, you!'

He spun to face the voice only to catch the briefest glimpse of a large man who sped towards him and tackled him at stomach-height. They both fell into the open pod, crushing the corpse inside against the back panel.

The impact left Julian winded. His aggressor pinned him into place with a firm grip on each shoulder, feet braced on the inside of the pod casing.

Trapped on all sides by metal and flesh, Julian could barely move. His arms were pinned to his sides and his legs kicked helplessly. He was unable to defend himself when the man restraining him lifted his right hand, balled it into a fist and slammed it into his cheek.

Julian recoiled, nearly headbutting the side of the pod. He remained there to allow the initial sting to subside a little, before lifting his head. But the fist was waiting.

A second blow caught him in the temple, the left side of his face burning as the flesh began to swell and bruise.

'You won't make it back to your cell, you piece o' shit!' He raised his fist again.

Suddenly he stopped. His eyes bulged and a haunting gurgle escaped his lips. His grip weakened and he slumped forward, revealing a long, thin blade that had followed his spine up into his brain. Sam floated behind him, a small splash of blood staining the white garb under her armour and her rifle still slung over her shoulder. She stared angrily down at Julian.

'Gunfire and brawling? Exactly what part of that was subtle?' she hissed.

'It was going really well until that last bit.'

'That shot was one hell of a gamble.'

Julian ignored her, pushing his way out from between the two corpses. 'I take it you handled your side of the room?'

'I've done a quick pass through the whole chamber. We're good. You handle the bodies, make sure they're properly stowed away. I'll go get Hayley. I'm pretty sure I've found an armour set more her size.'

'Good. Get her suited up. I'll be right over.'

* * *

Sam had apparently covered her side of the chamber much quicker than Julian had by leaving the bodies floating freely in the air, waiting to be hidden away afterwards. That meant it took a little longer to get them all wrapped up inconspicuously in their sleeping bags.

In the end it was for the best. It kept him busy while Sam and Hayley visited various lockers in the hopes of finding suitable armour components. Sam had found pads for Hayley's arms and legs, but she was simply too small for most of the vests and boots.

While they never found a perfect fit, they did eventually stumble across some pieces that would at least stay in more or less the right place. They just wouldn't be very comfortable. On the plus side, she only needed to endure the one boot.

Sam had also managed to find a handful of electrified stun batons, which she distributed. Now everyone had a slightly more discreet option for taking people out.

They'd stayed out of sight all the while and despite a mercenary or two passing along the chamber on their way through the vessel, they remained undiscovered.

After a short period of preparation, all three of them were suitably equipped, though as the most able and experienced fighters, Sam and Julian took point as they flanked the foremost entrance to the room.

They were close to the bridge now. Their exfiltration was nearly complete.

With no time to waste, they slipped around the corners and moved up the tunnel. Most of the vessel behind them, along with any number of raiders they'd passed by. They would have to watch their backs now.

No alarms were raised as they closed the distance to the flight deck.

The door they were faced with was much like every other door on the ship, meaning it would rattle and rumble as it slid along its rails. There would be no chance of a silent entrance. Instead they would just have to be quick.

They also had no way of knowing the shape, size or layout of the bridge, nor did they know how many people might be inside. They could assume that as long as they were cruising there would be no need for a full complement manning their posts, so there might only be one or two. That said, they were probably going to be re-entering normal space before long. Perhaps they would all be in there, preparing for the final stages of their voyage.

They would have to prepare for either eventuality. If their numbers were few, they could catch the raiders off guard and overpower them. Otherwise they would have no choice but to open fire.

Again, Sam counted down from three. At zero she slammed the door open and pushed inside, and Julian followed closely.

One figure manned the central console. She swivelled to face the sound of intrusion. In an instant, Sam readied a small knife. She pinched its tiny blade between her thumb and index finger and threw it hard and fast. It buried itself up to the hilt in the pilot's stomach. Then she followed up with a swift strike to the temple with her stun baton.

The impact knocked the pilot unconscious. Her head and limbs drifted freely, anchored by the torso strapped into the seat.

'You didn't need to do that!' Hayley pushed past them and examined the throwing knife lodged between her ribs. 'She wasn't going to put up a fight. The baton would have been enough.'

'Uhh, yeah, you're probably right,' Sam said, staring at the knife with guilt on her face. 'Sorry, I- I was on autopilot.'

Julian looked at the body, then turned to Sam. 'Don't worry about it. It's life and death right now. She chose her side.'

Hayley didn't look so convinced. Even Julian wasn't sure he believed what he was saying. He just knew he didn't need remorse weighing him down right now.

'Alright, Sam, we'll get over to the *Veteran* and finish this,' Julian said. 'I hope their superspace drive doesn't give you any trouble. By the look of this ship it's probably a bit rickety. In any case, just try not to crash. At these speeds you won't have the kind of error margin you're used to.'

'I know. Don't worry, I'll sort it out. You just try not to attract too much attention. I know what you're like.'

'I'd have been quieter if I had a stun stick back then. I'm sure we'll be fine now.'

'I hope so.' Sam floated over towards Hayley and placed a hand on her shoulder. 'Go ahead. Time's ticking.'

Julian led Hayley back to the door, then turned back to give Sam one last look. 'Good luck,' he said.

'You need it more than I do,' she replied.

CHAPTER 24

Down a ladder and along a short corridor to starboard, Hayley and Julian found themselves in the bowels of the *Shameless Renegade*, peering down into the tunnel that connected the two starships.

They could hear murmuring from the other side.

'This isn't going to be easy,' Hayley said.

'No joke. That cargo bay is far too open. We'll never get in there undetected.'

They'd seen how the raiders had stripped the cargo hold clean. Any kind of cover they might once have been able to use would be tucked away at the edges. They, however, would emerge from the airlock in the centre of the enormous floorspace. Chances were they would be spotted immediately, and dead soon after that.

'Let me go in,' Hayley said.

'What? No, absolutely not!'

'I'll only take a quick look. Just enough to get an idea of how many people are in there and where they are. Then we can work out a plan.'

Julian opened his mouth to argue, but didn't see any other way. He looked down into the airlock again and scratched his chin.

'Okay, fine,' he said. 'But have your gun handy just in case.'

She nodded and grabbed her rifle. Then she turned upside down and climbed cautiously up through the tunnel.

Julian watched her go, his mouth dry and his gun at the ready.

She slowed as she neared the other side. She looked around, then hopped across to the other side of the tunnel and continued to push through.

She was within reach of the threshold now, ducking her head just beneath it. Then she reached up further. Julian nearly called out to her. He wanted to tell her to stop, that she was being too reckless, but that would only make things worse. He bit his tongue and crossed his fingers.

Much to his relief she soon retreated and made her way back down the length of the tunnel.

'That was way too far, Hayley! You could have been seen!' Julian hissed.

'I couldn't see anyone from lower down and I wasn't coming back with nothing. We needed to know where they were. And don't pretend it's not already dangerous. I know what I'm doing.'

'Now's not the time to argue about this. What did you see?'

'As far as I could tell, there was a group of about six, maybe seven. They're all together on that side.'

'Really? That many?' Julian exhaled sharply. 'Were they armed?'

'Some of them at least, but their weapons are holstered. We'd have the first shot.'

'That always helps. Still, we probably ought to thin their numbers a little first. I don't like the idea of being outnumbered three to one.'

'Alright, makes sense. What did you have in mind?'

He considered throwing something through to grab their attention, but while it might have worked as a distraction in a pinch it almost certainly wouldn't split their group as intended.

Then he hit upon an idea.

He positioned himself directly over the entrance to the

tunnel and with an effort to imitate one of the mercenary's voices from earlier, he called through, 'Oi! Any of you lot up there wanna lend a hand with some 'eavy lifting? Our client's bought some cargo and wants it took to 'is room.'

The murmuring stopped.

Hayley stared at him urgently. 'What the hell are you doing?' she whispered.

Julian hushed her with a finger.

He was relieved to hear a deep, irritated moan followed by the reply, 'Yeah, alright, we'll be right there.'

He allowed himself a moment of victory before moving out of the way and readying his stun baton. Hayley did the same, pressing herself against the surface beside the opening.

'How much money's this bloke got anyway?' the raiders muttered on their way down.

'Apparently not enough to just buy his own ship.'

'How much do these things cost, anyway?'

Julian tightened his grip on the baton. Two had spoken, but there could be more on the way. His hand began to shake. He already missed having Sam with him.

Two figures emerged from the tunnel and, after allowing them to move a little further into the open, Julian and Hayley electrified their batons and aimed for the raiders' heads.

As they went down, a third raider came through. He cursed as his comrades fell, then lunged at Julian, who swung his weapon wildly at the large man. The mercenary dodged aside and grabbed Julian's wrists.

The mercenary's grip was vice-like and Julian's struggles didn't faze him. The raider slammed him against the wall, twisting Julian's arm until the baton dropped. Only then was one of his wrists released as the raider grabbed his gun.

Julian saw something swipe towards the raider's head. He

felt a shock as the current passed through the hand that grasped him, but the other man took the worst of it. His grip weakened and he fell away to join the others.

Hayley held her baton with confidence and smiled as she rested it on her shoulder. 'Don't worry, I got you,' she said.

'Thanks for that.' Julian smiled back. He didn't know where her newfound confidence had come from, but he was glad for it. He had hoped she would find the strength to fight back, but now it was hard to believe this was the same person who'd been in the cell with him. He felt proud of her.

He looked at the incapacitated mercenaries. Three down. 'That's about half of them, right? Maybe we can take a couple more.'

'Let's do it,' Hayley replied.

Julian called up again with his disguised voice, 'Anyone else? There's a lot of stuff!'

He was certain he heard someone curse. He and Hayley moved out of the way again as one more raider came down and was swiftly taken out of the picture.

'There should only be a couple left,' Hayley said. 'We can take them.'

'You think so? How far in are they?'

'Not too far. I reckon we could charge them.'

'Are you sure?'

She bobbed her head enthusiastically.

'That's not the adrenaline talking?'

'We can do it!' she insisted.

'Alright. Let's go then.'

They moved up the tunnel until they were right at the threshold. Julian let out a quiet breath, then peeked over the edge to judge the distance for himself.

He was spotted.

There were three left and all of them were looking right at him. They cried out, scattered and reached for their weapons. They even managed to fire off a few wild shots before Julian was able to duck back into cover.

'For fuck's sake,' he cursed, holstering his baton and grabbing for his rifle. 'Couldn't even get on board the ship without making a ruckus.'

'Well they've found us now,' Hayley said, readying her own weapon and flicking the safety off.

They looked up again just in time to see one of their targets floating above them, trying to get a clear shot through the airlock. A spray of bullets ricocheted down the tunnel, but Hayley and Julian responded quickly, each returning a flurry of rounds. A handful of shots struck the man's body, some glancing off his armour while others bit into his flesh.

The impacts sent him into a spin, blood spraying out in crimson spirals as he rolled through the air. The raider dropped his gun, grasping at the wounds with both hands in a vain attempt at halting the flow of blood. His writhing and kicking gradually petered out and his body fell limp.

Hayley raised herself up a little, placing her gun against the deck and peering over the top while the rest of her body hung down into cover. Julian did the same, aiming in a different direction.

He managed to catch a glimpse of one of the remaining raiders, hidden behind Winter's car. The mercenary leaned out and fired off a burst before retreating back into cover. Julian ducked his head down and the rounds pinged harmlessly against the deck plating.

He peeked again. He made a mental note of where his target's head had been and lined up a shot, expecting him to lean out of cover in the same way.

The target poked his head out to fire another burst. Julian fired off a round and struck the raider in the eye. He fell back, his body continuing to spin in the air long after his quick death.

Julian turned to his left in time to see Hayley hit the last target in the leg. The raider yelped with pain and clutched at the wound. Hayley dropped her gun and drew her stun baton. She leapt out of cover, charged him down and smashed it over the back of his head.

'Good job,' Julian said. 'But they'll be on to us now. We have to move fast.' He snatched up Hayley's gun and threw it in her direction as he pushed himself out from the airlock, leading the way towards the door nearest to the aft of the ship.

Another door opened on the far side of the bay and a handful of raiders pushed their way in. Julian pulled Hayley into the corridor out of harm's way and closed the door just as the assailants began to open fire.

'Yup, definitely on to us.' With no time to lose, he pushed himself away from the door and down the corridor. 'Keep an eye out behind us and shoot on sight. I'm hoping we can outrun them though.'

The *Redemptive Veteran* wasn't a large ship, so there wasn't far to go, but it also meant the raiders' mercenary force was more concentrated than they would have liked.

Hayley and Julian powered their way through the corridors like torpedoes, mowing down any resistance they encountered with a quick flurry of gunfire as they rounded each corner. Most of the opposition was caught by surprise, with no time to bring their weapons to bear before they were shot down, left to spin as geysers of blood squirted out and stained the bulkheads.

The pair rounded one final corner and were faced with a

short hallway that terminated with a double door. They'd reached the bridge.

Julian's heart leaped. They were going to make it out free and alive, he could taste it now.

He cast a glance towards Hayley and found she was already looking at him. He smiled at her, then they both turned their attention to the doors.

They approached slowly, drifting along the final stretch. Hayley covered Julian as he reached for the door controls. Before he could touch the button, he heard a hiss and the doors parted. His head snapped around to look and saw two more mercenaries coming through. They looked just as shocked to see him.

Julian reached for his gun but they were one step ahead, as theirs were already in hand. Yet before they managed to clear the doorway, a spray of rounds tore through cloth and flesh. They fell back the way they'd come.

Hayley charged past him into the bridge. He had to double take before he could follow.

He looked over to the far side of the deck and his heart sank. Gram was here, squared up and staring them down. She held Winter in front of her, a handgun pressed against her head.

'Julian, lock the door. We don't want any surprises,' Hayley ordered.

He wasn't used to her taking charge, but she had the right idea. He moved to the door control panel and locked it before re-joining Hayley. They levelled their guns but didn't fire for fear of hitting Winter.

'Well, well,' Gram said, peering over Winter's shoulder. 'Look at us. Seems we just can't avoid these little stalemates, can we?'

'It's over, Gram, you've lost. Just let her go,' Julian said.

'Of all the crews I've ever raided you've certainly caused me the most problems, but I haven't lost yet, boy. Not while I have her.'

A succession of loud beeps emanated from a console manned by one of the raider crew, who half-turned towards Gram.

'Gram, we're undocking.'

'What? Why are you doing that?'

'No, it's not me! Someone on the *Renegade*'s doing it.'

'Open a comm link. Find out what they're up to.'

'I don't think I need to. They're locking weapons on to us!'

Gram turned her furious glare back to Julian and Hayley. 'What are you doing?'

'We've made our choice,' Julian said proudly. 'We'd rather die than become slaves. Your choice is a lot easier. Would you rather die, or give us our ship back?'

She pressed the barrel of her gun harder against Winter, who grunted in response.

'Exactly how many people do you speak for? I'll kill the girl, destroy her message. How many lives are you willing to risk just for a chance at getting your little spaceship back?'

Orson was right. She was still using the message to her advantage. It had to be a trick. It was all too perfect for her.

'I'm not falling for that, Gram,' Julian said. 'It doesn't make any sense. You kill her and all you're going to do is lose the only thing you still have on us. Let her go and give up.'

Gram squinted at him and tilted her head. 'You think I'm lying to you?'

'She isn't,' Winter quickly added. Her fear looked genuine enough.

'Just stop, Gram,' Hayley begged her. 'No-one else needs to die. Surrender and we'll drop you off on Earth completely unharmed.'

Julian side-eyed Hayley. They could discuss later whether to honour that promise, but first they had to win.

'Bullshit. You'd hand me over to the Conglomerate, first chance you got.'

'I can't speak for everyone else, but I'm willing to forgive,' Hayley continued. 'Nothing can bring back our dead. If you give us our ship back and let us go, we'll offer you the same thing.'

The bridge fell silent as everyone considered their options, but the quiet was soon interrupted once more by the hiss of the doors as they slid apart.

Julian spun to face them, expecting to be caught by raider reinforcements. Instead he saw the face of Edward Orson.

He pushed his way across the threshold and closed the door behind him. 'You can't lock me out of my own bridge,' he said casually, rifle in hand.

'Orson! You've come at the perfect time. We've just about got your ship back.' Julian turned to face Gram again, a smug grin spreading across his face. 'You'll want to surrender now, Gram. Orson won't like you threatening that message.'

Quite to his surprise, she was also smiling now. 'Indeed he won't. So you might want to watch your back, boy.'

Julian squinted at her in confusion, then felt the cold metal of a gun barrel pressing into his spine.

'Lay down your arms, Julian,' Orson growled into his ear.

Hayley shifted her attention to her captain. 'What are you doing?'

'You lot have become far too reckless. Think how many lives you've jeopardised. I will not see that message threatened. Drop your weapons and surrender to them.'

'What the hell? Are you mad?' Julian held defiantly on to his rifle and kept it trained on Gram. 'We were just coming to an agreement. We could have finished this peacefully. No more blood spilled.'

'Not anymore,' Gram interjected. 'Deal's off.'

Julian seethed. 'Don't do this! We were getting somewhere!'

'Listen to your captain, boy,' she mocked.

'You bitch!'

Orson slammed the butt of the rifle against the back of his head. Julian quickly recovered but his head throbbed from the impact. He brought his weapon up again, this time trained on his old captain, but the impact left him dazed. His aim was far from steady.

'Stand down!' Orson barked.

'And if I don't?'

'This gun's not for show, boy. If you don't surrender, I'll end you right here.'

'You're insane!'

'If this is insanity then so be it. Now do the smart thing and drop your gun!'

CHAPTER 25

Once again, Winter felt powerless. She continued to drag down the people she wanted to consider her friends. Allies, at the very least.

But with so many other lives to consider, she couldn't risk helping them. This standoff could have gone so many ways and most of them started with her death. No wonder Gram was so confident.

She didn't want to admit it, but it had been a relief when Orson had arrived. Perhaps they never would reclaim their ship, but at least no-one else would have to die.

'Now do the smart thing and drop your gun!' Orson ordered.

Julian's face was burning with anger but he clicked on his rifle's safety and cast it across the flight deck. Any conviction left on Hayley's face soon seeped away too as she followed his lead.

Orson's face began to relax as the danger passed, replaced with the unmistakable expression of sorrow.

'You too,' Gram said.

Orson threw his rifle aside.

'Good man.' Gram tapped a nearby seat with her foot to get the pilot's attention. 'Take their weapons.'

The pilot slipped out of his harness, collected the discarded firearms and stripped all three of the intruders of their weapons. Once they were disarmed, he returned to his seat.

Gram gave Winter a hard shove, launching her across the room to join the others.

'Broadcast on comms. Get a couple of guards up here to keep this lot in check,' she told her crew before turning back to her captives. She kept her gun loosely pointed at them while cradling her head. 'I can't tell you how difficult you've made this job, I really can't. But I must tell you how thankful I am to have you here, Winter. Don't get me wrong, you're a pain in the arse, but it seems you're the only thing I have that can cripple this crew.'

'You don't have me, Gram,' Winter protested.

'Oh, no, of course. Paul has you. In any case, you guys picked one hell of a time to make your escape because we're re-entering normal space any minute now.'

'More like any second,' the pilot corrected.

'You'd better hope whoever you left in charge of the *Renegade* knows what they're doing. I'd quite like my ship to still be in one piece when this is over.'

'It'll be fine,' Julian said.

'Let's find out.'

Gram turned her back on them to stare out into the swirling purple of superspace and the pilot began the countdown.

'Five. Four. Three. Two. One.'

Space began to quiver at a point in front of the vessels. Ribbons of distortion streamed along their hulls. The flight deck started to rattle and shake. Winter had to get a grip on the nearest bulkhead for support.

From the origin of the distortions in space, something began to split. A white light rippled out, glowing brighter and brighter. Then an almighty crack flashed out, carving its way through space and around the *Redemptive Veteran*. The ship shuddered violently and Winter had to use all of her strength to keep herself from being thrown around the room.

The shaking came to a sudden stop. Winter took a moment

to recover, then pulled away from the bulkhead and looked out. The purple clouds of superspace had vanished, replaced by the comforting and familiar sight of stars twinkling brightly in the inky black abyss.

Taking centre stage was a beautiful blue planet. Its vast oceans sparkled in the pale sunlight beneath a thin veil of white cloud. It was every bit as stunning as Winter had been led to believe, yet under the circumstances she felt more relieved than awestruck.

Gram looked over her shoulder. 'It looks like the *Renegade*'s still intact, after all. Your pilot knows her stuff, I'll give her that.' There was almost a look of respect on her face which she quickly wiped away. She turned to her helmsman. 'Bring us into orbit. Don't bother shedding any speed before then. I just want to get there as soon as possible.'

All you need to do is arrive in a wide orbit and your little machine will do the rest.

Winter had been given that instruction back on Arali. It felt like a lifetime ago, yet it still echoed around her head like an earworm.

She could see the planet now. How close did she need to be? Had she done it? Was her mission complete?

A familiar hiss. The doors to the bridge parted again and two armed raiders entered the room, their faces beaten and bloody. Apparently they had already seen some action.

'Ah, about time,' Gram said as she faced them. 'Keep these four under guard, will you?'

'Back to their cells?'

'The cells are on the other ship! Doesn't matter, we'll be landing soon.'

Something clicked inside Winter's neck, like a tiny switch had been flipped, and just like that she stopped listening. She simply found herself unable to pay any more attention. Gram was probably still talking, but she no longer had the capacity to care.

Instead she found herself straightening up and turning to face her new guards. They raised their rifles in perfect synchronisation. Normally that would be enough to make her back down.

This time, she did the opposite.

She flashed forward, smashing one in the face with a right hook and yanking his gun away with the other hand. Following through in a single motion, she brought the butt of the rifle into contact with the second guard's cheek, knocking his aim off centre and causing a round to fire into the bullet-resistant cockpit glass. Then she swung back at lightning speed, enough to drive the weapon barrel straight through his armour and his skin, carving a bloody path directly into his stomach. He screamed in both astonishment and agony.

Gram readied her pistol again, aiming and firing with blistering speed, but Winter was quicker. She withdrew her stolen rifle from the mercenary's wound and brought its broad side up to shield her face. The bullet ricocheted off at a shallow angle and struck the second guard in the thigh.

She charged forward and grabbed Gram's arm, pulling her aim towards the ceiling before she could unleash another round. She twisted until Gram's grip on the pistol loosened. Winter brought the rifle up and to the right, smashing Gram in the chin and causing her to spin. Then she brought it back down the same way and clubbed her over the back of her skull with enough force to knock her out cold.

Winter adjusted her grip on the gun, finally placing a finger on the trigger. She turned and fired a single shot into each of the guards' heads.

Her eyes snapped to the pilot who'd snatched up a rifle of his own. She took him down, delivering a punch to the cheek, then slamming his face down into the control console.

The fight was over in seconds. Winter towered over her fallen foes, but she felt nothing besides ambivalence. They had been in her way. They weren't anymore.

'Bloody hell, Winter!' Orson exclaimed. 'Why didn't you tell us you could do that before? Hell, why didn't you actually *do* that before?'

Winter didn't respond.

Orson hesitated. 'Well, let's not waste any time. You two, grab a weapon. Get these raiders under guard.'

The crew obeyed their captain. Julian took up the rifle of one of the fallen guards while Hayley moved forward to take back her confiscated stun baton.

Winter felt a tension growing inside of her as the crew rearmed themselves. She lunged forward, wrenched the baton out of Hayley's hand and with a flurry of sharp swipes she had beaten all three of them unconscious.

She didn't know why she had done it, nor did she feel remorse. Instead she dropped the baton and readied her rifle again before charging out of the room.

She swung herself around the various turns in the corridor as she hurtled through the ship. She'd barely registered a pair of raiders along the way, before she'd raised her gun and neutralised them with a bullet each. She sped past their bodies, not paying them a second thought.

She'd returned to the cargo bay. No hostiles in sight.

She launched herself into the centre of the room where she grabbed a handhold and slowed herself to a stop. There, she moved to the side of the airlock, now sealed shut, and pried open a hatch set into the floor. She'd never known it was there before, yet somehow she wasn't surprised to find it. Nor was she amazed that it contained exactly what she needed: an equipment rack with a handful of spacesuits.

But what did she need them for? How could she not know?

Each had been custom fit to a different member of the *Veteran*'s crew. She helped herself to Sam's, seeing as she was the closest in size to her, and began to pull it on over her smuggling attire.

Part way through the process of getting changed she grabbed for her gun. As if by coincidence one of the cargo bay doors opened and an armed raider entered, but she was already aiming in his direction.

She fired. He fell. She dropped the gun and continued getting changed. As soon as the helmet was on she was ready to go.

Go where?

She located a control pad inside the equipment locker. She had no idea which buttons she was pressing or why, but when she was finished the first door into the airlock slid open and she flung herself inside, the rifle slung over her shoulder.

She'd passed through here on her way to the *Shameless Renegade* before, so at least she recognised this second control panel when she saw it. A few button presses and the door slid shut behind her, sealing her in.

She continued to tap away at the controls, a strange blend of mystery and familiarity to their touch and function. She never understood what she was doing until after she'd done it, at which point it felt as if she had always known. She wasn't at all surprised as the air leaked away from the sealed chamber and the second set of doors silently parted, revealing the speckled black space beyond.

The *Renegade* was out there, the edges of its silhouette

highlighted as the white sunlight shone against the angular shape of its hull. Somewhere in the middle, hidden in the shadows, was her way in.

Despite the other ship's airlock being invisible to her, she knew precisely where to aim, in the same way she'd taken out the raider who'd discovered her in the cargo bay. She hadn't known where he was. She'd simply known where to point her gun.

She held herself firmly against the hull, her feet flat against the solid metal plating, and she aimed.

She kicked away hard and flew deep into the void, the *Redemptive Veteran* shrinking away behind her while the looming shadow of the *Shameless Renegade* grew larger, blotting out the stars behind it until all was darkness.

Winter could hear nothing beyond her own steady breathing in the vacuum of space. She couldn't quite believe how calm she was. No-one in their right mind would attempt anything like this without a cable connecting them to their ship or some form of manoeuvre gear. One mistake and she would be sailing off into eternity, never to be seen again.

Yet much like everything else she had done in the last few minutes, she knew without a doubt that she would succeed. She would reach the other ship alive and intact and everything that might get in her way would be turned to her advantage.

She reached forward, grabbing on to the airlock frame and bringing herself to a stop. She couldn't see the controls as everything on this side of the vessel was bathed in perfect darkness, yet somehow she found and utilised them. The doors parted, she slipped inside and began re-pressurising the chamber.

The familiar rumbling and clunking of the raider ship returned to her ears. She didn't bother to remove the spacesuit.

Instead she pried open the interior lock and made her way into the belly of the ship.

The ship's central tunnel was directly above her, accessible by two identical walkways, each ending in a short ladder. She picked the nearest one and launched herself through at breakneck speed. She took the upward turn with expert precision and kicked away when she reached the top. She didn't even bother to look as she unslung her rifle, aimed over her shoulder and fired a shot towards the back of the ship. She already knew it would find its mark in the face of a potential troublemaker.

The door to the bridge was mere feet in front of her. She holstered her gun again and began to remove her helmet as she reached for the door handle.

She threw the door along its rails and it clanged into place. She recognised Sam in the pilot's seat who, startled by the sudden noise, brought her weapon around to face it. Winter didn't wait for her to shoot and instead threw her helmet towards Sam's face.

A burst of fire belched out from Sam's rifle, each bullet striking against the incoming helmet and throwing it back towards Winter. Winter anticipated its return trajectory. She readied a fist and punched it, forcing it to reverse its direction a second time. It struck Sam square in the forehead. Winter charged forward and followed it closely with a hard blow to the back of the head.

Winter took another seat nearby and fastened herself in. She pulled engine control over to her console and forced the vessel into a much more rapid deceleration. Her upper body immediately launched forward as the reverse engines burned. Her vision began to darken and her head throbbed, but she didn't care. Taking hold of the manoeuvring thrusters, she tightened the vessel's orbital curve, angling the *Shameless Renegade* towards the planet's surface.

They were already travelling at high speed and much of the distance to Earth had been covered during Winter's escape. They were right above the planet now, so it wasn't long before orange tongues of plasma began to lick at the corners of the canopy as the upper atmosphere began to ignite.

The vessel rattled and quaked. The reverse thrusters managed to maintain their deceleration despite gravity steadily taking hold. It wouldn't be enough to bring them to a stop before ground level, but Winter had a plan.

She just didn't know what it was yet.

The clouds sizzled away as the *Shameless Renegade* ploughed through them. A vast mountain range in the distance bordered a wide expanse of farmland. In the very centre of the land was an enormous lake. The water would be her best hope of making the landing survivable.

Winter made some last-minute adjustments to the ship's trajectory and angled the nose up a little, making sure that the *Renegade* would land on its belly. Once confident that nothing more needed to be done, she moved her seat away from the control console and rested her hands in her lap. Then she waited, watching the lake grow closer and closer.

The impact sent an earth-shattering bang echoing through the mountains. The ship shook violently. Despite the harness her body was thrown around wildly beyond her control. Her head beat against the seat and her arms and legs flailed out in front of her. Angry white water blinded her to everything beyond the glass.

The dizzying motions didn't cease immediately. The vessel continued to rock as the waves it sent outwards moved back in, pushing and pulling against its hull. The danger had passed.

That was when truth suddenly began to sink in.

Another sharp click in her neck and Winter's mind returned. She was left to see all that she had done, and started to hyperventilate. She looked outside at the unfamiliar scenery, then down at her blood-spattered hands.

Then she remembered Sam. Horrified, she turned and saw her strapped into her seat, blood trickling from a gash across her face.

Winter began to scream, but soon her lungs felt weak. She couldn't scream anymore. Everything below her neck felt as if it was fading away.

'No,' she said, panic rising. 'No!' She hurried to unstrap herself from her seat, fumbling with the buckle in her desperation. She tried to stand in the gravity, real gravity for the first time in weeks, but her legs collapsed beneath her. She felt weak and achy.

She tried to drag herself towards the door. She didn't know where she was going, but she definitely wasn't staying here. She had to leave.

Her movements slowed. All too soon sensation in her legs faded completely. Her arms too. She lost all control and her head fell to the floor. Her eyes felt heavy and her head hurt.

All you need to do is arrive in a wide orbit and your little machine will do the rest.

Is this what he meant? Had she completed her mission?

Sensation abandoned her. Darkness engulfed her.

Her eyes closed.

All she wanted now was to sleep.

CHAPTER 26

Orson awoke to a hard pounding in the back of his head. His eyes fluttered open and he reached a hand back to cradle the wound.

He drifted through the *Veteran*'s flight deck, staring up at the ceiling. He twisted and turned in an effort to bring himself upright.

The room felt smaller than ever with the number of bodies drifting through the air. Dead mercenaries, still leaking blood, though most of the free-floating droplets had settled on the bulkheads by now.

Recalling the events took him some effort, and the images that came to mind didn't make sense. In his mind's eye he saw Winter beating Gram unconscious with the butt of a rifle. Then her fingers curled around the hilt of a stun baton. The rest was a blur.

Those batons were painful but reliable ways of neutralising someone without causing lasting damage. It seemed also that their effects wore off a little sooner than a bludgeoning such as the one Gram had received. She remained secured to her seat, blood streaked across her face and matted into her hair, but a quick check of her pulse confirmed she still lived.

Then he looked past her, out into space. He allowed himself to relax a little when his eyes settled on the glistening planet Earth outside. He was home now. This nightmare would soon be over.

He turned back into the cockpit to check that his crew were recovering, but Julian's eyes were already open.

'She alive?' he asked, gesturing at Gram.

Orson paid her a glance then turned back to his engineer. 'Just out cold.'

There was a twitch in Julian's brow and his piercing gaze angled down at her bloodied face. Then he turned away, looking around the space until his eyes settled on Gram's pistol. 'Then let's put an end to that.' He reached for it, checked that the safety was off and placed a finger on the trigger. His arm stretched out as he aimed for her head.

Orson lashed out, grabbing Julian's wrist with both hands and pulling the gun off to the side.

Julian's voice was dark. 'What's wrong? Worried I'll get brains on the chair? I wouldn't worry about it, this place needs a clean anyway.'

The lines on Orson's face deepened. He spoke with rekindled authority. 'You will not kill her.'

Julian coughed as he choked on his shock. 'You're serious? Look again. Do I have to remind you that's the bitch who hijacked your ship, threatened to sell us as slaves and damn near killed us when we resisted? You've wanted her dead ever since she slithered on board.'

'You forget your place, boy,' Orson snarled. 'This ship sails in the name of the Solar Conglomerate. Now take a look out that window.' He waited for Julian to peer over his shoulder before continuing. 'That's right, son. Welcome to Earth. We're not fighting for our lives anymore, which means we respect the righteous authority of Solar law. We'll make her face the music and she may yet hang, but she will do so in an official capacity. You understand me?'

'At least a dozen of her lackeys are already dead. What does it matter if she goes with them? She should be dead by now anyway. She doesn't deserve a trial.'

'Everyone deserves a trial,' Orson retorted. He tilted his head. 'Need I remind you of that mutiny of yours? If we were still far from civilisation I could have you shot, but under the law of the Conglomerate I'd be the one in the wrong, so I'll tell you what. If you want to help me uphold the law then she lives and so do you. But if you cast those rules aside, then so will I. I hope I've made myself clear.'

Julian's anger simmered, but begrudgingly he surrendered and handed over the gun. 'Yeah, old man. Crystal clear.'

'Call me Captain,' he said. 'I've got my ship back, after all.'

'You're welcome,' Julian muttered as Orson returned to the front of the bridge.

'Check on Hayley,' the captain ordered. 'If we're awake she ought to be recovering soon as well. And get rid of these bodies, for crying out loud.'

He left Julian to work and returned to Gram. He let out a sigh as he leaned over her. The time to kill her had unfortunately passed. He could still play the legal system though and make her life hell until her dying breath.

He moved closer and patted her down, searching for any hidden armaments but finding none. In a skin-tight flight suit like hers, weapons would be hard to conceal anyway. Then he moved on to the pilot sitting next to her. Winter had slammed his head down into his console and it hadn't moved since. Orson reached forward and placed his hand atop the man's head. He pulled back on it gently to begin with, but when it refused to move he tightened his grip and yanked harder.

The head snapped back with a cracking sound, revealing a face shredded into bloody ribbons by the broken glass that had held it in place. The workstation had shattered and the sharp, jagged remains of the display made way for a face-shaped hole.

Orson released the body and withdrew his hand. He shook

his head and whispered to Gram, 'She killed everyone else. Why couldn't she kill you too?'

'She's awake,' Julian called.

'What?' Orson's mind was still on Gram.

'Hayley. She's awake,' Julian said, his arms supporting the technician as she recovered. 'It's alright,' he told her. 'Just a stun weapon. You'll be fine.'

Hayley groaned as she awoke, squeezing her eyes shut as she winced with pain. 'Winter …'

'Yes, it was her. Don't ask me why.'

She looked up into Julian's face with confusion. 'Where did she go?'

Julian looked up and his eyes darted around the cockpit. 'Good question. I don't know that either.' He turned to address Orson. 'Did you see where she went?'

The captain's head was still fuzzy, but even so he cursed for not having asked himself that question already. He didn't waste time replying, instead pushing his way through the bridge towards Julian's usual workstation – still operational unlike the helm.

He called up the surveillance feeds from around the *Veteran* and searched the ship. There were corpses all over the place, drifting through almost every room and corridor. The only living people he could find were the raiders' commissioner, Paul Narn, and a single raider guard escorting him. Apparently they had ducked into an SSR suite to avoid the chaos. No sign of Winter though.

'I don't see her anywhere.'

'Are you sure she's still on board?' Hayley asked.

'What, are you serious? You think she got off somehow?' Julian said. 'We undocked from the *Renegade* so she can't be on there. Where else could she have gone?'

Orson made a quick check of the ship's inventory. 'One of our spacesuits is gone. Sam's. The two are about the same size, wouldn't you say? She could have taken that and gone–'

'Gone where? She'd have had to make an impossible jump to get to the raiders' ship from here.'

'Maybe not. Their ship may be closer than you think.' Orson said, looking at the latest sensor data, then pulling back in surprise. 'Huh. That's weird.'

'What's weird?' Hayley asked.

'The *Renegade*'s gone. I'm not seeing it out there at all.'

'Well maybe … Maybe she did jump,' Hayley suggested. 'Maybe she missed and Sam saw. Maybe she's following Winter and trying to collect her.'

'There's an easy way to find out,' Julian said, making his way to Hayley's usual console. 'I can check the sensor logs and see where the ship went.'

He sat tapping at the computer screen for a minute or two. Orson grew impatient. Time was wasting.

'I think we can rule out your theory, Hayley. If Winter tried to jump across, Sam would have followed on a course heading directly away from us. Instead they made a beeline straight for the planet.'

'They're on Earth?'

'Seems so.' Julian sat quietly for a moment, then thumped the console in frustration. 'It still doesn't tell us where Winter went.'

'I think it does,' Orson said. 'I think she's on that ship. Or at least she was.'

'I already told you that's not possible.'

'Think about it. She was a completely different person when we last saw her. The Winter we knew could never have taken out everyone on this bridge, and I don't believe for one minute she would have attacked us. She had dexterity and speed like I've never seen before. I don't doubt she could have made that jump. Hell, she might have even taken the *Renegade* to Earth by herself for all we know. That's where she was heading anyway, to deliver that message of hers.'

Julian and Hayley looked uneasy. They exchanged glances, then turned back to Orson.

'This doesn't add up. None of this makes sense,' Hayley said.

'If you're right, it sounds like she's been hiding far too much information from us.' Julian shook his head. 'I don't trust her.'

'That doesn't matter. She has a mission to get that message of hers to the Conglomerate and we need to make sure that happens.'

'With what she's apparently capable of I doubt she'll have any trouble from here. Besides, with all these lies and secrets, who's to say the message is for the Conglomerate anyway? Who's to say there's a message at all, for that matter?'

'I promised to see Winter's job through to the end, and to the end is where I'll see it!' Orson screamed, his rage once again getting the better of him. 'Julian, take Gram down to SSR suite one. You'll find the raiders' client in there with a guard. Keep them secure. Seal them in the pods if you have to. Tell them I'm watching and that if they give you any trouble, I'll self destruct this ship before they have a chance to take it from me again. That ought to keep them in line.'

'What are you–?'

'Not another word, boy, just do it!'

Julian swallowed his pride and did as he was told, making his way over to Gram, unbuckling her from her seat and lugging her out of the door.

Orson turned his attention to Hayley. 'You stay here. You're going to help me find that ship.'

'Okay, Captain, but … well, Julian would know how to do that far better than I would.'

'Hayley, listen to me. He's an engineer, you're a technician. I know you're going to tell me they're not the same thing but right now they have to be, okay? I'm not leaving you in charge of those thugs, so that means your job is to track the *Renegade*. Just do whatever Julian would do, okay? Just without all the mouthing off. Find a way.'

Hayley silently obeyed, taking her place at the seat that Julian had just left behind. She sat staring at the screen for a moment, then said, 'I think I've got an idea.'

'Don't leave me in suspense, let's hear it.'

'When Julian said they made a beeline for the planet, he wasn't wrong. Their course was a perfect straight line right up until gravity took hold. At that point it's pretty predictable. What I'm trying to say is I can map their path all the way down to the planet's surface. I can rewind the ship's clock back a little way too, until Earth is in the exact same orientation it was at the time. That should tell us more or less where they made touchdown. It's not the best way to track them, but at least I know how to do it. I think.'

'See, Hayley? I knew you wouldn't disappoint. Get it done and I'll get us ready to follow.'

Orson moved the piloting controls to his console and began plotting an approach to the planet. The *Redemptive Veteran* was already in a wide orbit, but they'd need to get a fair bit closer if they were going to follow the *Shameless Renegade* down with any kind of haste.

He angled the ship's trajectory towards the planet to tighten their orbital path. He wondered how the authorities might react to an unresponsive vessel coming this close to the planet without announcing. He pushed the thought aside. He didn't have the time to worry about such things.

Once the course was plotted and their orbit had begun to shrink, all Orson could do was wait for Hayley's update. A few minutes passed and the silence grew tenser.

'Oh,' Hayley murmured.

'Oh?' Orson repeated. 'What does that mean? Have you found it?'

'I think so, Captain, but you're not going to like it.'

'Then hurry up and tell me! I don't want to be kept waiting any longer.'

'If this data's right, and I don't see any reason why it wouldn't be, then the *Renegade* went down somewhere in East Africa. I'm seeing mountains and … It doesn't look good, Captain.'

Orson fell silent. They both knew the implications. She was right. It didn't look good at all.

'How long ago did they land?' he asked, a slight shake in his voice. He was nervous. Winter's message could be in jeopardy.

'An hour ago. Maybe two.'

Orson's hands launched back to the controls and he turned the ship sharply towards the planet. There was no time to lose. There could already be people out searching the wreckage. Perhaps they'd already found the message? No, he couldn't entertain that possibility. He just had to act as fast as he was able.

He checked the live footage of the SSR suite where Julian had gathered the raiders. They floated inside the open pods while Julian guarded them from outside. Orson keyed open a commlink and spoke to them.

'This is your captain speaking. We've lined up a course for the planet and are making a very rapid approach. Things are going to get a little bumpy, to say the least. Just hang tight and keep your bitching to yourselves.' He closed the comms and called across the bridge. 'Hayley, I want you surveying the ground. We're going to make a pass over those mountains and I want you to keep your eyes open for that ship. You see anything that might tell us where it went, you let me know. Understand?'

'Yes, Captain.'

He turned his attention back to their approach and watched as the hull began to heat. Ribbons of red hot plasma cascaded over the bow of the vessel as the air burned around the *Redemptive Veteran*, hurtling towards the planet's surface. 'I won't ask you to see this to the end with me, Hayley. I don't know what's going to happen when we get down there, but if it gets rough I'm going it alone. This is my fight.'

'We've come this far. I don't want to leave you now.'

'I'm not arguing with you about this. You will stay put. That's an order.'

Hayley didn't utter another word. Orson would have persisted but his attention was needed elsewhere. He would have to insist further once they were down. She didn't need to be involved any more than she was and he was sure that no-one was out of harm's way just yet.

CHAPTER 27

Winter returned to consciousness, roused by searing aches and pains all through her body. She leapt in her seat as her most recent memories flooded back and her breaths became rapid and irregular.

She knew there was no point in panicking though – a lesson she'd learned many years ago. She breathed deeply and revisited each event in turn, hoping to sharpen her blurry recollection.

As she did so, it became clear that whatever had driven her actions had also ensured that her thoughts – which had felt more like digital computations rather than mental processes – had been burned into her mind with perfect clarity. She knew precisely how much force she had exerted with every attack she'd made and exactly how fatal the results had been.

Her thoughts went to the *Veteran*'s crew. She had beaten three of them down with a stun weapon. They'd be out cold for an hour or so but they'd certainly live. Sam on the other hand had taken a high-velocity space helmet to the face. She'd certainly feel the effects of that for a little while longer.

Of course Winter had also taken Gram down with a strike to the back of the head. Again, it hadn't been enough to kill her, though on some level she wished that it had.

Her own thoughts repulsed her. She never wanted to wish death upon someone, as much as she wanted to convince herself that this was different.

She tried to bring her hands up in front of her face to see

the blood on her palms and knuckles again, but they didn't move. Now the truth of the present began to set in.

Her hands were cuffed behind her back, pressed against a seat that felt different to her chair on the *Renegade* bridge. This one was made of a rougher leather, the padding underneath squashed and worn from use.

Finally ready to face the world once again, she opened her eyes, but quickly shut them again, dazzled by bright light. Slowly, she tried again. Her eyes adjusted gradually and she began to take in her surroundings.

She was bound hand and foot inside a dingy military troop carrier. She sat against the wall, with sunlight pouring through the rear entrance immediately to her left. She leaned out as far as she could to look around. A distant range of mountains set against the blue sky, stood as the backdrop to a sprawling green grassland. As she turned her head, she saw an enormous lake. Out towards the centre of it was the dark, smoking silhouette of a ruined starship.

Winter almost completely overlooked a small group of people standing by the water, blending in with the wet earth. She squinted, trying to see more. Most of their features were indistinguishable, but some of them were in loose-fitting apparel and well-armed. An organised military force, it would seem, which made sense considering the vehicle they were keeping her in.

That was all she was able to determine before she realised that one of them was pointing at her and that others were beginning to turn in her direction. She ducked her head back into the vehicle.

Was escape an option? Perhaps she could find something to break open her cuffs. It wasn't until she looked into the darkness of the truck that she saw Sam, similarly bound, sitting against the same wall. She was still unconscious, a swelling darkening on her forehead. Winter gulped, hoping to swallow the guilt welling up inside her.

Even if escape were possible, she couldn't abandon Sam. She didn't even know who they were, but her implant had brought her here and they had gone all the way into the middle of the lake to get her. It would be a safe bet that they were the intended recipients of her message, in which case it was even more important that she stay. She needed to know what she'd been carrying all this time and that it was worth the sacrifices she'd made.

Footsteps could be heard squelching in the dirt as someone approached the vehicle. Winter sat up straight and a large man came into view, standing just outside the opening. His head was round, as was his nose, and he had little more than stubble decorating his scalp. He looked Winter up and down.

There was a soft expression on his face. Was that pity?

'You didn't need to cuff me, you know,' Winter said. 'I chose to come here.'

'Even if that were true, my hands are tied, no pun intended. Anyone who lands their ship like that, I'd consider to be more than a little unstable.'

'What do you mean "if that were true"?'

'You didn't choose to come, did you?' He stepped up into the vehicle and sat on the seat across from her, then leant forward with his hands in his lap. 'That thing in your neck is a remarkable little device, isn't it? Life support, storage device and a beacon. Led us right to you.'

This was the first Winter had heard of it being a beacon. Once again she was reminded of how little she had actually been allowed to know. It was infuriating.

'I take it you've got your message then?' she asked, trying to mask her anger.

'Yeah, we got it.' He averted his gaze, looking outside. 'Already transmitted it back to base.'

After a few seconds of silence, Winter looked at him expectantly. 'Well? You going to tell me what it said?'

'You're not going to like it.'

'For god's sake, tell me,' she growled. 'I've been carrying this thing for two weeks and that smoking wreck out there pretty much sums up my journey. I don't care what the message is. It really doesn't concern me in the slightest, but getting it here has been the single most traumatic experience of my life. I have every right to know.'

'Well, I guess you'll find out sooner or later anyway,' the soldier said, still avoiding eye contact. 'This message was a test. A new way to transport confidential information without it falling into the wrong hands. You were basically a … proof of concept.'

Winter couldn't quite believe what she was hearing. Her mouth fell open as she tried to make sense of it. All this time, she hadn't been carrying anything important at all.

'But …' She struggled to find the words she needed.

'We didn't know you were coming,' he continued. 'Guess they would have had to send a message to tell us in the first place, which would have defeated the point.'

'I need more than this,' Winter said, too shocked to shout. 'Who are you? Who sent the message?'

The soldier gulped. 'I wish I could tell you.'

'Why can't you?'

'We were told not to.'

'By who?'

'I'm sorry but you can't know. Your whole mission was

based on you not knowing these things. If you knew, you could have taken the message to the wrong people.'

'That doesn't matter anymore. You've got the message. The mission is over.'

He shook his head. 'No,' he said quietly. 'No, I'm afraid it isn't.'

Winter didn't think her heart could sink any further. 'I don't want to ask any more questions. Just tell me what I need to know.'

The soldier turned to face her. His eyes kept finding hers, then drifting away again. 'It takes a certain kind of spine injury to need an implant like that. There aren't many others with one, on Earth or Arali, and you're far more physically capable than the rest. That makes you special, which means we're going to have to keep using you to deliver messages. After all, if your journey was really that bad, it's a good thing you were there to protect the message, wouldn't you say?'

He paused, giving Winter a chance to respond. She didn't take it.

He looked outside again, in the direction of the lake. 'We'll need to send you back to Arali to confirm that everything worked and then we can start communicating properly.'

Her mind was racing. Of all the things she'd been led to think, of all the things she'd let herself believe, how much of it had ever been true?

'I have family on Arali. Whoever sent your message is holding them hostage, but told me if I finished the job they'd be set free,' she told him. 'Will he set them free?'

'Probably not,' he said. 'He wants you to keep working for him. If they're released you could turn away. Right now he has what he needs.'

He opened his mouth to continue, but hesitated.

'What?'

The soldier's head swivelled to face Sam. 'She a friend of yours?'

Winter looked at her. She was slumped forward in her seat, her hands cuffed behind her back. Dark patches of dried blood were caked on to her face. Winter felt another pang of guilt.

'I guess you could say that.' She turned back to the soldier. 'Why?'

'Because apparently, having your family hostage on Arali isn't enough. We need to have some incentive for you on Earth too, just in case you try anything while you're here.'

'You really think I'm stupid enough to try and sabotage this mission with so much at stake?'

'It's just a precaution. We don't know what you'll try.'

'It's barbaric and unnecessary! She's been fighting for her freedom the whole way here and the last thing she needs is for you to take it from her anyway! I'm already doing your job. Just let her go.'

'It's not my decision!'

Winter fell silent. His face was stern but it quickly softened.

'I agree, it is barbaric. We're turning people into tools. Everything about it is wrong, but we're at war and there are people out there more powerful than either of us who think this is what needs to be done. War is turning us into monsters. It's all I can do to try and retain a little humanity until it ends.'

Winter stared at him with cold eyes. 'If you don't like it, why don't you do something about it?'

He looked down at his feet. Then he rose slowly from his seat and climbed out of the truck, stepping down into the mud. He hovered at the opening before turning back to face Winter.

'You understand I was just passing on a message, don't you? Not that I wanted to. Only that I had to. In that sense we're quite alike,' he said, this time managing to look her directly in the eye. 'Maybe you're right. Maybe there is something more I could be doing. But you know what? If you think there's hope for me, I reckon there must be hope for you too.'

He smiled at her. Winter wasn't sure what to make of him. She couldn't believe their situations were at all comparable, but maybe he was right. She still had time on her side and no matter what they made her do, her mind was free. Perhaps there was still hope.

'Good luck,' he said, then turned to trudge away,

Before he could get too far, Winter called out to him. 'Wait!'

He stopped and looked back over his shoulder.

'I was told the message could save lives. Was that true, or was that a lie as well?'

'One message can only do so much on its own, but that's just the start,' he replied. 'We are trying to end a war. Try looking at the big picture. You might feel better.'

Then he carried on walking.

Winter watched him go, then turned around to face Sam. She hadn't moved at all and her breaths were so shallow they were almost impossible to see. If she weren't to be used for blackmail, Winter would have suspected her to be dead. After all, everyone else was.

Could that really be true? There must have still been a few raiders on that ship, not to mention the passengers from the *Veteran*, still sealed away in their cell. They were probably all killed in the crash.

A pulse of nausea punched through her stomach. She tried to push the thought aside.

Instead her mind drifted to Isaac. His body had been a gruesome sight, but he was almost certainly more intact than his mother right now.

The thought occurred that his fate was sealed the second he had stepped on board the *Veteran*. Even if Gram hadn't been the one to kill him, he still would have failed to reach Earth alive. He was always doomed to fall victim to her failure.

Could it be that Winter now had more blood on her hands than Gram? What did that make her?

Her eyes started to well up as she tried to fight the guilt. She gritted her teeth in an attempt at keeping the tears at bay. When that proved futile, she tried to redirect her attention.

She had delivered the message, at long last. And she was alive. Surely that was something to be celebrated.

Her first trip through space had been a hard one, but it was bound to have been an exceptional journey. It was the first time the crew of the *Redemptive Veteran* had experienced anything like it and with all of the journeys they had made in the past, that had to count for something.

Even though there was so much more still to be done, she was sure that she'd be spending a lot of her time alone in space. She could still think of a plan. She had to believe that it could be done.

The first step would be trying to solve some of the mysteries that remained. Most importantly, she needed to know who she was working for and where she could find him.

She'd long considered what she might do with him if she ever got her hands on him. Once again she found herself wishing death upon someone who surely deserved nothing less.

Winter could only hope that one day, she would have the luxury to choose what should be done with him.

The seat shook beneath her as the vehicle grumbled to life. The chains around her wrists and ankles rattled and the wheels began to roll. Water pooled in the deep tire tracks left in their wake, seeping in from the mud in which they made their impressions. The sunlight glistened in the puddles, dazzling Winter and forcing her to turn away, back to the dark interior of the transport.

She was surprised that no soldiers had joined her in here for the journey, but thankful for the relative peace and quiet. Perhaps they had prepared to find more survivors in the shipwreck. That supposition did nothing to improve her mood.

Sam's head fell about limply as they wobbled over the uneven terrain. Winter could only hope that she would wake up soon. She didn't want her to suffer any more injuries and a road through the mountains wasn't likely to get a great deal smoother.

Of course, when she did wake up, she was going to feel much the same way Winter did: lost, confused and afraid. At that time, there was only going to be one person around to explain their predicament.

That sounded far worse to Winter than the prospect of a return journey.

CHAPTER 28

'I can see black smoke rising from Lake Tana. That's got to be where they went but …' Hayley's voice trembled. 'They must have come in very fast. I can't see how bad it is from here but it definitely isn't good. We need to get closer.'

Orson had managed to lose enough speed on entry to keep their descent steady. They were falling much faster than he would normally like, but these were unusual circumstances and time was of the essence. On this occasion he wished he could go faster.

An obscure shadow rested on the rippling water, shimmering under thin rays of light that managed to break through the overcast sky. As they got closer, the shape was unmistakable. Two enormous engines mounted on a shock-absorbing frame, bolted on to either side of a spear-shaped hull. Even half-submerged in water and heavily damaged, it was undeniably the *Shameless Renegade*.

'A short-range beacon was active here only an hour ago. There are still echoes coming back from the mountains. I don't see any reason why it should have stopped broadcasting unless someone turned it off.'

'You think Sam might have done that? Or Winter, maybe?' Orson speculated.

'I doubt it. In fact, they probably turned it on in the first place. It could have broken, but … I think someone else might have gotten to them first.'

Orson swore. 'Find out where they went. I want to catch up to them as soon as possible.'

'Aye, Captain.'

If the Conglomerate had been here, or even within a few kilometres of here, there would have been signs of conflict with the resistance, but there were none. The only others who could have found them so quickly out here, and have the tools to retrieve them, would be the resistance fighters themselves. If there was still a chance to keep Winter's message out of the hands of the enemy, they would have to catch up immediately.

'Now, Hayley! I need an update now!'

'I-I think I have something. Abnormal heat signatures on the lakeside. Tyre tracks in the mud.'

'Where do they go?'

'I can only follow them a short distance before they dry up, but they're heading towards the mountains. Our best bet's to just follow them in a straight line and keep an eye on the roads.'

'Is that really the best choice we've got?'

'I'll keep trying but there's not a lot I can do. These are public roads.'

'God dammit,' he cursed, forcing the ship into a tight turn to face the direction of the tracks. Then he slammed the main engines to full and began to power the ship towards the mountains, steadily ascending to bring them back over the peaks.

There wasn't a lot to keep an eye on. The roads here were long, but few and straight. There were newer routes that followed the contours, leading right through the middle of the mountain range. They could be wasting valuable time by going this way, though it was the only clue they had. Fortunately, they still had the advantage of speed. It would take them less than an hour to pass from one side of the mountains to the other, unhindered by roads and the limited engine power of an automobile. The people they were following would take far longer.

Orson's patience wore thin as he waited for an update from Hayley. He found himself glancing out through the main viewport at the front of the bridge, desperate to spot some sign that they were heading the right way, even though he could see no more through the window than he could on his displays.

'There!' Hayley almost screamed. 'There's a road leading through a canyon over to port. I'm seeing four heat signatures moving in tight formation. Looks just like a small military convoy.'

'That's our target,' Orson barked, pulling the ship into a tight turn.

The road was little more than a dirt trail following the cliff face. There was no way off it for miles besides a sheer drop into the rocky valley. It was a narrow road too, so turning a vehicle back the other way would be dangerous at best.

That was perfect. They would have nowhere to run.

With the *Veteran*'s size and the roar of its engines, they had no way to do this stealthily. The ship slowed as it moved into position, a kilometre or two out into the canyon, at a right angle to the road and slightly above it. The convoy accelerated. They were apparently attempting to get to safety, or at least some form of cover. Orson held his position.

At this distance he could distinguish the individual vehicles. There was a large gun turret mounted atop the leader, followed closely by a flatbed carrying an airboat. Two troop carriers took the rear, meaning a single squad of soldiers. Possibly two.

His first target was obvious. He'd have to start by taking out the firepower. The *Redemptive Veteran* had no weapons of its own, so he'd have to take a cruder approach.

'Captain? What are we waiting for? Do you have a plan?' Hayley asked nervously.

Orson watched the convoy. 'Yeah, no time to explain though,' he said in a low tone. The cockpit was quiet enough for him to hear his sweat-soaked fingers drumming against the touch screen's digital throttle. 'Just brace for impact.'

He pushed the throttle to maximum. The engines ignited and the ship gathered speed, heading for the lead vehicle. Its weapon was already aimed in their direction and a rapid succession of shots began striking against the *Veteran*'s hull, though their effect was minimal against the vessel designed to cope with the intense stresses of moving between spatial planes.

The inaccuracy of the weapon quickly became evident, the rate of impacts increasing as the distance between the ship and the cliffside closed.

At the last instant, Orson cut power to the engines and buried his head in his lap. The ship's momentum carried it the rest of the way, thundering into the rocky wall. A deafening cacophony shook the ship, which groaned as the collision stressed the steel frame beneath the hull. The storming clatter of rocks tumbling down from above shook the bulkheads, smashing hard against the buckling metal and the glass canopy.

With his body strapped to the seat, Orson's head threatened to abandon him entirely as the force of the impact snatched it from the safety of his hands. While his neck managed to remain intact until the shaking stopped, the jolt from the whiplash speared through him.

He grunted with the pain and rubbed at his neck. Behind him he could hear Hayley making similar noises. He cast her a sideways glance. She'd be fine.

Falling chunks of earth continued to drum against the hull

even after the *Redemptive Veteran* came to a complete stop, but Orson had no time to lose. He unstrapped his restraints and stood, briefly testing his strength against the planet's gravity. He tapped on his console and spoke over the intercom. 'You still alive, Julian?'

'Just about,' the engineer groaned, his voice crackled through the damaged communication system. 'You want to tell me what happened?'

'Stay where you are and keep an eye on the prisoners. I'm going for a walk.' He closed the comm, snatched one of several rifles from the deck and made a move for the door.

'Orson!' Hayley called after him, reaching for the crutches she had slung over her back.

'Stay here, Hayley.'

'But I can help.'

'No!' He whirled around to face her and watched as she recoiled in fear. He glanced down at the rifle in his hand and found it pointed in her direction. He lowered it to hip-level, clicked the safety on and took a deep breath. He forced his anger down as much as he could before turning back to the door and marching out.

Panels had fallen from the bulkheads in the impact and debris littered the corridors. Orson stepped through crumpled metal and ducked under hanging wire as he stalked through his ship. The damage it had sustained from his manoeuvre was extensive, but he hoped they could make it fly again, if only enough to get off this continent and into friendlier territory.

That bridge would have to be crossed later. Right now, Orson's focus was on the present.

He entered the cargo bay. Girders and support struts had broken loose. Some leaned against the bay walls and others lay across the floor.

He ignored the chaos and headed to the main door. It was sealed shut, but the controls set into the wall still appeared to be intact. He slammed a fist against the largest button on the panel and a whirring sound filled the chamber as enormous motors hidden behind the bulkheads came to life.

A series of metallic clangs burst out from behind the walls as the door seals disengaged. Then came a loud screeching noise that filled Orson's ears. The doors slowly began to part, stuttering as they scraped along their damaged mountings and revealing the armoured vehicle he had obliterated in his landing. It looked like a tin can that had been crushed underfoot.

The doors almost completely opened before coming to an abrupt halt, leaving very little room either side of the wreck to get through. With few other options, Orson brought his gun to bear and attempted to squeeze through a small gap on the left, gritting his teeth as jagged plates of ruined alloy jabbed and scraped at his legs and back.

The soldiers outside had already emerged from their transports and were inspecting the ship. No-one had yet spotted Orson. He sensed his opportunity as they stood in the open. Even before he could free himself from the wreckage, he raised his weapon and released a torrent of automatic gunfire into their loose formation.

Four of them, about half their number, fell immediately and the rest dove into cover behind the trucks.

He switched his weapon's firing mode to single shot and popped another round, taking out the driver of the first vehicle. He had bought himself at least a few seconds to free himself while they regrouped. He grasped at the *Veteran*'s hull and tried to yank himself out into the open, avoiding the serrated metal of the debris.

He was nearly free when out of the corner of his eye he spotted a head poking out from behind the flatbed, trying to identify the source of the gunfire. Orson lifted his gun again and brought him down.

His advantage wouldn't last much longer. With a bit more pulling and some careful footwork, he pried himself free. He made a break for the front of the flatbed, threw himself to the ground and crawled underneath it.

Towards the back he saw the boots of four soldiers standing in the dirt. The ones on either side looked to be leaning out, presumably trying to locate Orson. All the while he was silently inching forward. He switched his weapon back to automatic fire, then replaced his half-empty clip, gently placing the old magazine in the dirt.

As he neared the far side of the truck he rolled on to his back. With his gun at the ready and his feet flat against the gritty rock, he pushed himself out into the open, in between the middle two soldiers. They were distracted, far too busy looking around their cover to notice him. He squeezed the trigger and passed the gun over his body from right to left. The four targets fell to the ground, each with a spread of holes in their backs, blooming dark and red.

Orson picked himself up. By his count, nine had been neutralised, discounting the driver, but a full squadron could still have one or two more. He kept his weapon raised and moved forward to inspect the troop carriers.

He rounded the first one and looked inside. Empty, save for the last two drivers who quickly fell under another burst of fire. That only left one more place for Sam and Winter to be held.

He kept up his aim as he moved to the rear of the final vehicle. He braced himself, then whipped around the corner.

A flash of movement inside, followed by a bang as Orson fired. The soldier stumbled back against the far side, then collapsed to the floor.

He dropped the gun to his waist when he laid eyes on the two women chained up inside.

'Orson!' Sam tried to stand but was stopped by a set of cuffs attached to her seat. 'How did you find us?'

He ignored the question. He tossed his gun to the dirt, then jumped inside and released their restraints.

Winter stood and rubbed her newly freed wrists. 'Do I want to know how you stopped the convoy?'

'No you don't, but you're about to see anyway. Right now we don't have a second to lose. Back to the *Veteran*, double time.'

'Where are we going?'

'Exactly where you were meant to. Now get a move on!'

'What's that supposed to mean?' she asked, but Orson didn't stay to listen. When he turned the corner to go back the way he had come, he saw his handiwork from the outside for the first time. He stopped and beheld the battered vessel, its bow resting against the cliffside while the rest was kept aloft by a continuous burn from its ventral thrusters. Then he continued moving towards it.

'Captain!' Sam called. 'All due respect, but what the fuck have you done to the ship?'

Orson didn't slow down as he looked back at her over his shoulder. 'The engines still work, so as long as you can get us to the Conglomerate HQ you've still got a job to do.'

'Wait, Conglomerate HQ?' Winter said. 'Why there?'

Orson stopped again. He turned and saw her standing still, just ahead of Sam. 'So you can deliver that message,' he said.

She hesitated. 'But … I've already delivered the message.'

His eye twitched. 'What do you mean you've already delivered it? Delivered to who?'

'This lot,' Winter said, gesturing to the trucks lined up in the road. 'It's fine, we don't need to worry about it now. If the message was for the Conglomerate, they've got it now.'

'Winter,' Sam said. 'They weren't Conglomerate.'

Orson breathed deeply through his gritted teeth. He paced in quick circles in the spot with one hand slapped against his forehead, fingering his receding hairline. With a roar of anger he dropped to his knees beside a fallen resistance fighter. He paused, then whipped a sidearm from a holster on the corpse's thigh. He charged back towards Winter with fire in his eyes. He caught her by the neck as she stumbled backwards and pressed the barrel of the gun between her eyes.

'What the fuck?' she gasped, trying to pull his hand away in a panic.

'You've been working against me the whole time?' Orson's furious voice shook almost as much as his hands. 'You wanted to make me trust you just so you can stab me in the back?'

'Let go of her!' Sam screamed.

Orson didn't listen, instead continuing to interrogate Winter. 'If this was the Conglomerate, why do you think I attacked them? Why would they take my pilot hostage?'

'Then the message wasn't for the Conglomerate,' Winter wheezed, straining to get her words out.

'Orson, let her go!' Sam ran towards him but stopped short as he turned the gun on her.

'Stay back, Sam! Just stay out of my way! Get back on the ship!'

Sam tore her gaze away from the gun and looked Orson dead in the eye. She took a deep breath and said in a level tone, 'You're going to shoot me now, are you?'

The captain had no such restraint, his dry, calloused finger wrapped firmly around the trigger. 'My allegiance is to the Solar Conglomerate, Sam. It always has been. Now, if you want to stand between me and victory, you should do so knowing that I take no prisoners.'

'I don't have a place in this war and, like it or not, neither do you. You're not a soldier anymore. Give Winter a chance to speak and you might hear the same thing.'

'If you're trying to play me for a fool it's gone on long enough. You're with her and she's with them! I'm not blind and I'm certainly not an idiot! Now, get on the goddamn ship and I'll join you once I'm finished with our Aralian operative.'

Sam refused the command. She took a slow confident step towards Orson.

'I gave you an order!' Orson screamed, his voice cracking under the intensity of his fury. His hands gripped tighter. His attention was so fixed on Sam that he almost couldn't hear Winter struggling to gulp down some much-needed oxygen.

Sam took another step forward.

'One more step and I swear I will blow your brains out, Sam!'

She pushed her luck as far as it would go, closing the distance to point-blank range. Steeling himself for the shot he'd never wanted to take, he pointed the gun at Sam's heart. Before he could force himself to squeeze the trigger, Winter delivered a quick strike to his cheek. It wasn't much, but enough to catch him off guard and cause him to stagger.

Sam lunged forward, reaching for the gun that was now pointed at the ground. Orson reacted quickly though, bringing it back up with a quick swipe. He tore a gash in Sam's face with the iron sights, knocking her off her balance and on to her back.

He then turned to Winter. With his gun already raised, he slammed the butt down hard against her forehead. He released his grip and allowed her to fall to the ground, coughing and gasping for air. He followed her down, crouching over her and placing the gun against her head once more. He didn't have the time to taunt her further. He had no choice now.

He looked her in the eye and squeezed the trigger.

CHAPTER 29

While Hayley could still hear the occasional crackle of gunfire outside, she could at least take a little comfort in knowing that someone was still alive.

Her crutches had been laid across her lap since Orson left, the urge to pursue him still tugging her towards the door. Yet only now that it had all fallen silent outside did Hayley know she had to listen to her instincts. If the conflict was over, a victor had been decided. She wasn't going to wait around when she could go now and find out who it was.

She slung one crutch over her back, took the other in her right hand and used it to drag a rifle towards her. She picked it up with her free hand, then pushed away from her seat, wobbling a little as she grew accustomed to the gravity. She pushed the crutch into her armpit and made her way towards the door.

Negotiating the corridors was a challenge. With large chunks of debris scattered across the floor it wasn't easy to pick a path through the ship. On several occasions she found herself having to stop and push a damaged panel aside with her gun just so she'd have a stable surface for her crutch. Exhausted, she made her way almost to the cargo bay, pausing only to poke her head into the SSR suite.

Julian looked at her as the doors parted. 'Hayley!' he exclaimed. He staggered to his feet and moved to the doorway, using the handholds in the bulkhead to keep himself upright. A large bruise was blooming on his temple. Apparently the landing had been a bit rougher for him.

The raiders, on the other hand, looked to be relatively uninjured. Narn and his guard stood enclosed in their pods, both looking shaken. Megan Gram, now awake and sporting two fresh wounds on her face, sat leaning against the back of her own pod with folded arms. She watched Hayley inquisitively.

'You'll have to bring me up to speed,' Julian said. 'Orson doesn't tell me anything.'

'Okay, well we found Winter and Sam. We followed them down to Earth but I think we were too late. They were captured but we found their convoy–'

'Hold up,' Gram interrupted from behind the glass. 'Your friends went to Earth without you? How did they do that?'

'With your ship.'

Gram's face hardened. She tilted her head downwards and fixed Hayley with a threatening gaze. 'They stole my ship?'

'Oh, not so nice when it happens to you, is it?' Julian taunted. 'Excellent, you're a hypocrite as well. I ought to be keeping a list.'

'Julian, Orson went out there on his own,' Hayley blurted. 'I don't know what he was up against, but he went out there alone and I heard gunshots.'

'He wasn't exactly thinking straight on the bridge. I don't believe he could mount much of an offensive in that state. Especially not on his own.'

'You think he's dead?'

'I think he's lucky to have lasted as long as he has. One way or another, he's gone. We need to move on without him.'

'So what now? We go out there and get Sam and Winter ourselves? We won't do any better than him.'

'If I might interrupt?' Hayley and Julian turned to Paul Narn, who had stepped to the front of his pod, his hands pressed against the glass. 'I think I may have exactly what you need to help save your friends.'

'Oh, fuck off,' Julian spat. 'I know desperation when I see it. Don't think you can wriggle out of this.'

'I'd listen to him, if I were you,' Gram suggested. 'He bought Winter, remember? He obviously has a fondness for her.'

'Sure, but does he strike you as the kind of guy who'd be lugging around a bag of grenades? Give me a break, he's useless.'

'I may not have grenades, but I do have money,' Paul said confidently. 'I also happen to know someone who can make impossible things happen, if the price is right.'

Gram chuckled. 'I'm not a complete sap. A little cash isn't going to make me put my neck on the line for anyone.'

'You know, this ship's looking a little worse for wear,' Paul said. 'I think its value might have gone down a tad, don't you?'

Though she couldn't see him from her angle, Gram glared in the direction of his pod. Then she turned back to Julian. 'You're right. I should've stopped listening to him ages ago. He's going to get me killed some day.'

* * *

The shot should have gone off by now. Winter stopped struggling long enough to see Orson glaring at the pistol with frustration and his index finger shaking violently as it tried to force the trigger to move.

He pulled the weapon away to inspect it. She took in a deep breath as he moved his other hand from her throat in order to flick off the safety; something he had forgotten when he scavenged it from the soldier's corpse.

All the while, Sam had been climbing to her feet. She

recovered quickly and just before Orson was able to turn the gun on Winter once more, she bent down and charged, tackling him to the ground. He fired off a shot that made Winter's ears ring, the bullet throwing up a plume of dust as it struck the ground mere inches from her head.

Now free from his grasp, Winter felt the scrape of rough coughs through her damaged throat. She rolled over and watched as Orson landed on his back with a grunt, but Sam's momentum carried on, forcing them both into a roll that carried them dangerously close to the cliff edge.

Winter dragged herself a short distance away from the brawl, then staggered as she pushed herself upright once more.

They now lay parallel to the edge, less than a metre from the deadly plummet. Sam was on her stomach, trying to claw herself towards the gun that had fallen just out of reach. Orson was on top of her, his arms wrapped around her legs to slow her down.

He grabbed at the back of her clothes, pulling himself along her body. As he released her legs she tried to kick at him, but it did little to shake him off.

The soldiers who littered the road had armaments to be scavenged. Winter dashed to a corpse lying behind the flatbed and snapped up his sidearm, making sure to release the safety.

She couldn't make the shot from here, fearing she might hit Sam. Even so, she lined her target up in the iron sights, her arms outstretched and her cheek resting upon her shoulder, and marched towards the fight.

'Orson, stop!' she called, hoping at the very least to offer a source of distraction.

Orson immediately rolled away but kept his grip on Sam, pulling her around with him. She landed on top of him, providing Orson with a layer of fleshy cover as he was now sandwiched between her and the ground. He gripped Sam tightly against him, all the while feeling out with one arm, hoping to scoop up the gun.

Winter hurried over to the weapon, keeping her aim on Orson. At this range, even with Sam acting as a shield, she had a clear shot at his head.

'Give up,' she said. 'It's over.'

Still he reached for the gun. He only withdrew his arm when Winter fired a bullet into the ground inches from his hand. He tightened his grasp on Sam, holding her arms to her sides.

'Let her go.'

He silently refused, adjusting his grip to keep Sam's struggling arms restrained.

Winter fired another shot into the dirt. 'I said let her go!'

He must have loosened his hold a little as Sam freed an arm and stretched it out past her head. She patted the ground with her hand, searching for the gun she couldn't see. It was still out of her reach.

'Go on, Sam. It's yours,' Winter encouraged her. She pushed it towards Sam with a toe until her hand finally fell upon the grip.

Just as her fingers began to curl around the weapon, Orson bellowed out a cry. He lifted Sam into the air and threw her off to the right with such power that she cleared the remaining distance to the cliff edge, and plummeted down the steep descent, taking the gun with her.

'Sam!' Winter watched in horror her as she fell, reaching an arm out as if to catch her, but it was far too little and far too late.

Orson wasted no time, pushing himself quickly towards Winter then grabbing at her outstretched ankle. He yanked it out from under her before she had a chance to understand what had just happened. She fell to the ground with a yelp and Orson swiped the gun from her hand.

He didn't keep her pinned for long though as Winter, fuelled by almost as much adrenaline as her adversary, delivered a blow to his face with the heel of her boot.

He staggered back in the direction of his ship, using the force of the strike to bring himself to his feet. He swivelled around, bringing the gun up to aim at Winter once more. By the time his eyes were on her again she was already standing.

The distance between them was too great. She wouldn't be able to close it before he'd have a chance to fire. Alone now, there would be no more distractions to save her.

She cast her eyes back to the cliff edge, looking down into the rocky depths. Sam's body was lost now, though its path could be followed by a series of red stains on the stone.

Sam had lost her life and Winter was still alive. They had barely known each other. Winter regretted never making the time to get to know her better.

She felt herself welling up, but wouldn't let Orson see her wiping away any tears. He, meanwhile, was using his sleeve to wipe a drop of blood from his nose.

'This is it, Winter,' he panted, his aim wavering slightly. 'There's no-one left to save you anymore. Now tell me what was in that message.'

'The message …' Winter trailed off. How could she tell him?

'Tell me!' he shrieked, his hands shaking.

'I'm sorry, but I was lied to!' she blurted out. 'It wasn't a message, it was just a test. They wanted to know if I could carry messages for them in the future and now they know I can.'

'No you can't. I forbid it!'

'Why? Who are these people? Aren't they with the Solar Conglomerate too?'

'Are you kidding? They're the precise opposite! They're Aralian sympathisers and you're delivering them top-secret information straight from Pioneer HQ!'

Winter took a step back. With her memories of the terrorism at Port Jova she should have considered that sympathisers would be at work here too. She wasn't doing much to regain Orson's trust, but getting back in his good graces was a long shot at this point.

'I don't know what you're hoping to get out of me, Orson. You obviously know more than I do.'

'I told you, I want that message! Spill it!'

'There was no message! There's nothing more to tell you!'

'You said there were lives at stake. Was that a lie too?'

'I didn't know it was a lie when I told you. I promise, I believed every word I said.'

'Bullshit! You're a traitor! You've been lying to me since you first stepped on board. You're working for the Pioneers!'

There was no way to convince him.

'If you don't tell me I'll have to pay a visit to their base and find it for myself.' His eyes grew wild as fury twisted his countenance.

'You'd get yourself killed. Why not report what you know to the Conglomerate?'

'They wouldn't listen to me unless I had something concrete. As far as they'd be concerned, I'd just be an old soldier begging for his job back.'

Winter didn't know how true that really was, but she had no doubt he believed it. 'Then let me come with you. I'll help you get it back from their base.'

'You still think I'm a complete dumbass! You'd turn me over to them the first chance you got!'

'They had me chained up in the back of a truck!'

'A show!' Orson insisted with a scream. 'It was all an elaborate show to trick me but it didn't work!'

His knuckles were whitening as his grip on the gun tightened. With him being so close to pulling the trigger, Winter had no intention of dragging it out anymore.

'You're deluded!' she screamed in an attempt at provoking his trigger finger.

'Shut the hell up!' he shrieked, shaking the gun towards her. 'Just tell me what you told them!'

'I already have.'

'Liar!'

There was a scraping noise behind him. Winter watched Julian dash out from in front of the flatbed truck, then skid to a halt as he saw what was going on.

'What the hell?' he cried.

Orson swivelled to face the other way, dropped to his knee and fired a shot. The force of the impact threw Julian down into the dust. Winter's hands flew to her mouth in horror.

A short distance behind, Hayley cried out. She flew to his side with all the haste she could muster, throwing her rifle and her crutch aside and falling to the ground beside him. She leaned over and tried to rouse him in a panic.

'Happy accident,' Orson loudly asserted as he climbed back to his feet and turned back to face Winter, pacing slowly towards her. He relaxed his gun arm a little, but kept it pointed in her direction. 'I've been tempted to shoot him for the longest time. Any time he's ever opened his mouth.'

'You're killing your own crew, Orson,' Winter growled at him. 'And you were lecturing me about betrayal?'

He stayed silent, red-faced and closing in like a predator.

Hayley looked away from Julian, her tear-stricken glare aimed at Orson. She lunged for her discarded rifle and lined him up in the sights. The instant that she could be heard scrambling in the dirt however, Orson surged forward and grabbed Winter, holding her between him and Hayley, his gun pressed to her temple.

'Are you willing to see Winter vanish from this reality? Because I don't think she'll be able to re-join us again once she meets up with Julian on the other side. Now, think about your next move very carefully. Get back on the ship, Hayley.'

Hayley's breaths were heavy and angry. 'Julian's alive,' she snarled. 'And he's not going anywhere.'

Orson grunted. 'As stubborn in death …' He stretched out his arm to aim at Julian. 'In that case, I'll just finish him off. I don't care anymore.'

Hayley's aim began to falter, her eyes darting between Orson and Julian.

'Just get back on the goddamn ship. Take him with you. That wound's only going to get infected if he stays out here. Go get him patched up.'

She hesitated, then threw down the gun. She picked up her crutch and pushed herself back on to her foot. 'I can't carry him on my own,' she said. 'Where's Sam?'

Orson remained silent. Hayley's face slowly changed from one of hatred, to one of shock and fear.

'Go on,' Winter taunted him over her shoulder. 'Tell her what you did to Sam.'

She felt him take a slow breath in past her ear, but before he could make a sound, the loud crack of a gunshot rang out through the valley. Orson unleashed a scream of pain as blood erupted from his outstretched gun arm. His pistol fired, but the shot went wide.

His grip on Winter loosened. She reacted by driving an elbow into his gut, then broke free with a sharp turn. He stumbled backward, winded but still cradling his bloody arm.

Winter swiped for him, grabbing his wrist and securing a grip by squeezing her fingers into the fresh wound. She swung him around and threw him towards the cliff edge. He collapsed to the ground and rolled towards the sharp drop, blood trailing in patches and pooling on the dry earth. He stopped just before the edge, using his good arm to try to claw himself away.

Winter stalked towards him, his blood dripping from her fingers.

'W-wait a second,' he gasped, almost looking feeble for once.

'Stop this, Orson,' Winter begged him. 'Come back with me. We'll figure something out together.'

He took some haggard breaths. 'I'm sorry. I don't know why I …' He lifted his head to look straight into Winter's eyes. 'Will you help me?'

Winter found it hard to believe him, but she didn't want to kill him. What else could she do? She stepped towards him. Carefully. Suspiciously.

She was only a few steps away when he leapt into motion, jumping to his feet and barrelling towards her. Winter braced herself to take the hit.

Another distant gunshot and a plume of crimson burst from Orson's chest. The force threw him back and he tumbled over the precipice.

Winter ran forwards and gazed over the edge. She watched as he fell down the sharp slope. He stopped screaming as his body lurched from side to side, battered by the rocky outcrops.

She continued to follow his descent until he vanished from sight. Then she turned back to the road to see where the bullet had come from. She was amazed to see Megan Gram standing behind the flatbed, rifle in hand.

The two shared a look, unsure what to say to each other. After a few seconds, Gram nodded slowly. Winter wasn't certain what it meant, but she returned the gesture.

Gram discarded the gun and walked over to Julian. She kneeled down, grabbed him roughly and draped him over her shoulder.

'Come on,' Gram called as she began marching back to the ship. 'Or I'm leaving you behind.'

CHAPTER 30

Soft yellow sunlight settled over the landscape. Fine dust permeated the rippling air, thrown up by the ventral thrusters that slowed the *Redemptive Veteran*'s descent. The craft touched down with a jolt and the thrusters cut out. Everything fell silent. The world was still.

Gram had managed to pry the ship free of the wreckage on the cliffside road and managed to fly it, despite the litany of failing systems. She set it down on a small plateau on the outskirts of the Simien mountain range.

Winter walked through the vessel's bloodstained hallways, slowed in part by the aches and stings of her wounds, and in part by the knowledge that these could be her last moments on board. She wasn't sorry to see this journey come to an end.

The doors slid apart and she stepped into the cargo bay. Aside from a few beams and panels that had fallen from the ceiling it was still mostly intact. The only other noteworthy point was the main door which had refused to close since the impact. The outer hull had crumpled and the mechanisms behind the bulkheads were damaged. The cargo bay had to be evacuated while the *Veteran* was in flight.

The bright rays of the setting sun poured through the opening. Winter shielded her eyes, giving them time to adjust as she stepped off the boarding ramp and on to the solid rocky shelf.

Mountains towered over her to the north and east, but everywhere else was flat. It could have been a trick of the sunlight, but the entire environment appeared to have been stained a brownish-grey. With the heat and the dust, she could have been back on Arali. She recalled tales of Earth, the beautiful shining blue gem. A paradise hidden away in the vast expanse of space. A diamond in the rough.

That was not what Winter saw now.

'We may not have picked the most scenic spot.'

She turned slowly to see Julian casually descending the ramp, a thick bandage tied over his left shoulder and another wrapped around his forehead.

'Not that this is the best day to go sightseeing though, eh?' he added.

Winter chuckled, facing towards the rolling brown farmland to the south as he stood beside her. 'With what we've seen today, I think anything would look bleak.'

Julian's head turned down to the ground. 'Yeah.' He sighed. 'It's been a bleak day.' He sounded tired.

They stood in silence. It was the first time in days they could stop. No more thinking, no more deceiving, no more killing. Yet, as welcome as the silence was, Winter didn't feel ready for it yet. There was an awkwardness that needed lifting.

'I suppose I won't have to pay for the trip, at least?' she said, nudging Julian's good arm with a smirk.

He continued to stare off towards the horizon. 'I think you've paid enough,' he muttered.

She hesitated, not sure if she should say anything, but decided that now was the time to speak her mind. 'Not as much as others. In fact, I think I may have come away best out of all of us.'

'Not quite,' Julian interjected. 'What about that prick, Paul? He's got himself a new starship.' He continued to avoid looking at Winter, now turning his gaze towards the *Veteran*.

'Well, kinda. Bit of a fixer-upper though.'

'Eh, he's got the money. She'll be space-worthy again in a couple of weeks.' He paused, staring at the craft for a little longer, then spun to face Winter. 'I wanted to thank you, truly, for everything you've done. I'm still not sure I believe everything I've heard about that message of yours and I'm not sure it matters anymore. I just want to thank you for doing everything you could in an impossible situation.'

'You don't need to thank me. In fact, I'd rather you didn't. Too many people have died on my account.'

'None of this was your fault,' he said, placing a hand gently on her arm. 'Gram may have swooped in to save you at the last moment but if you think that all of this was anyone's fault besides hers, you're wrong.' He stopped for a beat, then added, 'Unless you want to blame the bastard who paid her to do it. That's fine too. But you really mustn't blame yourself. That implant of yours threw you in the deep end on this trip. That's all.'

Winter felt her eyes beginning to water. She looked up at him and said, 'Thanks. It means a lot to hear you say it.'

'I'm not just saying it. It's the truth.' He let his hand fall back to his side and smiled at her.

Winter wiped the tears from her eyes before they had a chance to run down her cheeks.

'Everything alright?'

Winter looked past Julian. She had almost missed the sound of Hayley's crutches on the boarding ramp as she made her way towards them.

Winter rubbed her eyes once more to ensure they were dry before replying, 'Yeah, fine,' as casually as possible.

'Yeah,' Julian said. 'I was just, uhh, congratulating Winter on a job well done.'

'Not sure we should be calling it over just yet,' Hayley said. She looked back to see Paul and Gram approaching. Gram stopped at the foot of the ramp as Paul strode right up to the group.

'Can't you give us one second alone?' Julian spat.

'I can give you more than that. In fact, I've no choice in the matter. I fear that if I let you back on board my first mate may kill you herself.'

'First mate?' asked Winter, looking past him to see a look of cold spite chiselled into Gram's face.

'Indeed. With the unfortunate loss of the *Shameless Renegade*, it seems she's without a ship. I've already parted with the money I owed her for the *Veteran* and so the craft is mine, but I am of course short of a crew.' He smirked as he made an exaggerated shrug. 'It seemed only fitting.'

'She'll stab you in the back, you know,' Julian said, looking down his nose at Paul.

'I think not,' he insisted. 'In fact, Megan is no different from her mercenaries. Her loyalty is bought, not earned. As long as I keep the money coming, she'll stay in line.'

She was surely able to hear everything he was saying, but her expression remained unchanged.

'Believe what you like, mate. It's your funeral.' Julian said dismissively.

'Just watch your back,' Winter said. As much as she hated to admit it, he had saved her life.

'I surely will. I'm sorry to abandon you so far from civilisation, but frankly with the ship in this condition I can't be sure we'd even make it to port. Besides, I'm sure there will be plenty of tedious questions and paperwork assuming we do arrive in as many pieces, so I can at least spare you that.'

'Terrific,' Hayley said flatly.

'There is one thing I can do for you though. I have a gift.'

'What's that?' Winter asked.

'I'm willing to offer you some of the goods that were left behind on the *Veteran*. I managed to find a couple of crates of asareyite, which Megan had apparently been hoping to secretly liberate for herself. That should more or less pay for the repairs here, I believe. But there's also a quaint little vehicle which you're welcome to take with you. Apparently, it was too big to get through the airlock. Probably for the best, considering what happened to the rest of the inventory.' He cast a glance towards the thin stream of dark smoke that could still be seen in the distance.

'Not much of a gift,' Winter said. 'You do know that's my car, right?'

'And so it is again, though I believe Megan had her eyes on it for a time, as well. I'm not sure you'll all be able to fit inside, but I'm afraid I have little more to offer you.'

'We'll make it work.'

'I've no doubt.' He turned back to see the one surviving mercenary driving the car out of the cargo bay and on to the plateau. Then he hopped out and hurried back on board.

Gram looked, then turned her glare on Paul once more.

'Well, I shan't linger,' said Paul. 'I don't suppose I'm wanted here any longer. Besides, I must see the ship to a starport for repairs. Don't want to let it sit like this for too long. Heaven only knows what might fall off next.' He chuckled to himself, but no-one else joined in. 'I bid you a fond farewell and a safe journey. I would hope for our paths to cross again, though I fear these wounds may take some time to heal.'

'Oh, fuck off,' Julian cursed, pinching the skin of his forehead. 'Take your shiny new ship and go.'

'As you wish.' He didn't stop smiling as he backed away,

delivering a mocking bow before turning and hurrying back on board.

Gram, still standing on the ramp, waited for him to pass her before calling out, 'Hey Winter, try not to get yourself killed out there.'

'Uhh, thanks?'

'But if someone has to kill you, come find me. I've got dibs.'

That was the closest she was ever going to get to a friendly send-off. She offered a half-hearted salute and watched Gram turn around, strolling back into the ship and out of sight.

'So,' Julian said, looking to Winter and Hayley with a clap of his hands. 'What's next?'

Hayley opened her mouth to speak but stopped short. She looked away, then back again. 'I hadn't really thought this far ahead.'

'Well, we can't stay here.' He strolled a few steps away, looking out towards the west. The sun had nearly finished setting, the orange sky darkening to black. 'At least we've got a car, I guess.'

The *Redemptive Veteran*'s engines roared to life once more. The boarding ramp retracted and the ventral thrusters sputtered as they ignited. Dust kicked up from the ground forcing Winter to shield her eyes as the vessel gained altitude.

As it lifted higher, it became visible only by its great black silhouette, blotting out the stars of the night sky. Then, an orange flame erupted from the main engine that propelled it forwards. The craft accelerated over their heads, turning steadily to the north and shrinking into the distance. It wasn't long before the plateau was once again bathed in silence.

'Well, that's that,' Winter said. She watched the dwindling light of the distant engine, then returned to the matter at hand.

'I don't know about you two, but I need to get back to Arali. I have unfinished business there.'

'Really? You want to get back into space so soon?' Julian said with a tone of bewilderment. 'After all that's happened, don't you want a break from all that?'

'Well, I'd hope that the next trip will be a little less eventful. But yes, I have to get back soon. With all that happened on the cliffside, I'm probably racing against the clock now.'

'What could be so important?' Hayley asked. 'You've only just finished your mission.'

'Yes,' Winter said, looking to the stars above her. 'Now I need to claim my reward.'

EPILOGUE

The office was grand. So grand, in fact, that it might be better described as a hall. It had no windows and was illuminated instead by a pair of glimmering chandeliers.

The walls and furnishings were built of dark polished hardwoods, as was the floor. That was, with the exception of the raised walkway, built from polished blue Aralian asareyite, that covered the thirty-metre distance between the doors and the desk.

To the right of this walkway was an open platform, atop which sat a small table with ornate chaise lounges at either end, angled towards a fireplace nestled amid sprawling bookshelves. To the left, a meeting area with a mighty table sparsely encircled by executive chairs. The entire affair was complete with marble busts of historical figures, rippling water features and potted plants that had to be replaced daily due to the lack of natural sunlight.

The entire chamber shone with extravagance and wealth that might intimidate a common person. The minister, however, was far from common.

He sat behind his desk, a handful of dim white holograms suspended above it. Each was a report, an article or a memo. A plethora of information, far more than any one person could manage at once. Yet the minister reclined, rearranging the information with slow, disinterested waves of his hand.

Masked somewhat by the crackle of the flames and the trickle of the water, was the sound of distant footsteps at the far side of the room. They grew louder, then stopped.

A click, followed by a creak as one of the dark wood doors began to open. A soft voice came through.

'Permission to–'

'Enter,' the minister interrupted, his voice deep and authoritative. He swiped one of the holograms aside to get a clearer look at the visitor.

A young woman closed the door behind her and began the long walk to the minister's desk. Her polished black shoes clacked against the asareyite underfoot in a rapid rhythm. A glass tablet rested upon the smooth grey sleeve of her jacket. She carried the formal look well, for a commoner.

The minister held up a palm. 'That's close enough,' he instructed. She stopped a few metres short of his workspace. 'What do you have?'

'A message, sir,' she said. 'The source wished to remain anonymous.'

'Very well, young miss.'

'It says, "Code: Frost".'

The minister leaned back in his mighty leather chair. 'Intriguing,' he said. 'Was there anything more?'

'There is a brief addendum.'

'Let's hear it, then.'

She looked back down at her screen and read. 'Target escaped.'

He furrowed his brow and stroked his chin, but otherwise remained unmoved. 'Interesting,' he said flatly. 'Kindly delete that message on your way out, would you?'

'Of course, minister.' The woman turned on her heel and tapped at her device as she marched towards the door. As she left, the minister called up some files from little over three weeks ago.

It shouldn't surprise him that she had escaped. Everything

about her background would suggest she could be resourceful when a situation required it. Her disappearance was unfortunate, however. That implant of hers would have made her a valuable instrument.

Then again, perhaps she still could be. His power over her remained, not to mention the key to the implant itself. With everything he needed to bring her to heel, or to bring her to her knees, the odds were stacked in his favour. Before long, she would be coming back all on her own.

That transmission may have beaten her here, but she could be following it very closely. He would have to keep his eyes open for her imminent return.

He hadn't heard the last of Winter Starling, nor she the last of him.

* * *

ABOUT THE AUTHOR

James Vigor is a computer games programmer from Bristol, UK. He enjoys sci-fi and fantasy, orchestral music, role-playing games and capybaras. He would like to go to space but he can't, so instead he writes books to try and convince himself that it's probably more trouble than it's worth.

If you have enjoyed this book, please leave a review for James to let him know what you thought of his work.

You can find out more about James on his author page on the Fantastic Books Store. While you're there, why not browse our delightful tales and wonderfully woven prose?

www.fantasticbooksstore.com

Printed in Great Britain
by Amazon